The experts speak about
Jasper's Foul Tongue!

"The only thing we have to fear is fear itself...
and Kroenung's prose. Am I right?"
—*FDR*

"Let us sit upon the ground and tell sad stories
of the death of literature."
—*King Richard II*

"Persons attempting to find a motive
in this narrative will be prosecuted;
persons attempting to find a moral in it will be banished;
persons attempting to find a plot in it will be shot."
Mark Twain

"And they say **I** made a monster?"
—-*Dr. Frankenstein*

"Now you know why I do so much opium.
And this giant shroom I'm sitting on is next."
—*A certain caterpillar*

"I really made a mistake taking this one."
-*The Book Thief*

Also by Terry Kroenung
www.terrykroenungink.com

<u>Novels</u>
Brimstone and Lily: A Blade of Dubious Glory
Brimstone and Lily: Beware the Sword of Mirth
Jasper's Foul Tongue: The Avenging Arm of Sarcasm
Jasper's Magick Corset
Paragon of the Eccentric
Rapiers & Rogues
The Gaze of Zeus

<u>Drama</u>
The Three Musketeers
Coolness and Courage
Blood and Beauty
Gentle Rain

<u>Nonfiction</u>
HeartSnark

<u>Anthologies</u> (contributor)
Customs, Castles, and Kings, v. 2
Broken Links, Mended Lives
False Faces
Found (Colorado Book Award winner)

<u>Awards</u>
Colorado Gold Literary Award
Paragon of the Eccentric (winner)
Brimstone and Lily (finalist)

Independent Publishers Book Award
Brimstone and Lily (Bronze Medal)

Next Generation Indie Book Award
HeartSnark (finalist)

Colorado Short Story Contest
"The Day the Earth Couldn't Stand Still"
(winner)

The Legacy Stone
Book Two: Part Two

JASPER'S FOUL TONGUE: How Sharper Than a Serpent's Tush

The adventures of Verity Sauveur
and her most Righteous Blade of Wrath,
the Fell Sword Morphageus,
hereafter known as Jasper

Terry Kroenung

RARE MOON PRESS
Longmont, Colorado

Jasper's Foul Tongue:

How Sharper Than a Serpent's Tush:

(revised edition)

Printed in the United States of America

Cover image by Solarbearstudio

ISBN: 978-1-7378947-7-3

www.terrykroenungink.com

To
Douglas Adams and Monty Python

I didn't steal a bunch of your stuff for this book,
it was an, um, homage

Attention all students, teachers, and other crazed literature geeks!

There are several dozen references to famous books in *Jasper's Foul Tongue*. Twain's *The Adventures of Huckleberry Finn* is most represented, along with some Charles Dickens, but so are *To Kill A Mockingbird, The Odyssey, King Lear, Don Quixote, Monty Python*, and *The Hitchhiker's Guide to the Galaxy*, among others. I even made a joke about a Willams James book of Theology from 1902 (as one does).

See how many you can spot! Sponsor *JFT* Lit Parties!
Amaze your friends! Kick butt on *Jeopardy*!
Be smarter than a 5th grader!

Contents

*<u>**Another howdy-do from y'all's intrepid narrator**</u>*

So after those first two looney books, Ma's right insistent that I oughta make extra-double-sure y'all understand about this here one. I still hafta admit it sure looked like the stinky end of a polecat when I first scribbled it (sorta like this here introduction). I swear I get purty good grades in readin' and writin' but Miz Finch threw up her pudgy hands and declared that the Pennsylvania State Normal School sure never prepared her for my grammar. Thought she'd expire o' the vapors when she first eyed the rough copy. But betwixt her and Ma and Sha'ira (Jasper volunteered but that was a road I sure enough didn't want to go down), they wrassled the words into a rough sort o' shape that swanky, educated folks like yerselves kin read without too much eyestrain. We cleaned up the narration parts some but tried to leave most o' the dialogue stuff alone, so y'all get the flavor o' the thing. Jasper says it's sorta a castor oil flavor.

Took a month o' Sundays t' put lipstick on this here pig, let me tell ya. Miz Finch might be contemplatin' a career change, maybe cleanin' out the Washington Canal, where there'd be less stress on her nerves. If I'd known what a trouble it was to write a book I never would o' tackled it. Shoulda got on my raft and gone fishin' with Romulus.

I guess I oughta apologize in advance for Jasper. You'll see what I mean.

Thanks,
Verity

JASPER'S FOUL TONGUE: How Sharper Than a Serpent's Tush

"Close your cake-hole before a moth flies in it,"
suggested the dog.

24 / Lost in Lusitania
Tuesday, July 9, 703 B.C.

Once again my Stone-boosted night vision saved me. That and the fact that Carrasco's cavalry wanted a prisoner, not a skewered kid. I'm pretty sure that I had fear on my side, too. Unlike other folks accused of witchcraft in their world, I'd been seen actually slinging magick about. None of the knights seemed to want to get too close to the freckle-faced sorceress. Especially not in the graveyard-dark of the hilly patch of woods I darted into. *Fine by me. Looks like everybody's singin' the same tune here. Go back and tell yer captain you lost me. I won't say no different.*

Just in case one of my pursuers hankered after a promotion, I slung Morphageus across my back in Norman kite-shield form. That covered me head to knee. It'd take a miracle sword-slash or arrow-shot to bring me down. Of course, they might choose to just trample me under their horses' hooves. The longer I eluded them, the more frustrated they'd get. I'd had enough experience outfoxing boys at school to know that. Pretty soon they'd forget their orders. Then all they'd want is my blood, for daring to make fools of them. But while that might make them more dangerous, it'd also make them easier to fight if I got cornered. Half of their training would get smothered by rage.

At that moment fighting wasn't an issue. Horses can't race through woods very easily except on a clear path. I kept to the thickest part of the forest, away from any hint of a track, bulling my way through briars and shrubs, accepting face-smacks from branches of all sorts. Since I took up so much less space than a horse and rider, and could see in the dark, I could make a lot better time than the knights. After fifteen or twenty minutes I'd left them far behind. That left me with a new worry, though.

I had no idea where I was.

Oh, this is swell. Probably shoulda paid attention to where I was goin'. That's what I get fer stayin' off the trails.

"I like it here", said Jasper, all perky and upbeat. "It's so Robin Hoody. You could round up some Merry Men, irritate the Sheriff of Nottingham, rob from the rich, and invest in railroad stock."

I tried to give a listen for bad guys while his voice filled my head. "Hmmm. I don't recall that last part in any of the stories I ever read."

"Well, I never liked that whole 'give to the poor' part. What're they gonna do with the extra greenbacks? Just waste it on food and shelter, most likely."

"And you have a better plan?"

"You betcha! Westward expansion is where the action is. The iron horse, the steamboat, gold mines!"

"Ain't them railroad tycoons and robber barons already loaded?"

"That's what I hear."

"So you plan to rob from the rich and then give to the...other rich?"

"More or less. I ain't got all the details worked out yet. Still cogitatin' on the exact particulars."

"Okay. You do that. Feel free to cogitate a bit on how to get us outta here, too. Looks like we're gonna have to do some westward expansion of our own."

I could tell from the terrain which way west lay. The hills grew steeper moving away from the castle. Since the soldiers no doubt still hunted me, I didn't want to head downhill yet. Though I could move north, keeping the high ground to my left, I'd still be traveling in Carrasco's domains for a considerable distance. His troops might have the same idea and move along the border to head me off. South was no darned good, either. Gaulle and the *Kiss* were in the other direction. So off west I went, in the one direction I wanted to avoid. If Lusitania scared Sha'ira then I knew that I'd want to spend as little time there as possible.

For an hour I crept through the woods. Unlike the scrubby trees and glorified shrubs of Iberion, this proved to be a real forest. The spooky kind you read about in fairy tales. *Heck, with the world so transmogrified from that Merchantry spell, I wouldn't bat an eye if Red Riding Hood showed up. Maybe she could point me toward a proper road.* Every gnarled trunk looked like a werewolf or ogre. Branches grabbed at my hair as if monsters were collecting scalps. *Gee, where are all the nifty helpful talkin' trees when a girl needs one?* After a while I had to collect myself, meditate, and banish those silly fears. Jasper telling his usual run of jokes helped.

Now that I didn't have to run, I tried to watch where I was going. It wouldn't do to twist an ankle or fall down an old well. I also kept my eyes peeled for any kind of path. Getting out of this weedy mess and finding my bearings would be a whole lot easier that way. But I found nothing except thicker trees and steeper hills. So monotonous did all that vegetation get that I started to hope for a murderous beast or two to liven things up, which just goes to show you how bizarre my life had become, that such a thought didn't even scare me anymore. And when I actually heard something stalking me, all I thought was *well, you oughta be more careful what you wish for.*

Whatever it was, it didn't try to be sneaky. Its great heavy feet stomped through the underbrush like a troll, kicking up leaves and snapping twigs. I could tell from the way it plowed through everything in its path that it had lots of muscle, that it had a dense body. Every few seconds it'd stop to scent me. Great powerful snorts rent the night. A predator of some kind. *Sha'ira said them Bacchantes is just crazy women, though. This must be somethin' else. Maybe Dionysus himself, lookin' to drive me outta my mind, too.* I grabbed the shield from my back and willed Morphageus into its true form, calming its runes so they wouldn't give me away. A touch at my neck relieved me. The Stone stayed warm. No black magick. Maybe I could take this beastie, then. Tired of running from shadows, I tucked myself behind a tree to wait for my stalker.

Only two minutes later it came into sight, sort of. Though I couldn't spot it directly, I spied its movement. Bushes and tall grass danced as the snuffling creature followed my trail. It must've been keeping itself low, to better smell my tracks and to keep out of sight. Well, two could play that game. I dropped down onto all fours, reaching my Stone-senses out to help get the drop on it. Circling around in a big loop to confuse its nose, I came up behind the monster. This burly killer might be an unholy demon from the Obverse, for all I knew, but I'd had as much cowardly fleeing I could handle for one night. Time to scare somebody else for a change.

I leaped at the behemoth, great magick blade raised high above my head. For effect and to buck up my spirits I shrieked like all the Furies of Hades. In the near total-silence of the forest I almost scared myself with the noise. There was no doubt that it terrified my foe. His ear-busting howl gave me proof of that.

His howl? Wait a minute...

At the last second I turned my sword aside. It bit into turf instead of my intended target. The droopy-eared hound stood frozen as I missed it by a whisker. Alarmed yowling nearly deafened me. I felt my mouth hang open in disbelief that I'd almost bisected the dog I'd worked so hard to save. But that amazement was nothing compared to the surprise I felt when the pooch's wailing turned into something completely different.

"Mon Dieu!" he cried. "Watch where you are waving that thing! I only have the one tail, child."

Yep, the dog spoke actual words, clear as day. In a snooty Gaullic accent, no less.

"Well, how the heck was I supposed to know it was you?" I snapped. "I figured it was—"

I sputtered to a stop as the talking mutt business sunk in.

"Ooh, this'll be fun," Jasper giggled. The talking sword business didn't faze me anymore.

"Close your cake-hole before a moth flies in it," suggested the dog.

"You're talkin'," I informed him.

"So are you. Do you see me staring at you as if you are a side-show exhibit? And you Americans say we Parisians are rude."

"I should sell tickets," Jasper announced with a laugh. "In this corner, weighing in at seventy-five pounds, the Dogue de Gaulle!"

"You could o' mentioned before that you could talk," I grumbled. "Saved me all that trouble makin' hand signals and such."

"And in this corner, defending her title of World's Grumpiest Kid—"

"Jasper, shut up!" I hollered.

One of the hound's eyebrows eased up. He managed to look up at me and down on me at the same time. "I beg your pardon? My name is not Jasper." I got the impression he'd rather have died first.

"I wasn't talkin' to you. I was..." With a wave of a hand I let my words trail off. Explaining Jasper would be too complicated. "What **are** you called, anyhow? You're obviously from Gaulle, so I'm bettin' that Rover, Fido, or Rex ain't likely."

Plopping his butt down and sitting up as tall as he could get, snoot aimed at the sky, the dog said with patrician pride, "I am Jean-Luc D'Arcy Evremonde, Le Duc du Ponteau!"

Now I raised an eyebrow and crossed my arms. "You're kiddin', right?"

The haughty hound sniffed. "Do I look like I am kidding?"

"He looks like he was designed by a committee, if you ask me," Jasper snickered.

I had to agree with that. "Okay, Duke it is. That's a good doggy name."

Our Parisian Pooch nearly choked. "You will address me as Your Grace!"

"I'll address you 'Special Delivery' and have you shipped to Merchantry headquarters if you don't get down off yer high horse."

Duke shook his big head. Those impressive ears slapped one another like somebody pounding slippers together. "Why, I ask myself, why did we bother to win your revolution for you peasants? My poor cousin Lafayette, how ashamed he would be now."

That got my attention. I shaped the sword back into a cup. "You're tellin' me you're related to the Marquis de Lafayette?

THE Lafayette?"

"Oui, THE Lafayette. Did I stutter?"

"I love this dog!" Jasper said. "He followed us home, mom. Can we keep him?"

I shoved that annoying voice to the back of my head. "It's just that you're a...you know."

"A hound? How well I do know." The dog scratched at his neck with a rear foot. "But, of course, I was not always so."

Aha. Figures. He's like Romulus, only in reverse. Or Roberta and Ernie, but of a different species. Awful lotta shape-shiftin' goin' around these days. I'm startin' to feel left out.

Jasper returned. "If it'll make you feel any better, I can turn you into a red-furred beaver again."

"No, I'm fine the way I am," I said in my thoughts. "Thanks anyway."

"Have it your way. Just tryin' to help."

I spoke to the mutt. "So you used to be human, like me?"

He rolled his big brown eyes. "A human, yes, but not like you. I was...am, an aristocrat of Gaulle, master of men, arbiter of taste for my entire generation. Women sighed when my wig and I entered a parlor. Many a man swooned at sight of my cravat."

A fop, sounds like. Probably best not to mention that. "What happened then, uh, Yer Grace? Some Merchantry mage take offense at yer manner? Toss a spell and turn you into a...what are you, exactly?"

"I shouldn't expect a freckled barbarian philistine such as yourself to recognize my pedigree." He stood and posed, legs spread fore and aft, nose lifted, tail curled forward over his long back. "You are looking at a most splendid example of the noble basset hound."

Huh? "A basket hound? Who'd name a breed that?"

"Open your ears, funny-looking child! Not basket. A **basset** hound. Meaning low to the ground."

"That's accurate enough, I guess. This sorta dog is common in Gaulle?"

"Among the higher orders, yes. Lafayette gave some to your General Washington, you know. Like my famous cousin, I owned several, before my tragic fall."

A scene from Shakespeare's *A Midsummer Night's Dream* came to mind. Mr. Ford brought in a troupe all the way from the Sceptr'd Isle to play it. *"My hounds are bred out of the Spartan kind. Their heads are hung with ears that sweep away the morning dew...slow in pursuit, but matched in mouth like bells."*

Though I dearly wanted to hear about how such a snooty specimen ended up as a saggy, baggy, floppy, sloppy, drooly beast, and how he came to be in medieval Iberion, we'd spent enough time jawing out in the open. No telling how many eyes and ears we'd attracted. My Stone-senses started to warn me that we weren't alone in these woods. We needed to scrounge up a good hiding place for the night. Someplace both invisible and protected. After taking a look and listen to satisfy myself that nobody was close by, I sent the Duke to scout for a secure spot. Uppity as he was, he didn't argue. His nose dropped to the ground and off he went. Not two minutes later he let out a low woof and I went to him.

An old tree had fallen over and rolled downhill. A big rock had stopped it, creating a sort of cave. *Perfect.* I tossed the rucksack in, rolled after it, and motioned for the hound to follow. He submitted to a few head pats and waited with admirable patience for me to open the magick bag. *When he ain't talkin' in that irritatin' voice and bein' all upper-crusty, he's an okay doggie.* We wriggled into it, fastened it closed behind us, and lay down together on a soft pile of blankets. As if we'd planned it, we both sighed together. It'd been a long, scary, tiring night. *This bein' at the point of horrible death all the time sure does wear a body out.* Before I knew it I was dead asleep.

Of course my strange dream returned. The disturbing one with Tommy, the demons, and those Shakespeare ravens. I'd expected it to. What I'd been hoping for, though, was a vision sent by Sha'ira and her soul-pen. I couldn't understand why she hadn't got hold of me that way yet. Shoot, she could send them as daydreams. She didn't need to wait till I was asleep. *Must be a powerful lotta trouble on the Kiss, then. Maybe she's spendin' all of her time fightin' and don't have a chance to prepare her rituals. Sendin' a dream's not a simple chore, like strollin' down to the local telegraph office. You need time and fire and blood.*

After that I just had normal dreams. You know what I mean: runnin' away from monsters in slow motion, flyin' over canyons, goin' over endless waterfalls over and over and...

I yanked myself awake. When you start seeing any kind of

non-stop water in a dream, it's time to listen to nature's call. Rubbing the sleep from my eyes, I opened the sack, blinking at the bright morning sun. Even though we were under the fallen tree and a lush canopy of green blocked a lot of the daylight, one beam managed to poke me right in my freckly face. The Duke still snored beside me, speckled belly in the air again. With a smile I let him be and hauled myself out.

Lusitania didn't seem scary at all with birds chirping and squirrels scampering through the treetops. Its dawn air smelled fresh, a darn sight better than Castle Carrasco. *Of course, not runnin' fer your life perks up your mood somethin' considerable.* I did my business, then returned to the sack. Shucking the Rom rags and going back to my good old overalls and straw hat, I felt plenty fine. All rested and un-terrified. Maybe I'd get through this day without any chases, battles, black magick, or creepiness. Wouldn't that be something to write home about?

Thinking of home sent a cloud across my sunny mood. No word from Ma or Roberta or anybody. Where were they all? I was lost in a strange and dangerous country, not knowing a soul. All I had was a talking sword and a talking hound, each with limited social skills. In maybe a week and a half time would run out for Tommy in his Scepter'd Isle dungeon. There was precious little time left and I hadn't much chance of getting there to spring him. And even if I could make it to London before the moon turned, how on earth did I expect to force my way into and out of Merchantry House, the most magick-fortified spot in the world?

It's enough to make you want to just jump in a river and end it all.

So I did just that. Well, the jumping in the river part, anyway. The 'ending it all' I figured on leaving to fate.

It turned out that we were only a hundred yards from a shallow creek. Though no Potomac, it proved deep enough to keep me wet and Jasper happy. I could feel his magick charge returning. Days of grime soaked off my skin. That filled me with cozy bliss.

Until the unearthly screaming started.

Talos discovered something even more
formidable than a baby Amazon's sword.
Half a bushel of fresh manure, straight from the horse…
and straight into his face.

25 / Two Rescues

Jasper ran through every pirate-approved cuss word he knew. "How come somebody's always interferin' with my jollies?" he wanted to know. "You're a jinx, you know that?" He was a simple metal band on my wrist, to make swimming easier without having to leave him on shore.

I ducked as low in the water as I could. "Funny, I was just thinkin' the same thing about a magick sword I know."

The screaming must've been farther away than I'd first thought, because I didn't see anybody or hear movement nearby. *Nope, not a soul in sight.* But me being submerged neck-deep in a creek with hills in all directions meant that whoever it was might only be a couple hundred yards off. I wouldn't see them until they got right on top of me. Not getting anywhere with eyes or ears, I tried smell. Nothing much. Just mud and bird poop. Since taste probably wasn't going to aid me a whole lot, that left feel. Using the boost the Stone gave to all my senses, I stretched out a wet hand to touch the mossy bank. Vibrations tingled up my arm.

Horses. Several of them. And one small person on foot. Heading straight for the creek, of course.

Time fer Jasper's skinny-dip to end. Gotta get outta here in case I need to use him. Water'll probably play heck with the magic.

I splashed back to where my clothes and towel lay. Quick as I could I dried off and stuck one foot into my drawers. Believe me, nothing makes you feel more exposed than being naked as a jaybird while an unknown threat rumbles toward you. Jasper cackling and pointing out that I had freckles **all** over didn't help, either. Despite his distracting commentary, I got my overalls, shirt, and hat on, tucked the towel under one arm, and lit out for my rucksack.

The Duke still snored and slobbered where I'd left him. Poking him did no good. Neither did shaking him. *Some guard dog you are.* I jammed a strip of salt pork under his nose and said, "Breakfast time!" He woofed and shot straight in the air as if he'd sat on a thumbtack. That meaty bit got snarfed down his gullet before his paws returned to earth. Then I got an expectant look.

"What?" I asked.

"That is the hors d'oeuvre," he complained in his Parisian voice, "but where is the entrée?"

Having dumped my burden, chewing on bacon myself to charge up Jasper some more, I already had wormed my way back out of the sack. "Look, Your Majesty—"

"No, no, no," he corrected, following me out, "that is only for the King. You shall call me merely 'Your Grace', if you please."

"It don't please me one little bit, to tell you the truth." I closed the pack and slung it across my shoulders. Now I could hear the steady thunder of hooves, not just feel them. "You can stay and chow down if you want, but a bunch of fellers on horses is about to crest that there hill. From the sound of the poor wretch they's chasin', you don't wanna get in their way. I sure don't. So move your fuzzy backside."

My keen logic persuaded him. Or maybe it was the sight of three mounted men with short spears and nets, galloping into view across the creek. We hunkered down beneath the fallen tree to see who we might be dealing with. I hoped it'd turn out to be just hunters. Somehow, though, I knew that my life could never turn out to be so simple. One look confirmed my worries. Oh, the riders were on a hunt, all right. But they didn't have any interest in your standard prey.

A girl about my age raced before them, darting in between trees, rocks, and thorn bushes to hinder their chase.

She had flowing strawberry-blonde hair and pale skin, which made her look a teeny bit like me. And she was barefoot, too. No freckles, though. Plus, she looked a lot smaller than yours truly. I'm plenty tall and husky for a twelve year-old gal. *Okay, so she don't look much like me at all. Fer starters, she looks like a girl.* The kid had on a peach-colored sleeveless linen gown, about knee-length, belted at the middle. Branches and prickles had sliced her up something fierce. Red welts and cuts covered her, as if she'd been lashed. Her gait had a limp in it, maybe from an ankle twist. Tears ran down her cheeks. All-in-all, she didn't look like she'd last much longer.

Those bearded, bareback riders sure thought so. With whoops of impending victory they urged their steeds on, spreading out to flank her now that they'd arrived at the clearing near the water. The girl sped up as she headed downhill, but so did the hunters. From what I could tell she planned to rush across a log to my right and put the creek between her and her pursuers. At five feet deep and thirty feet across, the stream would slow down the horses some and give her a chance to get over the next hill, or maybe lose them altogether.

But first she'd have to elude those nets. Both flanking riders were nearly upon her. The sneering fellow on her left whipped his mesh forward. It was weighted with lead at the corners. As if she sensed it, the panting girl dropped and rolled. His throw missed high. *She must have eyes in the back of her head. Heck, for all I know, that might be true in Lusitania.* For a moment I thought she'd get trampled, but the huge horse leapt over her before its owner could get his wits about him. Popping up, she sprinted in the opposite direction, straight at the third rider, the one lagging behind. Surprised, he had no chance to maneuver his spear across his horse's neck. In an eye-blink she'd got past him, running back uphill. All three hunters reined in their sweating mounts hard, yanking their heads around to change direction.

Their target guessed that they'd do so. As they got halfway turned, all their momentum gone, she spun and dashed back downhill again. Like a Minie ball she shot through their formation, so quick that the right-hand man's net fell far behind her. Light as a pixie, she hopped up onto the log bridge at full speed, head down, arms pumping like locomotive pistons. By the time the hunters got their own steam back up and could slog through the creek, she'd be long gone. *That's it. She beat 'em. Good for you, kid!*

Too bad for her, Lady Luck had other ideas. The log had been there a long time. Its bark, dry and loose, shredded beneath her feet and a huge hunk slid off. Her footing gone, the young girl yelped and fell hard. With a loud thunk her pretty noggin hit the log on the way down. Out cold, she crashed into the water, limp as the proverbial rag doll. Floating there like a hunk of pinkish driftwood, she'd drown in no time.

The three men cried out in victory and urged their horses forward to claim their prize. I only had maybe ten or fifteen seconds to act. With a thought to Jasper I burst out of my hidey-hole, telling the Duke to stay put. By the time I reached the log, coming at the hunters from their left, unnoticed, the motionless girl's head was starting to go under. I jabbed Morphageus into the soft ground of the bank with all of my might. It had the form of an anchor with a pulley attached. A steel cable ran through it and around my waist. Its other end stayed in my fist. Not caring if the bad guys saw me now, I plunged into the water. They hollered when they spotted me and sped up their horses.

I snatched up the sputtering kid, half-awake now, around her narrow waist. She weighed next to nothing. Tossing her over my shoulder like a bag of grain, I hauled away on the loose end of the cable. With the pulley's help and the Stone's strength we got back to the shore in the time it takes to swallow twice. By the time the trio of riders got to the other bank, I'd changed Morphageus into a Roman shield, hung it across my back, scooped up the girl, and was huffing my way up the hill to the waiting hound.

Behind me I heard the first horse go into the water. Wading across would be slow work, but it wouldn't take them forever. We weren't out of the woods yet, as they say. The girl had got enough of her senses back to use her own legs. Though she must've been plenty confused, not to mention scared and exhausted, she didn't get the vapors and faint. Didn't ask a bunch of fool questions, neither. She clung to me for support but jogged under her own power. When we'd made it to the fallen tree I whistled for the hound to follow and kept on slogging up the hill. I had no idea if safety lay there or merely a squadron of net-slinging cavalry, but we didn't have any other swell choices.

As we got to more level ground I risked a look behind us. All three horsemen had crossed the stream. Retrieved nets in hand, they bellowed at us in frustrated rage. Mud kicked up behind their steeds' hooves. The chase was still on, no doubt about it. I sighed and picked up our pace.

"So, how do you like your Europan vacation?" Jasper asked. It annoyed me that no matter how winded I got, he always managed to chatter away like some crazed monkey.

"Remind me to give my bookin' agent a piece of my mind

when we get home," I answered with a thought. A glance to my right showed me that the girl could stand without help, though she didn't have the energy for much more than a stagger. It amazed me that such a frail-seeming kid could have lasted as long as she had against trained hunters. I told Jasper I needed some translation juice.

"Come on," I said to her, " we can't quit just yet. They're gainin' on us. Is there a road hereabouts, or someplace to hide where they can't find us?"

"No road," she told me, her voice barely a child's breath. "Staying on the road would have been death. They'll ride you down in an instant that way."

"A cave, then? Or a house we can defend? Even a hole in the ground?"

"There is nothing. I took to the Wilds to slow down their horses in the thickets. It did not work for long." She sagged, all done in. "I am finished."

"Well, I ain't. I'll fight 'em till they quit. I swear I will."

The strange girl shook her head and dropped to her scuffed knees. "You are strong, whoever you are. But even if you were a warrior and not a child like me, it would do you no good. Please leave me. They do not want you." Her accent sounded something like Iberion, but with warmer vowels and fuzzier consonants. Why she had any accent at all was beyond me. Apparently Jasper's translation magick turned words into Britannic, but gave them a dialect sound so the hearer could tell what language was being spoken.

I tried to get her back onto her feet, but it was no good. She had nothing left and her legs turned to rubber as soon as she tried to use them. The chase must've been going on for a good long while before I'd seen her. While the Duke licked her face and tried to comfort her, I turned to make my stand. Morphageus flowed into its natural black recurved sword shape. I took a threatening stance that Sha'ira had taught me, blade high above my head, and tried to look as intimidating as a wet girl could manage.

That must not have been much, because all I got was laughter when the hunters arrived. They stopped their blown horses in a circle around us. The hill-climbing and other chase activities had worn the animals out, too. One of the men slid off of the bare back of his mount and landed right in front of me, just out of my reach. His clothes resembled those of the girl I guarded, except his was dyed dark blue. Sandals laced up nearly to the knee covered his feet. He held his spear lightly, unconcerned about my weapon. *I wonder if he'd be so sure of himself if he knew I can change it into a ten-foot medieval halberd with flame for a blade? Or into a giant fist that can squash him like a bug?* Tempting as those ideas were, I chose to wait and see what might happen. If I could get them to talk before they attacked, maybe I'd learn something about the situation.

"Look at the mighty warrior," he said to his friend. Everybody laughed again.

"An Amazon, perhaps," one of the other men suggested.

"A baby Amazon, possibly," sneered the third one.

The fellow on the ground cocked his head to look me over. "Yet a new-hatched adder can still sting."

I adopted the local accent, a trick Jasper's spell permitted me if I gave it some effort. "You are the wisest of the three," I nodded, keeping a wary eye on the mounted pair.

He shrugged. "In the land of the blind, the one-eyed man is king."

That earned him hoots from his friends. I took advantage of that. "They do not agree. I wonder that you keep company with such dullards. I—"

His spear licked out at me, testing my reflexes. He pulled only half of it back. The rest lay on the ground where Morphageus left it. *There's your answer, mister. Try that again and it'll be your arm lyin' in the dirt between us.*

Examining the remains of his lance, he raised an eyebrow. "Such speed! Perhaps your Amazon joke is not so funny now, eh, Pelias?"

"One oddly-dressed girl can cow you?" said the mounted man who'd first spoke of the warrior tribe. I noticed that he looked quite a bit like the fellow standing near me. Brothers, maybe.

"Let me have a go at her," chuckled the other rider, the one with the permanent haughty look on his ugly face. He was tall, muscled, and so tanned by the sun that he seemed made of weathered bronze. Dismounting, he hefted his net and eased up behind me. "When I've caught her, and taught her to respect her elders, I think I'll wear that straw hat as a trophy. It will keep this summer sun off nicely."

Mr. Half-Spear waved him forward and took a step back. *Awfully chivalrous of you, not to rush me together. But ain't nobody gettin' this hat.*

"You offer me battle, sir," I said to the new opponent. "Do offer me your name as well?"

"Talos." The net began to swing back and forth. "Remember it when you are a slave in my home, shoveling my horse's manure. And what does your mama call you?"

Tempting as it was to say 'Nobody', I had a better idea. "She named me Creusa." In a book of mythology I'd read that Creusa had wrestled a lion that had attacked her sheep. She'd impressed even the god Apollo. *Maybe that'll impress this guy, too.*

"Aw, you're mommy's little princess," Talos mocked. I hadn't known what the name literally meant. "Never had one of those for a slave. This is an occasion."

As the last word left his lips he tossed the net at me. It spread out wide like a great hand, eager to snatch at me. I'd dropped my sword tip low and to the rear, so it wouldn't snag on the mesh when he made his move. Sliding with Stone-aided speed to my right, I sliced the net in two with a flashy uppercut. Nothing made by the hand of man could withstand Morphageus, according to Jasper.

"By all the gods!" Talos cried.

I came within an inch of claiming I was at least a demi-goddess. But that might open a whole new Pandora's Box of unforeseen problems, so I passed. For all I knew, the actual Pandora's Box might be sitting on somebody's shelf hereabouts.

"With all respect, sir," I said, returning to my high guard, "I am eager to be no man's slave."

Saucy as I tried to sound, inside my pulse threatened to blow my head off. Pelias hopped down from the horse and hefted his own net and spear. Three armed men, well-trained, alert and on their home ground, wanted to take me down and get to my defenseless foundling friend. Despite a little fight training from Sha'ira and Pitcairn, and even with the help of the Stone, this looked to be a tall order. If they all went for me at once, which was clearly what they now planned, I didn't have much of a chance. Fear saps the muscles and softens the mind, Sha'ira had told me. While my opponents prepared for a final assault, I silently chanted the words of meditation she'd taught me. Almost like a spell of peace, they worked to slow my heart and breathing, almost to slow time itself.

While in this state I felt, as much as I saw, Talos slide around so he stood directly behind me. Pelias danced at my right front. The fellow whose spear I'd ruined hefted its remnant to my left. A slew of possibilities, various combinations of attack-defense-counterattack, filled my mind. As they started to move in on me I chose the most likely pattern that would protect me, keep the girl safe, and do the least damage to the three men. *That's supposin' I don't get pin-cushioned on the first pass, of course.*

As it turned out, I didn't have to do any of it. A huge shadow blotted out the scorching Lusitanian sun. I'd moved so that two of the three men would have it in their eyes. A strange pulsing wind buffeted me from behind. Pelias' eyes grew wide and he ran away from me like I had smallpox. Made of sterner stuff, his maybe-brother only retreated a few paces, muttering to his gods to protect him. Turning with a frown, I saw that Talos had done likewise and was raising his spear at a great winged form that hovered directly above him. Just as I recognized the new arrival Talos discovered something even more formidable than a baby Amazon's sword.

Half a bushel of fresh manure, straight from the horse...and straight into his face.

A Rebel yell split the air. Tyrell and Alcibiades had come to my rescue.

"She's awful cute. A comely lass, as they say in the romances."
"Down, you! I got enough to worry about
without an overheated boy in my noggin."
I really didn't want to consider what he might turn himself
into while in the throes of infatuation for this girl.
That don't bear thinkin' about.

26 / What Sha'ira Didn't Mention

"By all the gods! Pegasus!" blurbled Talos through his faceful of dung. "Bellerophon and the mighty Pegasus!"

I had to admit, if you were looking into the sun and saw a tall strapping fellow on a winged horse, that'd be your first reaction, especially if you were of the Hellenic persuasion. Of course, Al sported a golden coat instead of a white one, but that's the kind of detail you'd likely overlook with clumps of poop dripping into your eyes. Talos paid no attention to the manure. He didn't even try to wipe it off. No, he just gazed up with a crooked neck, mouth open, babbling 'Pegasus' over and over.

Okay, if that's what he believes, I'll git some use outta it.

"Yes, Pegasus!" I cried, waving Morphageus over my head like Joan of Arc in some overdone stage production. "You laughed, called me a baby Amazon. Well, here is the vanquisher of Amazons himself, astride the mount of the Muses, that spawn-steed of Poseidon and Medusa."

Jasper choked on my pretensions. "Whoa, if you'll pardon the expression! Somebody needs a good editor."

"I'd appreciate a little support here," I thought back to him. "Don't see you doin' much to improve the situation."

"Oh, sure. Sneer at the magick sword. I'm only tryin' to alleviate the worst excesses of your bombastic rhetoric."

"Look who's talkin'. And I'm not bein' bombastic. I'm embracin' the patois of the local inhabitants."

"Patois? Awful Gaullic of you, little girl. Where'd you read that?"

"Nowheres. Heard a theatre critic spout it at intermission at Ford's once. Seemed to mightily impress the snooty crowd he was with."

Our argument over orthography, a word I'd looked up when I'd seen it in Shakespeare's *Much Ado About Nothing*, got interrupted by the return of Talos' friends. Now that their feet had outrun their fear, they'd slunk back to hurl taunts at Talos and spears at 'Pegasus'. Pelias roared, maybe more at his own cowardice than at his new enemy. His sturdy arm sent the lance streaking toward Alcibiades. *Guess Pelias don't have as much respect for his gods as Talos does.*

And Al had even less respect for the Hellene's spear. With a jaw-snap like an alligator the Norn horse picked the shaft out of the air. It broke in two with a sharp crack as he bit down. The pieces fell to earth on either side of the startled Talos, who backpedaled toward his friends. They shook him hard to wake him from his amazement. Blinking, he looked around, saw where he was, and pulled a short sword from a baldrick hanging on his horse's neck.

With nobody below him now, Tyrell guided the winged beast down to earth next to me. Al tucked the wings along his flanks, hiding his rider's legs. Normally he'd make his own limbs—the feathery ones, anyhow—vanish, but with three angry armed men about to start a scrap he wanted to be ready for action. I gave his yellow-maned neck a big hug and rubbed his velvety nose. Like always, the great golden horse snuffled me all over, hunting for apples or sugar. Finding nothing, he snorted in disgust and glared at me.

"Hey, sorry!" I said with a shrug. "Didn't know you'd be droppin' in on me. Make an appointment next time."

Something small and furry swung on my ear. I reached up and plucked Ernie like a ripe peach. He stood in my hand, wearing the silly piratical tricorn hat Ma had made for him and carrying his knitting needle lance. Try as he might, he couldn't look fierce. Even squinting up at me and scowling didn't do the trick. Maybe it was his plump little belly hanging out, making him resemble a furry overstuffed toy.

"Appointment?" he growled in his Britannic accent. "We needs to see a bloomin' secretary to save yer arse now?"

"I'll see if I can pencil you in," said Jasper, turning into a notebook and adopting an upper-class sneer. That nobody could hear him but me didn't matter to him. "Thursday looks good, if you don't mind that we're repainting the front parlor."

He kept going, but I spoke over him to Ernie, aloud. "Hey, my backside was in good hands."

The notebook became a big cartoony exclamation point. "Ooh, bad choice of words," chuckled Jasper.

Tyrell agreed. "Yes, ma'am, and those hands were holding it nice and still so it'd be easier to hit with a lance." He cocked his behemoth of a pistol, a nine-shot .41 caliber LeMat with a shotgun barrel inside the cylinder. Aiming it at the Lusitanians, who showed signs of getting ready to rush us with net, sword, and spear remnant, he raised his voice to get their full attention. "I'd think twice about that, gents. This here beauty's got three balls apiece for you."

Though they didn't understand him, and had no idea what he held in his hand, that commanding tone froze their advance. *Smart decision, gents. Tyrell's fought demons. You ain't likely to intimidate him none.* Alcibiades rearing up and spreading his wings probably helped some, too. Those fellows weren't having the kind of day they'd expected. It'd gone from an easy hunt of a near-defenseless girl to another kid holding them at bay to having one of their fearsome myths drop on top of them. Stabbing his busted weapon into the hard dry ground, the nameless leader raised both hands in peace.

"Perhaps we should all start afresh," he said. "We have no quarrel with this warrior. Though he does not ride the true Pegasus, his mount is sired by some god. There can be no other explanation. Who are you, child, and how may we know your ally? Your garments proclaim that you are strangers to Lusitania."

By Tyrell's frown I could tell that he had no translation spell or magick talky charm or whatever you'd figure Redeemers ought to have. The words made no impression on him. After explaining what had been said, I replied to the hunter. "My true name is Callisto, daughter of Nisos. The god-horse is Xanthippus. His rider is called Cadmus and is my eldest brother."

Tyrell lifted an eyebrow at that, but played along. "She speaks truly. Little Callisto was abducted. It has taken me many months to finally find her."

I translated that for the others, then anticipated their natural question. "So long have I been in your land that I have your speech. Cadmus is only just arrived and knows naught but our native tongue. I will explain his words to you, and yours to him."

"You are welcome, then," said the leader of the trio. "I am Acastus. This one, who suffered such indignity from Xanthippus, is called Talos. And here is my own brother, Pelias." He nodded at the remains of his weapon. "It would seem that he and I are now bound by more than blood. You have shattered both our spears in a like manner. Perhaps the horse is not alone in being of Olympian parentage."

That's a good idea. Glad you thought of it, buster. Don't hurt to have an advantage. "Wisdom lives in the mouth of Acastus. There is a rumor that my true father is not Nisos, but Apollo, that he came unto my mother from a cloud, as a beam of springtime light. Soon she quickened and I entered the world with hair the color of the setting sun."

"Oh, brother," Jasper said, "those road-apples from

Alcibiades ain't the only pile of manure around here. We're gonna need hip boots if you tell any more stretchers."

That seemed to relax Acastus and his brother. "If true, it would explain much," the sun-baked Lusitanian muttered. "No ordinary girl could best either of us, let alone both." *Easier on their feelin's to lose to a god, I suppose. I won't bust yer bubble, then.*

"As I say, it is only a rumor. My mother would never confirm or deny it. Perhaps she did not know the full truth, herself." I nodded at the girl they'd been chasing. "Since we speak of truth, might you speak with candor as to why you hunt this child. She does seem an ordinary girl. Hardly fitting sport for strong men such as yourselves."

"Your eyes deceive you," Pelias broke in. "Or, rather, her craft deceives your eyes. This is no innocent maiden."

Talos agreed. "A monster, she is."

I gazed down at the kid, shivering on her knees as she clung to Duke. Her pale skin covered in filth and gashes, hair tangled and dress torn, she looked anything but horrifying. "A monster? Does she overpower your soul with her ferocious cuteness?"

Acastus glowered at my mockery. "Laughter will not protect you if she takes on her true form."

"She slew four of my men as they worked in the vineyard," Pelias assured me. "Burned them alive, then ate their flesh."

"You saw this?" I asked, squinting and trying to imagine any possible way for the pale girl to overwhelm a ladybug, let alone several men. "With your own eyes?"

"Those who see it die," answered Talos, staring at his prey as if she was an angry adder.

Tyrell made a *pthht* sound with his lips. "Awful convenient for you all, isn't it? No one can gainsay you."

I translated his comment for the accusers, as I'd been doing all along. They shrugged and stared at their sandaled feet. "She came from the dread underworld, Tartarus, from a fiery vent in the earth," Acastus claimed. "At certain times her form alters, and then the blood-lust takes hold. Many have said so."

"Many have said so?" Tyrell echoed. "But I thought you said that all who see it are killed?"

That made me wonder. "At certain times, you say? What do you mean? At midnight, or during an eclipse? Is there a pattern?"

I small hand snaked around my leg. The kid on the ground looked up at me with huge blue eyes and a quivering lip. Her pointed jaw and slightly-protruding top teeth made her look like an adorable little goat. "They lie!" she cried, with an accent that I now noticed sounded sort of Lusitanian, but with an undertone of something more rumbly. She shook that red-blonde lion's mane and gave the men a stare that could've curdled milk. "They fear what they do not understand and would rather slay a stranger than give heed to her warnings."

Okay, now this is gettin' complicated. "What warnings?" I asked.

"Maybe she's been tellin' 'em suitors should try bringin' her flowers instead of spears," Jasper suggested.

"You think this is that simple?" I asked him in my thoughts. "Just some barbaric courtin'?"

"Could be. She's awful cute. A comely lass, as they say in the romances."

"Down, you! I got enough to worry about without an overheated boy in my noggin." I really didn't want to consider what he might turn himself into while in the throes of infatuation for this girl. *That don't bear thinkin' about.*

She struggled to her feet. I had to hold her up when she started to wobble. The knot on her head from where she'd whacked into the log was the size of a hen's egg. "I have a godly gift," she said. "Or a curse. The knife cuts both ways."

"As do her claws!" Talos hissed, knuckles whitening on his sword hilt. He edged forward, shoulders tense.

I pointed Morphageus at him. "Just simmer down, buster," I warned him, forgetting my role for a second. My strange words seemed to give him more pause than the weapon did. Taking a breath, I translated for Tyrell and got back into character.

"What is this gift?" the Rebel cavalryman wanted to know. "And why do these men fear it so much?"

"I have a gift of prophecy," she told us, as if confessing to being a plague carrier. "It is, alas, very limited. I can only foretell disasters. Storms, shipwrecks, earthquakes, epidemics."

"She does not foretell them!" Pelias blurted out. "She causes them."

"Not so," the girl insisted in a pained voice. "My mother was a priestess of Poseidon. The power flows from him." She gave me that imploring look again. "A fit comes upon me and my eyes go dark. People say I speak what doom shall come, in a strange tongue."

Acastus pulled his shattered spear from the ground. "Then the monster comes, the beast that cannot be slain."

Talos drew new courage from his leader's re-arming himself. "And by the next moonrise, the prophecy comes to pass. Sailors perish on the wine-dark sea. Children and their mothers are swallowed up by steaming chasms in the earth. Temples are shaken into crumbs of marble."

"Yet you all admit that none has actually seen the passion come upon her," Tyrell pointed out. "Nor laid eyes on this monster you claim she turns into."

I turned his words into Lusitanian for them, adding my own two cents worth. "This sounds to me as if you are believing rumors and lashing out in blind panic. You would thrash your own servant girls for behaving thus." *I could get used to this fancy manner of talkin'. Mr. Ford's gonna be mighty impressed when me and Tommy get home...knock on wood.*

"Should we discount so much testimony, from so many of our friends and allies?" Acastus wanted to know. "Pillars of smoke must mean a fire is at hand." But I could see him starting to waver already. His fellow hunters, too. Despite their awful behavior toward the poor girl they'd nearly butchered, these weren't evil men at heart.

"I do not doubt that tragedies have struck your people," I said, lowering Morphageus. Then I gave Tyrell a look and he holstered his pistol. "But you are wise enough to know that a fearful drop in one ear becomes a great wave of terror soon after. People are too quick to think, and say, the worst when they are afraid. It is up to men of wisdom and vision such as yourselves to be the breakwater."

They all sagged at my words, then stood tall again as they made the collective decision to be what I had hoped they could, the dependable fathers and counselors of their city. Acastus and Pelias looked at one another, nodded as if speaking by wireless telegraph, and let their points droop. Talos, always the follower, did the same with his bronze sword. Beside me I felt the girl let out a long-held breath. She smooched the Duke on his big wet snoot.

Pelias said, "So much coolness of brain in one so young. Perhaps Athena is at work here."

"Her owl, at least," Ernie muttered so only I could here. He clung to the back of my neck, unseen by the Lusitanians.

"What's that supposed to mean?" I asked, just as quiet.

"You'll see. If our luck holds."

As if Dame Fortune watched our every move, a trumpet blast from some kind of large animal horn shook the air around us. Two other calls answered it, from different directions. High-pitched cackles commenced, out of dozens of feminine throats. Twigs cracked as scores of bodies began thrashing through the brush toward our hilltop.

Despite her exhaustion and cracked skull, the fair-skinned girl took off running like a deer fleeing Diana's pack. "Run, fools!

They've surprised us!"

I'd learned in my short time as Stone Warden that hesitating when told to run for your life was a sure way to end up as a notch on some icky monster's tally stick. What with all of the Bullies, Shades, demons, and poop monsters, my feet had learned how to scoot all on their own. And that's just what they did. Before I even had time to consider who might be after us, we were all sprinting after the girl. Duke led the way, howling as if the infernal regions had just opened up to spew out the damned. *Sure ain't nothin' wrong with his survival instincts.* Ernie deserted my neck to hop onto the galloping Alcibiades. When Tyrell tried to scoop me up onto the winged stallion I shook my head and shrugged him off.

"No! Hide Al's wings and pretend he's a normal horse. We may need to spring a surprise of our own soon. Keep an eye on our three friends. Make sure they don't change their minds again and grab the kid. I'll stick with her and find out what's up."

"Yes'm," the Reb said with a smile and a finger salute to his kepi.

I discovered that a fairly flat path ran along the top of the ridge. *Woulda been nice to have found this last night.* It made running a darned sight easier and quicker. Catching up with the streaking form of the girl, I asked her between breaths why we were fleeing.

"Bacchantes!" she answered, panting. "Acolytes of the god. Look!"

To my right, lurching through the trees, came a monstrous

regiment of women. Some old-timey guy had written that about politics, but in this case the phrase was dead-accurate. And I mean that literally. Those crazed followers of Dionysus, who slaughtered every living thing they encountered in a frenzy of religious ecstasy, were walking, rotting corpses.

The undead, some writers called them. Zombies was another term I'd heard used.

Jasper spoke in my head with a stuffy too-dry Britannic tone, as if he was noticing a missing shirt button. "Hmm. Looks like Sha'ira forgot to mention that little detail. Frightfully careless of her. You'll have to speak to her about the oversight."

Yeah, maybe I will...if we don't get torn apart in the next two minutes.

The Lusitanians clasped hands with Tyrell,
all of the men congratulating
themselves on their clever tactics.
No credit for the female who thought of it, I notice.
Why ain't I surprised?

27 / Hot Pursuit

I counted around sixty Bacchantes, but there might've been more. It's hard to be precise when you're expecting to have your innards strewn all over creation. Dressed in practically nothing, just tiny bits of goat skin, the living dead women swarmed at us from the right, the front, and the rear. Our only possible escape route lay back downhill, toward the stream. *That's just peachy. Pinned against a natural obstacle by a more clever foe. Makes me feel like every one of Lincoln's generals.*

We were about to play the scariest game of tag ever. And I knew enough tales about them to know that getting caught would have a lot worse consequences than in our schoolyard game. Our pursuers weren't slow and clumsy, like the undead Bully-raised Confederate soldiers we'd faced in Virginia. Whatever magick animated these things had made them a lot quicker than you'd expect the dead to be. Lacking the full agility and speed of a living person, they still posed a real threat. Though we managed to stay just ahead of them, we couldn't outrun the things to where we could totally escape, neither.

The bloodless exposed skin of the Maenads revealed wounds from animal bites, insects, and ordinary decomposition. Many also wore the marks of attacks from weapons, probably as their victims tried to defend themselves, and from one another. Plenty of them had been bitten or clawed by their fellow monsters. *Guess that frenzy that takes 'em ain't too choosy about its victims.* Between swords, spears, their sisters' teeth, and the normal effects of the grave, the Bacchantes' appearance churned the stomach. Rotting, discolored flesh, missing eyes and teeth, foul fluids oozing from places you didn't want to consider, arrows protruding from throats, limbs hacked off by desperate men. It all looked like Halloween at Dante's house, designed by Edgar Allan Poe. On top of that, they kept up that non-stop lunatic giggle. A screech like the Furies had made would've been easier to take. Their insane tittering ice-watered my backbone.

Mostly empty-handed, some of the Maenads carried staves with vines and foliage twined about the top, with a pine cone at the tip. They didn't seem to be weapons, but I couldn't guess what else they might be for. Emblems of rank, maybe, if the creatures had enough mind and organization for that sort of thing. I didn't aim to stick around long enough to find out. We had to scoot. The four horsemen had already got themselves down to the stream and were waiting for us. Me and the strange girl, with Duke dogging our heels, dashed down the steep hill. Only six paces behind us, the quickest of the risen dead followed.

Their horrid laughter reached out for us like the skeletal fingers of the Grim Reaper.

My mind raced as if it was an out-of-control locomotive, trying to come up with a brilliant plan of escape. There were way too many of them to fight, even if that had made sense. Judging by the damage they all had, we'd have to chop them up like so much sausage to get them to stop advancing. Whatever gave them a semblance of life didn't seem to be vulnerable to steel. Morphageus might make an impression, but I sure didn't want to face them with my back to a brook and bet our lives on it. *Maybe they'll stop at the creek's edge. Black magick don't do well with deep or flowin' water. Awful shallow, though. A risky proposition.*

Reaching the others, I waved for them to cross the stream. I boosted the girl up onto Alcibiades and put her in front of Tyrell. All the horses splashes their way to the other side. Duke hopped onto the log bridge, turning to *aarroo* at the rotting fiends who had almost caught up with us. Following the hound onto the fallen tree, I shooed him to the far side. Two Maenads, an old fat one and a scrawny kid, clawed their way onto the log before I got all the way over. Tyrell shouted a warning. The LeMat boomed, scaring the heck out of the Lusitanians. Chunks of bone splattered from the forehead of the heavy monster, but she didn't seem to notice. Still she came on, staggering her way toward me. With a gesture I told Tyrell to save his ammunition for somebody who might actually bleed. Instead, I reformed Morphageus into a medieval voulge, a sort of curved meat-cleaver on a ten-foot pole. We'd seen one at the Smithsonian on a school visit.

Time to see if water's our friend.

Reminding myself that my attacker was already dead and likely couldn't feel anything, I grit my teeth and swung the pole. My blade sheared off her plump left foot at the ankle. It slid into the creek with a plop. She frowned and stared at where her limb had been. Then, like a pine that had just felt the woodsman's axe, she slowly tilted to the side, gaining speed as she went. When her round body hit the water all animation left her and she became a corpse in the usual way, still and limp. *Hey, luck's finally runnin' our way.*

"Speak for yourself, kiddo," Jasper complained. "These things taste like road-killed possum. Yuck!"

I poked at the second Maenad until she lost her balance, flew into the creek, and also died a true death. "Quit yer whinin', you. If we'd stayed up top we'd have been the road-killed ones."

A couple more fiends tried to rush me, with the same results. Then the others stopped to consider other options. They may have been dead, but they weren't completely mindless. At first they looked like they'd just send everybody across the log in hopes I'd get tired or overwhelmed. But the bridge was only three feet thick, and since so much bark had fallen from it the surface was real slippery. For maybe a minute and a half we had us a standoff. I wanted to just run away, but that would've left us right where we'd been before, just one step ahead of disaster.

"Now what, god-child?" Acastus wanted to know. "Shall we

flee?"

"They will just come across this log and maintain pursuit," I said as Callisto. "We need to destroy the bridge first, and quickly."

Talos laughed at my suggestion. "How? Do you have a handy Titan to assist you?"

"We need not turn it into kindling," I told him, "just drag it to this side so that it is useless to the Bacchantes."

Pelias threw up his hands. "Four horses could do that, but we have no rope. These nets are too light for such weight."

"Leave that to me…and, uh, Apollo." Jumping down next to Alcibiades, I told Jasper what I wanted. My skinny-dipping must've worked, because I had the magick left for my purpose. The pole-arm melted into a thick, flat, four-horse harness, shining like quicksilver in the sunshine that filtered through the treetops. Before the undead women could comprehend what we were doing, I'd looped the back end around a thick broken limb of the tree. In no time the horses, led by Al's unearthly Norn power, dragged the ponderous log into the creek and then up onto our bank.

Now the creepy cackling turned into a mix of pathetic moans and bitter screams. Two or three Bacchantes threw themselves into the water in desperate pursuit, only to meet the same fate as the others. The Lusitanians clasped hands with Tyrell, all of the men congratulating themselves on their clever tactics. *No credit for the female who thought of it, I notice. Why ain't I surprised?* They waved at the writhing cluster of horrid women and turned their mounts away from the stream at a walk. After pausing a moment to make sure the creatures weren't going to suddenly sprout wings and come for us after all, I followed, the girl dropping from Al's back and joining me on foot.

"I owe you my life," she said, hugging me close.

I'm not much on hugging strangers, but I squeezed her anyhow. "Shoot, I was just savin' my own hide."

Her mouth curled up at one corner. "You like to pretend. It keeps you safe."

Oh-oh. "Pretend?"

"You wear a mask, like the actors in the springtime dramas. I would wager much that you are not named Callisto. In fact, you are not the offspring of a god, despite your wondrous powers, nor is that man on the winged horse your brother."

I still tried to keep it up. "Your eyes burn through to the soul."

She giggled. "Please speak as you do naturally, not as you believe you ought. It requires less effort, I think."

My new friend had a point. When you're caught in a net, struggling just wears you out. "Shoot, I thought I was doin' good, chatterin' all Lusitanian-like."

"But you were. I do not mean to offend. My gift from Poseidon is to prophesy doom, but I have learned to see into the hearts of others, as all women must do to survive. That requires no god's aid, only submission to our nature."

"You'll get no argument from me there."

"My name is Ino. And yours?"

I hesitated, but not for long. If she was a Merchantry spy, the

Proprietor possessed even more subtlety than I gave him credit for. Checking to make sure that the mounted hunters were too far away to hear, I told her, "Verity."

"Ver-it-ty," she repeated. "And what does it mean?"

"Truth."

Ino considered that, then nodded. "Your mother chose well, I think."

"Well, it sounds better than Ethel or Amaryllis, that's fer sure."

She laughed at that, stooping down to pet the Duke. He generously permitted her to worship him. "Your dog is…unusual. Such big ears. Such giant paws. Do you call him Oedipus, perhaps?"

Now it was my turn to chuckle. In school we'd learned that Oedipus meant 'swollen foot' in Hellene. "Naw. Actually, there's a difference of opinion on that. He claims he's some sort of royalty and that I should use a name as long as your arm. I just call him Duke."

"He does look like royalty. So proud and handsome."

"So drooly and arrogant," Jasper groaned. "And he smells like a pile of dirty socks."

"Thanks," I said in my mind as the hound rolled over for a belly rub from Ino. "I've been goin' crazy tryin' to figure out what he smells like. Old socks is it, exactly."

That mention of scent brought me up short. My other senses, especially hearing, were tingling. *Somethin' ain't right.* I turned to look back toward where we'd left the undead Maenads. Low chanting in a language my spell couldn't translate made its way to us. All four dozen half-decomposed creatures knelt in a circle around a tall tree that looked similar to the one that we'd dragged away. To and fro they swayed, like grass in a breeze. One of their number, the least-rotted and damaged, held her bushy staff horizontally above her with one arm. The other waved in an arc. She aimed her hand at her sisters. As she did so the chanting grew louder and faster. Just when it reached a peak she pounded the butt end of the staff into the ground between her feet. White and gold fountained up from the earth. Far away as I was, my witched nose could still make out the aroma of something that shouldn't have been there.

Milk. Milk and honey, spouting out of the dirt.

"Which reminds me, we ain't had lunch yet," Jasper pointed out.

"What're they doin'?" I asked Ino, pointing at the strange scene.

She squinted. Seeing that far was harder for her. "Summoning the fertile might of Dionysus, with the thyrsus."

"That's the stick she's holdin'?"

"It is. A staff of fennel, topped with a pine cone, decorated with ivy. When they combine their summonings thus they can harness the power of the earth and nature."

Another Maenad, one who'd been barely an adult in life, limped from the circle. She carried a huge bronze cup in her one remaining hand. The other looked like it'd been bitten off by some great beast. Dropping to a knee, she caught the gushing honey-milk mixture as it bubbled up between the staff-wielder's legs. Energy seemed to thrum through the standing creature's body. It made her vibrate as if she clutched live lightning. While the ecstasy held her, the younger Bacchante turned and staggered back to the circled women. One by one they took greedy guzzles of the sweet white drink. No sooner did each swallow her share than the god's fever seized her. With a yelp she'd thrash on her back in the grass, almost as if poisoned. Just when you'd expect her to gag and die, she'd rise up onto her feet again. If you didn't know better you'd think she'd returned to actual life again. But the wounds didn't heal, nor the putrefaction vanish. Then she'd squat beside one of her friends and commence to making that creepy laugh. In about three minutes they'd all drunk their fill. The cup-bearer slurped hers and held the vessel up to the Maenad with the thyrsus. Electric trance gone, she began behaving just like all the others.

Ino gasped. "This is bad. We must leave. Now." She spun and ran off toward the men.

Duke and I followed, me moving backward so I could keep the mob in sight. Good thing I did. That way I managed to see why the undead horrors had so scared Sha'ira. As one they all surged to the tree in the center of their formation. With strength that could only have come from the darkest of magicks they tore at the soil with their bare hands. Dirt flew faster than a battalion of army pioneers could've managed. In less than a minute the chief roots had been exposed. Pulling at them with insane grunts and squeals, the Maenads soon loosened the tree's hold on the earth. Triumphant cries reached me. Pushing on the trunk with their awful hands, the walking dead women tipped it over with a mighty series of cracks and snaps. I felt the ground shake as the tree struck it. Only then did I wake up and understand just what the monsters had done.

They'd bridged the creek again.

"I advise retreat, child," the basset hound at my feet said in his Gaullic voice. "Even Bonaparte would agree, in such a circumstance."

"No argument here," I muttered.

Jasper spoke up. "If it'll make you feel any better, we could call it a Retrograde Advance."

The Maenads roared and started to swarm across the fallen trunk. "Gee, thanks. That makes all the difference. I may sing me a happy tune."

"We need to have a long heart-to-heart about your pessimistic attitude. It's really startin' to give me the hypos."

"No, what we need is to put some mileage between us and the crazies."

Ignoring the rest of Jasper's commentary, I caught up to Ino, with the pooch panting right next to me. Far ahead, where the woods grew thicker, all four horsemen waited, weapons at the ready. Branches snatched at my limbs as if they wanted to capture me for the pursuing horrors. Twice my hat fell off and I had to turn back to retrieve it. Everybody shouted for me to leave the thing and get to safety. Shoot, no! *Heck with that. I really like this hat. Reminds me of the fight with the ravens near*

Richmond and how I first knew I had real friends.

Those friends came to my aid again. Good thing, too. I plopped the straw hat back onto my noggin for the second time and lit out for the Lusitanians. Ducking under some overhanging brush, I stopped dead. My feet still moved, my arms still pumped, but I made no progress. The howling Maenads increased their speed when they saw me stuck fast. A look over my shoulder showed me my predicament. My overalls had snagged on a wicked thorn bush. Just as I considered shucking them and escaping in my hat and drawers, help arrived. Ernie scampered up my leg, along my struggling arm, and onto the branch. His knife-sharp rodent's teeth made short work of it and I popped loose. Stuffing him under my hat, I headed for Tyrell and the hunters lickety-split.

Too late. The Maenads had found new reserves of speed now that their prey was so close. Loathsome rotting fingers slid off of my overalls. Breath smelling of decay came near to overwhelming me. Whipping Morphageus up as a round Viking shield, I bashed two of the undead away. A third lost her jaw to a fierce kick. I backpedaled to gain some space, but more thorny vines tripped me and down I went. Victory screams almost deafened me. Dead bodies lurched toward me from three directions. Several bounced off of the shield. Hands laid hold of my arms and legs. With incredible strength they began to pull. My joints began to cry and separate. In just a few seconds Verity's various pieces would cover about three acres of Lusitanian real estate.

"You speak to your god? The one who
gives you these marvelous powers?"
Jasper nearly melted my brain with his hooting at that.
I shook my sore noggin to clear it. "In a way.
Don't know if you'd call him a god.
More like a Muse of Mischief."

28 / Safety...Sort Of

Reforming my shield into its rune-sword shape didn't help much. So many disgusting cold hands held me down that I couldn't swing it. Despite my Stone-strength they held me fast, pulling ever harder. Sharp pains shot up my arms and legs. A slobbering Maenad gripped my head and started to twist. Stars burst like fireworks before my eyes. Then my air got cut off and things started to go dark. *This is it, then. Here endeth the great quest. Sorry, Tommy. I tried.*

Half a second before Ma would've lost her only child, the hands on my neck let go. Something round and heavy landed on my belly, just as I tried to suck in a desperate breath. With my blurred eyes I saw that it was a decaying head, eyes still open and moving around. Both of the creatures holding my arms released their holds, too, while a great wind washed over me from straight overhead.

"Get moving, girl!" Tyrell shouted from atop Al, hovering six feet in the air. He lopped off another head with his Confederate-issue saber. "They keep coming even when you slice them into bits. Can't do this forever."

He shot up out of range as three Maenads leaped at him. One got hold of Al's saddle and clung there like a cocklebur. Kicks from the Reb captain's boot didn't dislodge her. In fact, she began climbing up at him, her terrible teeth chomping at his leg. Tyrell couldn't swing his sword for fear of hitting Al's flapping wing. But Valkyrie horses are trained fighters, not just swanky transportation. Alcibiades cranked his neck around and latched onto the fiend's ear. A second later she tumbled to the ground, arms windmilling, to land on one of her sisters.

I took advantage of my reprieve to cut in half the Bacchante who still held my right foot. Each of her fallen parts kept feeling around for something to attack. The thing on the left foot I shook off with my waning strength. Free for the moment, but with a score of monsters reaching out for me, I crawled backward and stood, every muscle crying out. Ernie shot from under my hat, his sharpened knitting needle spear ready for action.

"That won't do us no good," I told him. "Shoot, even dynamite might not help much. These things don't stop. Get back and guard Ino."

The tiny Marshal didn't waste time debating my command. He hopped off my shoulder and skedaddled toward the others, me following as best I could. None of my joints worked too well. I noticed that the Lusitanian men still sat on their motionless mounts, unwilling to help me, or just plain afraid to. Ino punched their thighs and hollered, trying to shame them into action. Nothing doing. With a frustrated scream she ran off into the forest.

All up to me, as usual. Why would I expect anything different?

"That just means you get all the glory," Jasper said. "Look sharp, here comes your air support."

I tried to grab Tyrell's hand as he flew in low to pick me up. But just as I met his gloved fingers with my own I got tackled by half a dozen cackling Maenads. Down I went, their gooey slashing and clutching hands all over me again. The suffocating stench of the grave threatened to do me in before I could get ripped apart. Others stood guard over us, preventing the Redeemer from giving me any help. That settled it. They did learn from their mistakes. *Bad news for me. I just hope I don't turn into a Maenad when I'm dead. Nobody looks good in goat fur.*

About to go under for good this time, I felt something warm and wet land on my cheek. More drops washed my nose and hands. With a bright sunny sky I knew it couldn't be rain. The deadly pressure on my beaten body eased. Maenads deserted me, their wretched laughter turning to moans of satisfaction. Summer heat and light made me squint. Deep baying from my hound echoed through the trees. All of my assailants were gone.

Ino had come to the rescue. Not with her brawn, but with her brain. Somehow she'd managed to drive a pair of deer from the deep woods. With the Duke's help, the blonde girl had chased the buck and doe into our clearing. The frightened animals had run from the frying pan into the undead fire. Like ants pouncing on a bacon crumb the decaying monsters had swarmed onto the antlered hind, their preferred prey. Not having my magickal Stone-aided strength, he hadn't survived long. Bloody hunks of raw venison and deer guts flew through the air. His terrified mate bounded up the hill to live for another day.

Taking full advantage of my second miraculous rescue, I let Ino half-carry me over to the mounted men. The sword shrank into a bracelet on my wrist. I was all done in. Few of my parts worked like they should. Bruises, scrapes, and dirt covered me. Pain shrieked along every nerve. My whole body felt like a boiled noodle lying in burning coal oil. Jasper, who sensed everything I did, expressed his distinct dissatisfaction with the state of affairs.

"I'm suddenly reminded of how swell it was to not have a Stone Warden," he whined. "You humans are awful fragile."

"Looks like somebody don't recall how he used to be one of us breakable folks," I said. Wincing, I plopped myself down on a patch of soft grass. Duke slurped every square inch of battered skin with his sloppy basset tongue. You'd think I'd have tasted terrible, but the saggy hound didn't seem to mind.

"Looks like we're even in the life-savin' department," I told Ino. "Pretty quick-thinkin'."

"You are very welcome, Callisto," she smiled. "I saw the animals run away from us when we crossed the stream. Sneaking up on them and shooing them in your direction was not difficult. I have much practice in stealth."

"Well, much obliged, anyhow." I gave the three Lusitanian men a sour eye. "As for you fellers..."

They all looked ashamed, and rightfully so. All of a sudden they found plenty of stuff to look at besides me. But Acastus reminded me of a fair point. "Battling the favored children of Dionysus would not have saved you. You saw how even your valiant brother and his Olympian steed could not pry you from their clutches. We would have become offerings ourselves."

I turned my aching neck to look at the feasting Maenads. Gore covered their vile rotting faces. They munched on soft rubbery innards, foul juices running down their chins...those who had chins, anyhow. Only bones remained of the poor sacrificial buck. *He died so I could lie here. Sorry...and thanks. I hope you're rompin' in whatever Valhalla awaits a deer.*

"Besides," Pelias added, "the god does not reward the insolence of those who interfere with his rites. You are a stranger here. Believe me when I tell you that a dismal fate awaits any who assault a Maenad, even if they should survive that encounter."

Deciding that I needed my energy for more than glowering at them, and having to agree that they couldn't have helped me much, I took out my pipe and lit it. Four sets of eyebrows rose at that. They sniffed the tobacco smoke and made scornful faces. I returned their sour looks with interest. *Too bad if you don't like it. It don't thrill me none, neither. But Jasper needs this, which means I do, too.* Soon they all shrugged and seemed to decide that the weird kid wouldn't reward their insolence if they interfered with her rites.

Tyrell landed Alcibiades next to us. I'd expected that and had pulled goodies from my rucksack for them. Al caught the apple I lobbed his way, acting as if it was the least I could do for his service. His rider accepted a cigar and a swig from my whiskey flask. Jasper blubbered in my head that I was giving away what was rightfully his. By my way of thinking, though, anything that Tyrell consumed was that much less I'd have inflicted on me later.

Concerned that the dreadful Maenads might not settle for just the one deer, we slunk into the deepest part of the woods. I rode on Al, sitting in front of Tyrell, that miserable McClellan saddle rubbing my backside raw. But since I could barely stand without help I had no choice. Despite her own exhaustion, Ino walked, keeping the golden horse between her and the men who'd been hunting her not long before. From what I could tell, neither side really trusted the other yet. After a few minutes we happened upon a grassy track and headed back uphill again, westward.

I felt a little better after smoking my corncob pipe. The stuff tasted nasty and made my head swim, but Jasper thrived on it. It'd take a darned sight more than that to wipe away the damage done by the pack of walking corpse-women, though. In my future I foresaw plenty of whiskey-sipping, skinny-dipping, and sugar-gorging. *Which also means lots of headaches and queasy bellies. Which will make me feel terrible again. Which will require even more indulgence. It's a vicious cycle.*

Jasper had a different opinion. "You're lookin' at this all wrong," he insisted. "Remember, if it doesn't kill you, it makes you stronger."

"Maybe so, but it'll still make you mad as a hornet, if you catch my meanin'."

"Oooh! Sounds like a threat. Can you hear my knees shakin'?" He giggled. "Oh, that's right...I don't have any."

I willed the cup into the form of a rag doll. Since he had no choice, Jasper pouted and complied. Then I grabbed his cute little legs and knocked them together several times. "Look, I've struck fear into the heart of the deadliest weapon on earth."

"No, you've merely humiliated the deadliest weapon on earth. It ain't the same. And if you get him too upset, he'll suddenly forget how to speak Lusitanian. So choose your next sentence very carefully."

Grinning, I returned him to cup form. "Why, mighty Morphageus, I feel a strange cravin' for the licorice whips in my enchanted rucksack."

I felt him smile in my mind. "Hmm. That might just take away every pain in your entire freckled body. See how easy it is to twist me around your little finger?"

Ino had been watching the whole exchange. Though she couldn't hear Jasper, she could tell that some sort of conversation was taking place. "You speak to your god? The one who gives you these marvelous powers?"

Jasper nearly melted my brain with his hooting at that. I shook my sore noggin to clear it. "In a way. Don't know if you'd call him a god. More like a Muse of Mischief."

"What does he say to you, this muse?"

"Depends. Sometimes he helps me, gives me warnin' of danger or defends me against a surprise attack. Other times he advises me on what I should do next. Mostly he just insults me and cracks dumb jokes. Thinks he's real funny."

"Your muse sounds like the silly boys in my village back home."

Jasper made a disgusted sound. "Hey, watch who you're insultin', honey! I'll have you know I'm the Omnipotent Avenger of Injustice."

Yep, she's awful good at spottin' the truth, this one. She didn't exaggerate when she claimed to see into the hearts of others.

"That's because he used to be a boy, a long time ago. It's his spirit that lives in the sword."

She nodded as if she encountered one of those every day. "And he has unlimited power? He can do anything he wishes?"

"Naw. He has to do what I wish, unless he's protectin' me from sudden danger. And his magick has to be recharged."

"Recharged? You mean refilled, like an empty bucket?"

"That's about it." I explained about Jasper's limitations, about how he forced me to experience life's pleasures so he could feel kind of human again. The more I thought about it, the more irritated it made me. But since I couldn't change things, I shrugged and gave up stewing over it. Someday I'd learn how to safely use a Chauntline and then Jasper would have less of a hold on me.

"Don't fool yourself," he said, reading my thoughts. "You'd miss all those cigars and stiff drinks and chocolate-covered cakes. I can't wait till we get home and you can play hooky to go off fishin' with Tommy."

Tommy. You would have to mention him. I'm not much closer to gettin' him outta that dungeon. Thanks fer nothin', Jasper.

Forcing him to the back of my mind, I asked Ino, "Where are we headed?"

"To Cumae, the city of those brothers," she replied, pointing to Acastus and Pelias. "It has a double wall to keep the Maenads out. It works, most of the time."

"That's good. It's hard work dodgin' them girls. How many of 'em are there?" I prayed that the band we'd just escaped was all there were.

Ino dashed my hopes. "Lusitania is overrun with them. Three-quarters of our females. When a girl becomes a woman she is seized by the frenzy at the next full moon. Her lust for the god drives her insane. She prowls the forest with her sister devotees, consuming wine, raving, dancing. Soon she dies, either from self-destruction or at the hands of her mindless fellows. By the next moon Dionysus revives her. In the state of not-death she is even more uncontrolled than in life. Not iron nor steel may slay her. Fire merely causes mirth. Only deep running water can return her to the grave for good."

Boy, that's about as horrible as it gets. "But not all of the girls. Three-quarters, you said. Some escape?"

"The god spares enough so that they might marry and beget more children for his rites."

"How do you know if you're one of the lucky ones?"

"You do not. You wait for the first moon after your womanhood. If you awake sane the next morning, you have not been chosen."

I looked back over my shoulder, wondering if the Maenads might be following. Nobody in sight. "How do folks live with this?"

"Many do not. Some slay their girl children, rather than risk such a fate. But rare are the parents who can bring themselves to do such a deed. More often they kill themselves, unable to cope with the strain of attacks from the Sisterhood. But the Bacchantes prefer to prowl amongst trees, not towns. And human blood is not their drink of choice. As creatures of nature and vegetation, they mostly devour rabbits and other game during their rituals. That is why I drove the deer to them. You were a feast of last resort."

Good to know. Don't like bein' on a monster's menu. I got enough troubles with demons and Bullies as it is.

"So we'll be safe in this town we're headed for?"

Ino gave me a strange smile. "Safe from Maenads, anyhow."

We got through the woods with no more problems, if you don't count Jasper's horrid so-called singing. Silly songs from minstrel shows are fine in small doses, but not for two solid hours. As we neared the edge of the forest I had to make a face and take a gulp of whiskey to ease my pain. Jasper hadn't been too accurate when he'd claimed that my eating licorice would do the trick. It helped, sure enough, but nothing short of ether seemed likely to get rid of all of my agony.

The town of Acastus and Pelias sat in a little valley, with the same creek I'd bathed in running through it. Its buildings were of whitewashed stone and red-tiled roofs. Each citizen had painted bright murals along the edges of his house. Doors and shutters tended to be blue. A garden behind almost every home provided fruits and vegetables. Plenty of olive trees lined the dirt streets. Most of the public buildings of Cumae were on a middling-tall hill at the east end of the city. Just as Ino had said, a pair of high walls encircled the place, about thirty feet apart. In the space between them ran the stream, diverted through there as a Maenad trap. At the north and south ends of town sturdy wooden gates, guarded by strong men with spears and bronze helmets, provided the only way in or out.

Acastus and Pelias turned out to be well-known to the sentries. Those stern soldiers waved us through the south gate with ease, though the clothes Tyrell and I wore caused some comment. I made a note to change into the local rags as soon as I could. They'd surely be cooler than my overalls and heavy shirt. All of the nervous citizenry seemed to be comfortable. Everybody I passed looked like a figure on an ancient Hellene vase. Lean, dark, big-eyed, and clothed in light fabrics dyed in natural colors. Very Socrates and Plato-ish. That made sense, of course, considering the circumstances of Lusitania since the Affluxion. It had started as an Athenian colony.

Folks moseyed in all directions, nobody choosing to rush in the mind-numbing heat. Here, out of the shady forest, the sun tried its level best to fry you into a crispy piece of human bacon. Mothers shooed children out of the way so they could sweep or hang laundry. Cute donkeys hauled all manner of goods, either on their backs or in wagons pulled behind them. I wished I could ride one bareback instead of suffering on half of Al's saddle. Market stalls sold food, shoes, pottery. The sort of stuff you'd expect. Jasper ogled the edibles and kept reminding me about lunchtime. My belly joined the chorus. With any luck Acastus would soon deposit us in a cozy spot where we could rustle up some vittles.

The only trouble was, it suddenly struck me that I'd heard of the name of the town before. At school. Aeneas had visited it. My appetite vamoosed like a Union platoon in front of Lee's army. *Oh, this ain't good. Not by a darned sight.*

We were trapped in Cumae...the entrance to the Underworld.

"She? This...is a girl child?" the woman sneered, disbelieving.
A rough paw seized my chin and yanked it back and forth.
I found myself staring up an impressive beak of a nose
and into sharp gray eyes like those of a hunting hawk.
"What mother would allow her daughter
out of the house like this?"

29 / Lampade

Maybe I'd been hobnobbing with monsters and evil things for too long, but after jerking my head around a couple of times and seeing no sign of a fiery pit of doom, I shrugged. *Don't seem Underworldy. No columns of smoke. No wails of despair. No winged demons herdin' souls into everlastin' torment. Shoot, it might just be a different Cumae altogether.*

"Oh, that's right," snickered Jasper, taking a break from pining after fresh-baked bread, "this is that other Cumae. The one where puppies and bunnies frolic in meadows of Turkish Delight and sugarplums."

"Could be. There's magick afoot, you know."

"With your luck, the bunnies will have enormous teeth and gnaw people's heads off."

I rolled my eyes. "Yeah, that's real likely."

"Valiant knights perishin' by the dozen..."

"Kinda hard to swallow."

"Great heaps of bones in front of the bunny's lair..."

"Now you're just bein' ridiculous."

"Okay, just you wait. I'm tellin' you, killer rabbits are no myth."

By then I'd given up and was laughing half out loud. The locals smiled at me like I was the beloved village idiot. Acastus turned around on his horse to frown and ask an unspoken question. Tyrell threw up his hands in reply. For some reason, the idea of vicious beheading bunnies tickled me. I wiped snot off my snoot with the back of my sleeve and snorted myself quiet. Duke trotted along beside us, shaking his floppy head in aristocratic disgust. *He's one to talk. I just saw him rootin' through Lusitanian garbage not five minutes ago.*

Now all worries about the wretched Underworld had left my head. As I recovered myself the horses in front of us stopped at an impressive two-story home with a green-and-gold mural of Athena covering a side wall. Servants scooted out of the sea-blue door to hold our bridles as we dismounted. Well, Tyrell and the others dismounted. I more or less slumped along Al's neck and splatted onto the flagstones that covered the home's entrance. All of my leg muscles had stiffened during the two-hour ride. None of the rest me felt any better. Try as I might, I couldn't do much more than raise my head a few inches.

"It lies there like a waterlogged bag of barley," a woman's warm voice said from right above me. "I have seen wounded warriors return from a summer's campaign with more vitality."

Acastus spoke up with vigor and a touch of awe. "Make no

mistake, she **is** a wounded warrior." His strong hands hauled me to my feet and kept me from collapsing. "She saved us all from being devoured by the Sisterhood, then fought like Ares himself when they swarmed over her."

"She? This…is a girl child?" the woman sneered, disbelieving. A rough paw seized my chin and yanked it back and forth. I found myself staring up an impressive beak of a nose and into sharp gray eyes like those of a hunting hawk. "What mother would allow her daughter out of the house like this?"

Whipped as I was, I roused myself to go to Ma's defense. I jerked my face out of her grip and puffed up as much as I could. "The best mother in the world, that's who! And I'll thank you to not down-talk her, ma'am."

The lady of the house, for nobody else would've dared take such liberties with a guest, gave me the same look you'd give a kitten who tried to out-roar a lion. Tall, sun-dried, and slim, with her hair held in place by a complicated set of fancy bronze combs, she didn't seem to have heard much back-talk lately. Her long dress, bloused at the waist and held up by a blue-jeweled gold brooch at teach shoulder, was made of light yellow wool with black trim. Several expensive rings adorned her fingers. "Look, it speaks."

"Quit treatin' me like a trained parrot. I don't know who you're used to dealin' with around here, but I ain't about to—"

"Acastus, I like her!" the proud woman exclaimed with a wide grin that totally transformed her face. Where before she'd been a nasty shrew, now she put out more glee than a dozen kids' birthday parties. "Finally, someone with flame in her spine!" She pulled off my raggedy straw hat to peer at my short red hair. "And flame on her head, as well."

I had to admit that I probably did look a lot different than anybody else in Cumae. In Lusitania, for that matter. Other than the strawberry-blonde Ino, every head I'd seen since landing in Europa had been dark as coal. My constellation of freckles, pug nose, and denim overalls marked me as an outsider, too. Now I noticed the servants pointing at me and whispering. *Swell. Now I'm a carnival sideshow attraction.* If there were any Merchantry spies about, word would get to them real quick that I'd arrived.

"What did your fine mother name you?" asked my newest friend.

"Callisto." I figured I'd try to keep up my disguise, though I had my doubts it'd last long under this clever woman's scrutiny.

"Your mother venerated Artemis. She gave you the name of one of her nymphs."

"Uh...yes, ma'am." From school I knew that Artemis was the goddess of forests, hills, the moon, the hunt, and plenty of other stuff. *Not sure where this is goin', but I guess I'll have to hang on till I get bucked off.*

"A nymph who was later transformed into a bear. You aren't going to feast on any of my handmaidens, are you?"

Jasper broke in. "No promises, lady. Some of us are starvin' here."

I just smiled and held my tongue, unlike the Savage Sword of

Silliness. Apparently no answer was expected, because she patted my shoulder and grinned back. "I am Lampade, wife of Acastus. You and your friends are most welcome. Please introduce them."

I put on my best manners and presented Tyrell to her as my noble brother Cadmus. He flashed her that woman-melting smile and tipped his cap. Lampade didn't exactly dissolve, but she returned the favor. Al, as Xanthippus, also earned her admiration. Even with his wings made invisible, that was one impressive horsie. When I introduced Duke she took one look at him and giggled, a sound I would've bet good money she didn't know how to make. The low-slung hound swallowed his Gaullic pride and licked her hand anyway.

We had a tense moment when I got to Ino. From the hard look on Lampade's face I could tell that I was making a re-introduction. They'd met before. Judging by the bad energy thrumming the air between them, it'd been about as cordial as the Battle of Shiloh. Whatever had happened, Ino tried her best to get past it. She curtsied to Lampade, kept her eyes down, and generally played the contrite maiden. For her part, our hostess accepted the deference with good grace and no gloating. I took that as a cue to use whatever influence my spine's flame could provide me.

"Whatever may have passed between you, mistress, I must tell you that this girl used all of her wits to save me from certain annihilation. Dozens of Maenads bore me to the earth. Not even your heart-strong husband was able to effect a rescue. But, at no little risk to her own safety, Ino distracted the god's children long enough for me to escape."

Lampade took a deep breath and raised an eyebrow at her husband, his brother, and their friend. As one they all nodded their agreement with my statement. With a muttered, "*Humpf*!" he stood aside and waved us into her home. I got a hurried hug from the blonde prophet as she hustled past me. Duke followed her, no doubt smelling food inside. Jasper sure did, because he got all frisky in my head about cheese and olives and wine. Especially the wine. The four mounted men walked their horses around to the back of the gleaming white house, where a stable awaited them. That left just me, Lampade, and half a dozen attendants out front.

"Thank you, my lady," I said. "Graciousness and hospitality are never weaknesses, no matter who comes to your door."

"We will see if your wisdom matches your spirit," she sighed. "I pray to Hestia that my hearth and home are still in one piece when that girl departs."

As we entered the house I told her what Ino had said to me about her gift-curse from Poseidon, that she didn't actually cause the awful events that made people fear her. Lampade listened with respect, but I wasn't sure if I made enough of an impression to change her mind. Having only Ino's word to go by, I hoped that I wasn't letting my judgement get misdirected by sympathy for another kid. Acastus' wife didn't come off as somebody who could be easily fooled.

That concern for my skills at character-assessing took a back seat to admiration for the home. Though simple and uncluttered, as opposed to most of the living spaces in my time of 1862, Lampade's house still managed to feel welcoming. It was one and a half stories, built around a stone-floored courtyard, open to the sunny Lusitanian sky. Most of the walls boasted paintings of nature scenes or religious themes. Two or three sculptures of horses, in stone or bronze, decorated the space. What served as the kitchen took up a goodly amount of space to one side, where the smoke would rise through the roof opening. An iron tripod stood over the fire pit, soup simmering in a fat black pot hanging from it. A colorful altar to what I guessed was the goddess Hestia sat opposite it, against the other wall. Several openings, most with embroidered curtains as barriers, led to storerooms for food staples, fabrics, pottery, and such. One chamber did have an actual wooden door. Lampade explained that it was the andron, where the men lounged. We mere women weren't allowed in it. Our special place, the gynaeceum, was in the small upper story. That would be where I'd stay while visiting. They'd already taken bedding up there for me.

Word of our arrival spread real quick. Before I had a chance to mooch a hunk of cheese and shut up Jasper's pathetic whining, close to a dozen kids of all ages surrounded us. Two were the offspring of Acastus and Lampade, some were cousins, others were neighbors. I noticed one thing. Kids are pretty much the same no matter where or when you are. Just like the Rom children, the Lusitanians started off teasing me about my hair, freckles, and funny clothes and ended up inviting me to play their games. Nobody could touch me at tag, even as sore and tired as I was, because of all of my practice at dodging battalions of demons and Shades, not to mention the Maenad horde. They were better at knocking pottery shards off the top of a wall with a sling, since that was new to me. With Jasper's aid I could've done it, but cheating your hosts with magickal assistance is a pretty low-down trick, if you ask me.

After twenty minutes of that Lampade took me and Ino upstairs, where the servant girls had laid out a nice spread of barley and lentil soup, goat cheese, bread, honey, olives, and weak wine. That hit the spot, especially the last item. I thought Jasper would just about faint from ecstasy. To me it tasted like sour grape juice. Didn't have anything like the kick of whiskey and also didn't roil my belly. Though alcohol had been the last thing I'd wanted, Ino suggested that I avoid insulting my proud hostess and at least try the diluted wine. I recalled that President Lincoln's boy, Willie, had died from typhoid fever only three months earlier. *Maybe it's safer than pure water. Not too sure what their sanitation's like around here.* With that thought in mind I sipped the blood-red stuff, trying not to make a rude face and insult our host. It was only after I'd put away a big goblet of it that I discovered the jug of honeyed water, called hydromel, at the other end of the table. From then on that was my preferred drink.

We reclined sideways on uncomfortable couches and ate with our fingers. Being waited on by servants, especially knowing that they were slaves, stuck in my craw. I didn't want to think about what Romulus, who'd only recently been a slave himself, might have to say about it. But as he'd been a guard dog for the Emperor Hadrian, maybe he had a different idea about what was a normal part of life in ancient times. Since I was pretending to be of Hellene background I had to set my jaw and take it with a smile.

Lampade took the opportunity to ask loads of questions, of course. So did I. Most of hers were of the expected variety. Who was my family? How did I come to be in Lusitania? What lay behind my abduction? I spun her a long windy tale about coming from a land across the Great Sea, where I'd been the youngest child of a respectable merchant named Nisos. Slavers had stolen me at a crowded market when I'd become separated from my mother. For a great price I'd been sold to a prince in the far north of this land, as a companion for his only daughter. For many months I'd lived there, learning the language. But when I'd seen a chance to escape and get a message to my brother I'd taken it, eventually wandering to the south and Cumae. The story took a good fifteen minutes to tell and I put every bit of melodrama I could into it, all the while fearing that I'd either overdo the thing or make some fool mistake that'd give me away as not having lived in this country after all.

Apparently I touched the maternal side of Lampade, because she shed a couple of tears and pulled her own young daughter close to her as I spoke. Having no maternal side, or even a commonly decent side, Jasper did no such thing. Instead, he just jabbered on about the food and how my running my mouth with such a long story was preventing me from stuffing it full of cheese and bread and did I know there was **wine**?! After a while I considered sticking my finger down my throat and teaching him a lesson about who was in charge of Verity's stomach. But I saw no sense in punishing myself just to score a point on him. *That's the trouble with bein' bound to a magick spirit who feels everything you feel: it cuts both ways.*

"You have suffered much," Lampade said when I'd finished. "No doubt, your poor mother has felt even more misery. I am amazed that you did not slay me when I disparaged her so."

I waved that off. "Rage is a poison that twists the soul into knots. Does not Homer teach us this in the *Iliad*?" *Thanks fer that lesson, Miz Finch.*

"He does, indeed." She spread olive oil on a slice of dark bread. "Acastus spoke truly. You are wise much beyond your years."

"If that be so, it is a gift I inherited from my noble father." My stomach sunk a little. *No idea if I'm bein' honest about that. Ma won't talk much about Pa. My real one. No pictures in the house. Never a word about what he was like. Shoot, I don't even know his name. She just calls him 'your father.'* "And he would often insist that I judge others by what I experienced of their character, not by what rumors I heard at the market." I sent a glance Ino's way to make it plain what I meant.

Lampade sighed and nodded. "Fairly said. This girl has struck fear into our city and no one may honestly say it is because of anything she has been seen to do. We have taken the stories at face-value and driven her from our walls. But consider our plight before you think too harshly of us. The dead have risen in this land. Pitiless, cannibal, dead women. In every street mothers mourn their daughters, taken by the god for his cruel ends. Fathers wail for sons slain in their horrid rituals. We cower behind two high walls, guarded day and night by hoplites, always dreading an assault by the Sisterhood. Those in the far north have seen little of them. Here in the south they roam like enormous packs of ravening wolves. The difference is that a man may kill a wolf and it will remain dead.

So you can imagine our dread when this child appeared, preceded by tales from other cities of how she brought terror and ruin in her wake. That, in a dark trance, she predicted disastrous events which always came true. And that an invincible three-headed monster, breathing flame, appeared without fail the next day to add to the suffering. Is it any wonder that, in our state of mind-boiling terror, we behaved like bee-stung children, swatting at every flying thing?"

"Well, when she puts it like that..." said Jasper.

I gave her a sympathetic look, which I transferred to Ino. "You explain yourself well. And given that Ino admits that she does have the curse of foretelling dire happenings, no one could reasonably blame you for—"

My words got cut off by the bell-like clang of Lampade's bronze goblet hitting the floor. Her tiny daughter squealed and hid behind her mother's skirt. All of the slave girls crowded into the farthest corner of the room, away from me. *What did I do now?* I looked around to see what was happening. It wasn't me everybody was reacting to. It was Ino. The blonde girl shook as if lightning ran through her, back arched, foam leaking out of her pretty mouth.

"The Sisters are coming," she said in a frog-croak voice. "This very night they will destroy your puny city."

*"So, Evremonde, you betrayed the wrong people finally.
Look at you. From Duc to dog. What happened?
Get caught with a Merchantry colonel's daughter again?"*

30 / Grim Prophecy

"Well," said Jasper in a chipper voice, "it's been a lovely visit, but we really have to be goin' now. Feel free to call on us for dinner in Washington, if you don't get eaten alive tomorrow."

I caught Ino as she fell face-forward off of the couch, her every muscle taut. Gasping breaths filled my ears. Her blue eyes rolled back till only the whites showed. She shuddered, fists clenched and teeth bared. When I got her safely onto the floor, Lampade tossed me a cushion, which I slid beneath the stricken girl's head. It was just in time, too, because she started slamming her skull into the pillow as if she'd drive it to Hades. And the whole time that deep, raspy, unearthly voice kept saying over and over, "Destroyed Cumae shall be...they will breach your walls...all shall die...all shall die...all shall die...."

After about half a minute the whole thing ceased as suddenly as it'd started. Ino's muscles softened, her breathing slowed, and her eyes fluttered open. She blinked and looked up at me. "Is it morning already?" she asked. "Did I oversleep?"

"She has no idea what just happened?" Lampade asked, passing me a cup of hydromel. I pulled Ino up to vertical so she sip at the honeyed water.

"My throat hurts. So does my neck." She swallowed the drink and looked around at all the horrified faces. Then she buried her own in her hands and commenced to sobbing. I held her as best I could. *Comfortin' girls ain't my strong suit. Wonder if there's a magick pill I can take for that?*

She sniffed and rubbed her red eyes. "What did I say? How bad is it?"

I told her exactly what had gone on while she'd been tranced. All of the servants took the chance to scurry out of the room like rats heading for the rail of a stricken ship. None of us could blame them. From what I'd heard since arriving in Lusitania, the chances of Ino making an incorrect prophecy were close to zero. The forlorn look on Lampade's face told me that she was thinking the same thing. With barely-contained grief she surveyed her beautifully-decorated home, perhaps already seeing the night's flames consume it. Then she stroked her lovely young daughter's hair. What she might be imagining for her didn't bear thinking about.

"Mistress, I am so very sorry," Ino whispered. "Poseidon has spoken and he never lies."

Lampade clutched her child to her so tightly I feared for the little one's bones. "We shall all make sacrifice at his temple. Every man, woman, child in this city. Burnt offerings will blacken the sky."

Ino squeezed her eyes shut, turned away, and slowly shook her red-gold head. *No help there, then. Looks like you can't sway the god that easy.*

I stood up, joints creaking from the strain. They didn't hurt as much as before, thanks to Jasper getting his lunch. He'd renewed us a bit. "Sounds like we have only two choices: fight or flee."

The matron laughed, like a condemned criminal being offered her pick of noose or bullet. "That is no choice at all. Did you not hear her? 'Breach our walls...all shall die'. If we remain, we perish in Cumae. If we leave, we end our lives on the road. That is the only choice here."

"Surely not. Your walls are strong, your soldiers valiant and well-trained. The Maenads cannot—"

Acastus burst into the room, roaring like the Minotaur. He stopped halfway into the large room. Pelias, Talos, and Tyrell filled the entryway behind him. Handsome, muscular, with a full beard and long curls, he looked ready to do battle with Poseidon himself. "Speak!" he demanded to nobody in particular.

Lampade got to her feet with as much dignity as a queen. Flushing all fear from her face, she told him, "The god-trance took this child."

"And? What did she say? What new doom comes our way? Flood? Fire? Famine?"

"I only wish they could all fall upon us together, husband. Better that than the awful fate Poseidon has decreed."

Taking a long breath, Acastus considered the import of her words. "The Sisterhood, then. Naught else could so exceed your worst fears."

"The city shall fall, and all shall perish."

Gasps came from the men in the hall. Pelias and Talos vanished, probably to be with their own families. A few moments later hoof beats clattered from the rear of the house. Tyrell stood rooted to his spot, silently asking me what we should do. I just shook my head, unsure yet. We could easily escape on Alcibiades, of course, presuming the Cumaeans didn't slaughter us first for convincing them to bring Ino into the town. As Acastus' features darkened, I worried that he was planning that very thing.

Instead, he slapped his mighty bare thigh. In the confined space it sounded like a pistol shot. "If that is the god's decision, than running like scared mice will avail us nothing. Better to die in our city, amongst friends and family, in the city we erected with our own hands. The forest is where the Sisters draw their strength. Let them come to where we are strong. Let them try to walk on water. Let them break on our walls like waves on the shore. We will send many of them back to their graves, for eternity this time."

Lampade stepped to him, daughter in her arms. She touched her face with one jeweled hand. "I swore to die your wife, and I shall keep my word."

Kissing her palm, a surprisingly touching gesture from so tough a man, Acastus smiled as if going out for a night of drinking with his friends. "Think not of praying to Poseidon. He has never honored grovelers anyway. Make hecatombs to Ares instead. It is his aid we shall need."

I could see why everybody respected him. Already I was keen to man the walls with him and go down fighting. General McClellan could have used him in the Seven Days Battles before Richmond. If anybody in Cumae had the drive to defy Poseidon, Acastus might be the man. *Shoot, maybe they'll get out of this after all. Just because Ino's prophecies have always been right so far don't mean a miracle can't happen. Ares likes to help warriors. There's always a first time.*

Acastus roared out of the gynaeceum like a sea gale. Tyrell moved aside to let him go, then eased into the room. Nodding a greeting to Lampade, who was in such shock that she didn't express any outrage at his violation of the forbidden female quarters, he asked me what was going on. I'd forgotten that he couldn't understand any of the Hellenes. After a bow toward our hostess, who then sank back onto her couch, I tugged the Reb and Ino into the hall and closed the door. As quick as I could I caught him up on all of the latest reasons to have the heebie-jeebies.

"Besieged by raving lunatics who want to butcher us and destroy our way of life?" he said with a grin. "Why, Miss Verity, that's just another day at work for the Army of Northern Virginia."

"Righto! Give 'em what for!" a muffled voice added. Ernie pushed up the bill of Tyrell's gray cap. He stood atop the man's curly head. I'd wondered where he'd been hiding.

"Seems like somebody hasn't been listening'," Jasper snorted.

I agreed. "You fellers are bein' mighty selective with them ears of yours. Did you miss the part where I explained about the prophecies always comin' true?"

Tyrell made a *ppffth* sound. "I'm used to bringing ruination to fortune-tellers. My people have doing that ever since Fort Sumter." I reminded myself again to ask him why a French Redeemer was fighting for slavers. *Makes no sense to me.*

"You said it, boyo!" Ernie ran down his sleeve and hopped into my hand. "Who's this Poseidon think he is, anyways?"

"Uh, only the god of the sea and earthquakes," I reminded him. "Brother of Zeus and Hades, master of three-quarters of planet Earth."

As I led the way toward the narrow stairs, Tyrell asked, "What's his beef against Cumae?"

"He is not the one attacking the city," Ino explained, as if to a dim-witted child. I'd been translating as quick as I could. "Poseidon only gives warning of what will occur, speaking through me. The god who is bringing destruction is Dionysus."

"But ain't he just a fertility deity?" said Ernie. "And god of wine?"

I hesitated to translate that, but went ahead. Ino didn't bat an eye at there being a talking mouse in my hand. "Not completely. He represents frenzy, ritual madness, the kind that comes when people lose control of their emotions and journey to another state of existence. Wine can cause that, but so can many other things. Love, grief, actors performing a tragedy."

Tyrell frowned. "I have a good university education, but I

certainly don't recall any Maenads returned from the grave."

I chose not to translate that for Ino, since we were pretending to be from her time and explanations would just confuse things. "Must be the Affluxion. Dionysus is the only Hellene god to die and be reborn. When the Merchantry spell loused things up it must've mingled that part of him into the Lusitanian Maenads, just to add to the general misery. It'd give a boost to their dark magick, that's fer sure."

"No point in debatin' the why's and wherefore's," said Ernie. "A fight's comin' and that's a fact. Maybe it's a lost cause and maybe it ain't. But the city's defenses need to be manned."

"Where are we going?" Ino wanted to know, rubbing her neck.

"Stable," I whispered. Poking my head around a corner at the bottom of the steps, I saw that the house was empty. *Must all be out tryin' to appease whichever god they hope can get 'em through this. Good.* I waved Tyrell and the girl to follow. We all tiptoed through the courtyard and toward the small back hall. After checking again for any sign of servants or family, I shoved the Redeemer ahead, since he knew where the barn lay. He got us there without any trouble.

"What are we doing here?" Ino asked. She'd started to get real anxious. I couldn't much blame her, what with an army of crazy cannibals on the way and the whole town looking to blame her for it.

"Hidin', of course," I said, looking around for an empty stall. Handy for us, there was one next to Al's. We ducked into it and closed the low door. The Norn horse peeked over the wall, munching some oats. "The town's so panicky you shouldn't be seen until we can decide what to do."

Ino scratched at her arm. "You can all depart at will. Just take your winged horse and flee."

Jasper loved that advice. "Finally, some common sense. Let's jump on the flapper pony and high-tail it to the coast."

"Might not be that simple," I said aloud, pulling off my rucksack. "Maybe we're part of the prophecy now. Maybe runnin' won't get us anyplace but jumped by them Maenads somewheres else."

"Not exactly positive thinkin'," Ernie complained. "But stay or go, I'm ready to fight."

"As am I," Tyrell nodded, checking his pistol.

I screwed up face in thought. "Can Al fly us clear outta Lusitania in one go, if he has to?"

"Probably. He can take fallen Norse warriors to Valhalla."

"How far's that?"

The Redeemer shrugged. "You tell me. Since it's in a magickal realm, it could be a million leagues or a hundred yards. I do know that I've stayed in the air with him for twelve hours before. That's maybe four hundred miles at his top cruising speed."

"Wow. And how far to the beach in Gaulle where we need to meet the *Kiss*?"

"Not sure. A bit more than four hundred, though. And that's presuming that Pitcairn makes it that far."

Ouch. That don't sound good. "What do you mean? What's

goin' on?"

Tyrell holstered his gun and rubbed his horse's nose. "After you left, that underwater ship just sat there. There was some commotion beneath the surface, then its lights went out. Pitcairn wasted no time getting under way and putting that iron monster behind him. But either because that was the plan all along, or because we had blamed awful luck, we ran smack into three Merchantry-flagged men-o'-war, just waiting for us. Good thing the wind was right and the enemy had no steamships. All night we ran from them, staying barely a cannon-shot ahead. That Pitcairn is a wizard. Used every trick in the book. Maneuvered those enemy ships into one another in the dark. One lost its rudder. Another holed its bow. The third kept after us. Come dawn we spied yet another of them, just ahead, waiting for us like an anvil to be smashed upon. That's when I grabbed Mister Ernie here and mounted up to come find you. Figured you'd need information and maybe a way out of a jam."

"You guessed right about both," I told him, rummaging in my rucksack. "How's Ma and the rest?"

"All well, so far as I know. Your mother says to practice your magick, but to stay away from any Chauntlines. Also, to eat sensibly, and wash your feet."

"Oops," said Jasper. "Looks like I'm about to get turned into a bathtub."

"What about Roberta? She didn't fly with you?"

"She hopes to, later, when things calm down. Pitcairn has her flying patrols. Romulus and Sha'ira practice their battle tactics, in case the *Kiss* is boarded. They wish they could be here."

"I don't. There's enough of us in a pickle as it is." I excused myself and crawled all of the way inside my bag, drawing exclamations from all three of my friends. "A present from Ma. Right handy, ain't it?"

"Sure is, duckie," Ernie said, joining me. He marveled at the food stores and nearly dislocated his face chowing down on whatever he could get his little paws onto. I ignored his munching and grabbed some more of the potion pellets, making sure I also had the directions for them. Putting them in my front overalls pocket, I scooted backward. But before I could get back out of the sack I ran into something wet and rubbery. A curious look over my shoulder earned me a sloppy tongue slurp from Duke.

"Hey," I smiled, nuzzling his fuzzy snoot, "where've you been?"

He retreated so I could get out. "Foraging, of course. The Lusitanian dogs, they eat well." Sniffing, he poked his head into the sack. "Say, who's this feasting on my stores? Out, you interloper!"

Tyrell's eyebrows shot up. "Your funny-looking dog is speaking fluent Gaullic."

"Yep," I laughed. "That's somethin', huh?"

"Not only that, I've heard his voice before." Like a rattler striking, his pistol flashed from its holster to point straight at the hound. "So, Evremonde, you betrayed the wrong people finally. Look at you. From Duc to dog. What happened? Get caught with a Merchantry colonel's daughter again?"

Now my eyes goggled. Tyrell spoke in a Gaullic accent. I figured that he was speaking that tongue and the translation spell gave his Britannic words a tweak in my mind so I'd know.

The pooch shook his floppy ears till they flapped. "I knew I should have kept my mouth shut. As soon as I saw you land that horse I said to myself, 'Ah, Jean-Luc, that Bonapartist, he will be trouble'."

"I am no Bonapartist," Tyrell sneered.

"Finally saw the light, did you, Captain Tyrell? Or should I say, Lieutenant Defarge?"

I held up my hands. "Wait a gosh-darned minute! You two know each other? From Napoleon's time?"

"Well, in a way," Tyrell said with a shrug. "He was somewhat...taller, then."

"Peasant! I am still a bigger man than you! And always shall be!"

The Redeemer waved his hand-cannon. "Cur! You've finally found your natural form. Belly dragging the ground, eating garbage from the gutter."

I turned Morphageus into a long flexible hand and wrapped it around Tyrell's mouth. With one foot I shoved the Duke into the bag and sat on the opening. "Shush! Both of you. We ain't got time for this. Give a listen!" All of us turned our heads to catch a dreadful sound.

Maenads...thousands of them. All cackling in unison.

*"You know," Jasper said, "that may be the most pompous
and pretentious speech ever delivered
by a barefoot twelve year-old."
"Why, thanks. Comin' from somebody who likes to call
himself the 'Fell Cleaver of Righteous Wrath',
that's high praise, indeed."*

31 / Cumae Besieged

Great bronze bells boomed their warnings. In response, women wailed their own alarms and men shouted orders or encouragement to their fellows. Hoof beats thumped along the packed-dirt streets. As soldiers raced to their posts we could hear metal slap against leather.

"Times a-wastin'," I announced, as if anybody could be in doubt. I returned Morphageus to my belt in cup form. "Do we stay or do we go?"

Jasper voted first. "I'm perfectly happy with tucking my metaphorical tale between my spirit-boy legs and fleein' like a scared rabbit."

"Let's go down in a blaze of glory," Ernie suggested. "If it's absolutely necessary, that is."

Ino scratched at her legs now. *She's awful itchy. Must be allergic to the hay or somethin'.* "Go. Fly for your lives. There will be enough death here shortly without adding you to it."

Something tickled my brain. A page I'd read when we'd

studied Hellene mythology. I asked Ernie, "What did she say in her trance? What were the exact words?"

The mouse rolled his tiny eyes up as he tried to remember. "Umm...'the town will fall, and all in it will die.' Somethin' like that."

"No, 'somethin' like that' ain't good enough. We gotta know it word-fer-word."

"Why?" Tyrell wanted to know. "Bacchantes demolish the town, everybody gets eaten. The precise phrasing hardly matters."

I shook my head. That lesson was coming back to me nice and strong now. It'd been about the sneaky statements the Pythia would give out at Delphi. "But it does matter. If I'm right, then Poseidon's givin' us a clue that this time the disaster ain't gonna turn out to be what it's always been."

A low sad voice came from the other side of the stall door. "She said 'Destroyed Cumae shall be...they will breach your walls...all shall die."

Lampade pushed the door open. She held her two year-old daughter in her arms. Clutching her skirt, her son, who might have been five, looked at us with a mix of wonder and fear. Tears streamed down the poor mother's cheeks, dripping onto the straw that covered the stall floor. "Those are the very words. I do not mistake. They are burned on my heart with a hot iron."

"She's right," Jasper agreed. "That's the prophecy."

I stamped my foot. "Maybe you could've mentioned that a little earlier? Saved us some time arguin'?"

"I'd just thought you knew me well enough by now to ask when you want somethin'."

Ino needed more hands to attack all of her itchy places now. While she rubbed her back against the wall she asked, "What does your god say?"

"He ain't my god, he's just—" It occurred to me that as far as these folks were concerned, I could never convince them that Jasper wasn't a god. *Shoot, am I sure myself? He performs miracles, is pretty much all-knowin'. Hmm. That's a conversation for another time.* "He says you are correct. And that is most important to this city. Things may not be as bleak as we first feared."

A tiny flame of hope fluttered in Lampade's red eyes. "Then the city may be saved? The Sisterhood will be repelled?"

I let the Duke out of my rucksack and closed it up. He gave me a surly look. "I fear not, lady. Cumae will be a ruin. But if I am correct, its people will survive to rebuild it. Some of them, at any rate."

Lampade gave me a confused look, as did the others. I shrugged the pack onto my back and spoke to Tyrell and Ernie. "It don't specifically say that all of Cumae's people are doomed. It says 'they will breach your walls...all will die'. That could mean that the Maenads will die, if we stand and fight."

Tyrell let out a sour laugh. "It 'could'? It also 'could' mean just what it appears to mean. Seems to me you're wagering quite a bit on that one word."

"I'll allow that I am. But if there's any chance for these folks, that has to be it. The Sisters ain't gonna just fall over of their own accord. So if I'm right, we have to make a stand here, not run fer it and try to fight 'em on their own ground."

"So, assumin' you're not just indulgin' in a trainload of wishful thinkin'," Ernie said, "then the only real choice is to defend the city and lose, or defend the city and win."

"I still urge you to escape while there is still time," Ino urged. "You take a terrible risk."

Still she scratched every part of her. Ino's arms and legs bled from her nails scraping so much. I hoped I never got itches that bad. Once I'd blundered into some poison ivy. Wanted to jump off our roof, it'd driven me so crazy. That'd been nasty enough. Whatever she had was miles beyond my irritation.

"No," I announced, as certain as I dared be. "The prophecy has us in its fist. I can feel it. When we came to Lusitania we fell under the influence of Dionysus and Poseidon. Our fate is bound to yours. Only those who remain in the city have any chance of survival." I took the tin cup from my belt. With a snap of my wrist the sword Morphageus appeared, runes blazing. "My friends and I will help defend you and yours."

"You know," Jasper said, "that may be the most pompous and pretentious speech ever delivered by a barefoot twelve year-old."

"Why, thanks. Comin' from somebody who likes to call himself the 'Fell Cleaver of Righteous Wrath', that's high praise, indeed."

Hardly seeming to notice the magick I'd just done, Lampade

didn't grasp the situation as I'd explained it, that flight wasn't an option. She stepped to me and put a trembling hand on my shoulder. All of her pride and self-assurance had vanished when Ino had spoken for the god. "Acastus says that you have a hero-steed. With wings, like Pegasus. Can you not get my children out, at least? As recompense for my hospitality?"

You'd have needed Atlas himself to lift the heavy silence that fell over the stable then. Despite all that I'd just said, her woeful appeal melted me. *Shoot, maybe we can take the kids someplace safe, before the scrap starts. A high hill miles away, or even better, an island in the middle of a river. The Maenads surely couldn't get at 'em there.* But as soon as I let the idea flit through my mind, I knew it couldn't be. One thing my mythology lessons had taught me was that you didn't truck with fate. Even Zeus himself wouldn't try to buck it. Now that we were stuck in a place where all the Hellene legends were actual fact, we had to resign ourselves to playing by its rules.

"How I wish I could," I told her in as gentle a voice as I could manage. "But their fate is to remain here, as is mine. You are Hellene, lady. You know what happens to those who attempt to thwart the will of the gods."

Her whole body sagged at that. But a moment later she wiped away her tears, set her jaw, and said, "Right you are. If a stranger child from across the sea can risk her life, and that of her friends, for my family, then the least I can do is learn from her example." She set her daughter down and bowed to us all. "Go, then. Do what you must. Use your wonderful gifts. Aid my Acastus and the rest of the men. Make Poseidon's prophecy turn out the way you believe it shall."

I dipped my head in return. So did Tyrell and Ino. Even Ernie did, though he went whole-hog and gave her a fancy flourish of his tricorn hat. Duke, of course, did no such thing. Instead he gave the kids wet puppy-kisses. To each his own, I suppose. Turning to the itchy Ino, I said, "You'd best stay here fer now. You're no good to anybody if you get lynched by some panicky citizens."

Her arm was twisted way up behind her back, trying to scratch between her shoulder blades. She whimpered from her distress. "You may be right. I'll help watch them until something happens that requires me. Send word of events soon,"

"We will. Are you okay? Maybe you should go into the house. Looks like somethin' out here in this barn is disagreein' with you in a big way."

"It isn't that. It's..." She shook her blonde head and closed her eyes. "Never mind. Just go and repel the Maenads, if you can. If...when...they break through, come back so that we may fulfill the second part of the foretelling."

Tyrell started saddling Alcibiades. The Norn horse smelled battle coming. He'd quit trying to mooch goodies from us and began stamping his hooves and snorting. If I hadn't known better I'd have sworn he'd begun to glow. Valkyrie mounts are trained fighters, not just ferries for the honored warrior dead. As goofy as Al could be most of the time, he totally changed character when a scrap came his way.

"Sure wish we had Sha'ira and Romulus here fer this," I said, returning Morphageus to cup form. I hung it on my hip and smushed my straw hat down hard on my noggin. The rucksack settled nice and tight onto my back. "And Roberta."

Ernie hopped onto the Duke's shoulders. Amazingly, the floppy hound let him do it. I'd expected him to balk at having a member of the 'lower orders' ride him. *Maybe it makes him feel like a mighty war horse, instead of a Gaullic fop.* "You and me both, missy. Guess I'll have to settle for this saggy pair of wings." He patted the dog on the top of his pointy dome of a head. "Don't suppose you're some sort of magickal doggie? It'd be quite handy if you could flap these ears and fly."

"Learn to live with disappointment," the pooch told him.

"Who knows?" Tyrell said, pulling Al's cinch tight. "Maybe they'll show up. If they got free of those Merchantry ships and rendezvoused with the owls, they could be brought right to us. We sent one of Matilda's gulls back to the *Kiss*, saying we'd found you."

"How'd you manage that, anyhow?" I asked.

"Don't take a certified genius to spot an explodin' gunpowder shed in a medieval castle and deduce who caused it," Ernie laughed.

"Well, I'd kinda hoped that'd be the case when I did it, though my first thought was to make sure that Falcon wouldn't be able to use them weapons against his own people."

Ernie frowned. "Falcon? Who might that be?"

"I'll tell you on the way. Let's get movin'."

We left the barn, Tyrell on Al, Ernie on the Duke, and me on my bare feet. I still hurt all over from my previous tussle with the Maenads, but good food and a little rest made it at least tolerable. I didn't know how much magick-slinging and all-out fighting I had left in me, though. To take my mind off it, I went ahead and told my companions what had happened to me since I'd left the *Kiss*. They all seemed amazed at what I'd been through in so short a time. Had it only been three days? *Shoot, not even quite that long yet. Time sure flies when you're runnin' fer your life, I guess.*

Chaos filled the streets of Cumae. That came as no surprise to us. Distraught women dashed in every direction, looking for their men folk or their kids. Squads of bronze-armored men clanked toward the walls, spear tips glinting in the sun. Children and old people wailed, unable to do anything but stay out of the way and pray that all would be well. The odd looter took advantage of the confusion to help himself to goods from shops or stalls. But they were the exception. For the most part Cumae's citizens cooperated to face their imminent destruction.

"You sure we can't stop for a snack?" Jasper wanted to know as we passed a dairy dealer's place. "Those wheels of cheese sure look tasty."

"If you ain't careful you may taste death," I warned him. "We're in a heap of trouble here, bucko, in case you ain't noticed."

"Aw, it's only ten thousand soul-sucking, cannibalistic, undead Maenads, sent by the god of ecstatic revelation and mindless emotional frenzy."

"Gee, when you put it like that, I just feel like kickin' myself fer worryin' at all."

"Glad I could help. Can I have some cheese now?"

To shut him up I grabbed a handful of grapes from an overturned table and kept moving west, toward the wall most threatened by the Bacchantes. The Lusitanian sun was getting low enough to be in the eyes of the defenders. That was an inconvenience but if the gates got breached it'd be the least of our worries. Tyrell whistled. I followed him to our right, down a narrow street. Ernie and the Duke stuck with me. I noticed that the tiny Marshal of the Equity had managed to get hold of some of the same cheese that Jasper had ogled. He reached down and dropped some into the hound's mouth as they went. *Oh, there's the beginnin' of a beautiful friendship.*

A watchtower rose in a corner of the wall. Since the door hung wide open we ducked into it and climbed the stairs. Tyrell left Alcibiades below, of course, telling him to stay put. The Valkyrie horse would do just that. If anybody tried to steal him, it'd be the last thing they ever tried in this lifetime. All of the rest of us trudged to the top. Three armored men were already there, staring down at the sea of cackling monsters who pressed against the outer wall. One of them was Pelias.

"What are you doing here?" he demanded, though not with much vigor. Gone was the arrogance I'd seen in the forest. Now he had the look of a man who expected to be in the Underworld before dawn.

"Here to help," Tyrell said. "You'll need every hand that can hold a weapon."

"True enough, though I don't know what your silly dog and his pet mouse can do against such odds."

Ernie puffed up and waved his knitting needle at the sturdy Hellene. "Who's a pet? I'm a freedom fighter!"

I poked my nose over the edge of the tower wall to see what our situation was. It didn't look good. The Maenads pushed against a single spot in the stone barrier, hoping to weaken it with sheer weight of numbers. But as far as I could tell, even if they got through the first wall, the running water they'd encounter would kill them for good, as intended. Soldiers hurled javelins into the swarm, and fired innumerable arrows. That made no impression on the walking dead, of course. So far the wall held. Maybe they were just testing their strength. Or perhaps it was a diversion. Turning toward the south, I could see another huge gaggle of rotting women, making straight for the main gate. Though it appeared there were plenty of troops there, as well as immense bolts made of whole tree trunks, I worried that they'd find a way through. Wood is always weaker than stone.

Acastus clomped up the stairs at a dead run. "What are you doing here?" he asked.

"Popular question," I said. "Where should I be?"

"Back at my home, I fear. Talos has gone mad with rage. He swears he will slay the fair-haired girl, your Ino. Says she is to blame for our plight."

My jaw dropped. I could feel the blood rising into my face. "And you just stand here? Why ain't you off stoppin' him?"

"Because I have more important duties defending my sector. And because he is probably right in his belief."

I pushed him out of my way with all of my Stone-strength. His bronze breast plate clanged against Pelias'. "Fool men! Goin' around thumpin' yer chests and sayin' how brave you are, yet scared of one little girl." I took the stairs down two or three at a time, hitting the street at a sprint. After two blocks Tyrell swooped down with a winged Alcibiades and snatched me into the air. Leaving the Duke and Ernie to catch up as best they could, we flapped our way back to the house of Lampade. We got there just in time to see the enraged Talos, backed by half a dozen of his equally-maddened friends, kick in the barn door. Before I could do any more than dismount and take a couple of steps, they returned, dragging a screaming Ino by her strawberry-blonde hair.

Talos hurled her to the dusty ground, short sword in hand. "Sorceress!" he cried. "Monster!"

Though I wanted to help my helpless friend, I stopped in my tracks. Something was happening to Ino. Her golden hair flowed into a lion's mane, matching her new feline face. A tail grew from her back end, with an asp's venomous snout. From her back sprouted a third head, that of a goat. Flame spouted from its mouth, turning Talos into a shrieking torch.

Ino was a chimera.

"Just in case you're in doubt," Jasper said,
"I'm in need of a cigar, two stiff drinks,
three fistfuls of chocolate, and a nap."

32 / Monsters, Monsters, Everywhere...

"You know," said Jasper, "there's an awesome predictability to how the express train of your life tends to derail about every five minutes. It's really somethin' to watch."

I just stood there like a freckle-faced tree, gaping at the monster that had incinerated poor Talos. The thing had the head and body of an enormous lion, five yards long, its feet bigger than my head. Instead of a normal tail, though, that great green venomous snake thrashed back and forth, hissing and spitting at the Hellenes who tried to aid their doomed friend. Not trusting my first impression, I squinted at the head in the middle of the beast's spine. Sure enough, it actually was that of a black billy goat, complete with beard and horns. Its eyes, like those of the lion and snake, glowed redder than the fires of Tartarus. In none of the three pairs of eyes could I find any sign of the blonde girl I'd known. *No wonder she swore she didn't hurt nobody. She ain't actually in there that I can see. Somethin' else has replaced her.*

So shocked was I that I paid no attention to important stuff, like the angry ball of flame the goat spewed at me. Some part of my mind remained on alert, though, because a split-second before I became Verity-barbecue Morphageus flowed from my hip to cover every square inch of me in a giant fireman's helmet. Choking heat licked at me around its edges, but I stayed unscorched. That made me real glad that while Jasper could feel everything I did, it didn't work the other way around.

"You're welcome, Miss Sauveur," he said with a sigh. "And what might my next thankless task be? Polish your boots, perhaps? As if you ever bothered to wear any."

I was spared any need for a witty comeback, because I got knocked backside-over-tea kettle, rolling a good twenty feet. The chimera had pounced, swatting me like a cat batting a ball of yarn. Wide awake now, I shook my head and got up on one knee, holding Morphageus in front of me in Hellene hoplite shield form. Peeping around the edge, expecting to get toasted again, I saw that the creature had already forgotten about me and had moved on to Talos' shouting companions.

To their credit, they stood their ground. Swords out, they encircled the monster, not allowing it to dispatch them all at once. Now that they knew about the fire-spitting goat, they had a better chance of surviving the encounter. It let out a gurgling snort before it spewed fire. *Like a cat hackin' up a big old hairball.* With such obvious warning, twice the warriors managed to dodge such attacks. And while the snake tail looked terrifying, it had a limited reach if you kept an eye on it. More than once it struck at one of the men, only to be batted away by a parry. Serving as the controlling element of the chimera, the lion kept spinning as each Hellene fighter took a whack at it with his bronze blade. If it had just rushed each of them in turn the encounter would've ended in quick disaster for the Cumaeans. *Must be easy to confuse, with three competin' heads and all. I'll bear that in mind.*

Those six soldiers might have been able to defeat their horrific foe if they'd kept to their plan of confuse-and-strike. There was just one teeny problem. The chimera couldn't be hurt. Every time a sharp edge or point bit into its hide, nothing much happened. As far as I could tell, the creature felt pressure but no pain. It'd just swing round in response to each stab. And its skin couldn't be pierced at all. They might as well have been chopping at an ironclad warship.

With the chimera at bay, at least for a minute or two, I scooted sideways and headed for the barn, keeping my shield up. No telling when that flame-belching goat would take it in his head to send another merry greeting my way. I wanted to find Lampade and her kids before the beast did. Above me, Alcibiades flapped his wings and circled us all, Tyrell having launched him back into the air as soon as Ino had changed shape. After hollering at him to be careful not to get singed, I dove through an unshuttered window and landed in the same stall that we'd hid in before. Now nobody was there. But elsewhere in the stable I could hear crying and struggling going on.

Sticking my snoot out the door, I looked both ways. Nothing

in sight. Just more stalls and a pile of feed. But the strained sounds and whimpers weren't my imagination. They came from the right. I snuck into the musky passageway. It reeked of horse and donkey. Right then a body hit the outside wall with a sickening wet thump. *Score one for the unholy monster, I guess.* The goat's flame had set something alight. My witched nose picked up the smell of burning weeds. *Here's hopin' it don't catch this barn. We'd go up in a second.* With that cheery thought I hustled to the last stall, the only one with a door hanging open. When I got there I almost wished I'd gone the other way.

Lampade was killing her kids.

Trying, anyhow. Her eldest, the boy, struggled with a grim face as she fought to control him and slit his throat with a farm knife. It looked like the same instrument that the family used on all the livestock. In a far corner, tiny palms bloody where she'd been badly cut defending herself, the little girl sobbed. To me it seemed that Lampade had tried to kill her daughter first, but hadn't counted on her son's interference. Now she had her hands full, despite the size and weight advantage. Just like the other Cumaean men, he didn't plan on going easily. Before I could make a move to help, the distraught mother managed to fling the boy against the wall. Breath whooshed out of him and he sagged half-unconscious to the straw-covered floor. Gasping from effort and anguish, Lampade raised her long blade high, preparing to plunge it into her only son.

But the wicked point never reached him. Instead, it shattered against a hefty frying pan, courtesy of yours truly and Morphageus. It'd been quicker and safer to put the thing there with a thought than to try to jump between them. I held it by an eight-foot handle, wary of what Lampade might do next. In her trance of despair, anything was possible. For an instant I thought she'd just slump where she stood. From the way she paused and swayed, that looked likely. But whatever inner devil drove her to such desperation hadn't let go. She flung herself at the senseless kid, hands set to throttle the life out of him.

Again I had to act. This time Lampade's attack met a steel fishnet, like the ones her husband and his cronies had thrown at Ino. Despite my Stone-strength, I had a tough time hanging onto her. Those clawed fingers shot through the gaps in my net and came to near to snatching the boy. With a grunt I heaved my burden to the opposite corner of the stall. The kids clung to one another and wailed for their papa. I yelled until they stopped blubbering and paid attention to me. After a long minute of trying to contain the crazed Lampade and also trying to talk sense to them at the same time, I got them to go into the house in search of a servant. They were in pretty bad shape, both from cuts and bruises and from the shock of having their own mother try to butcher them like hogs.

Foam bubbled out of the Hellene woman's mouth. Every muscle felt as taut as a steel bridge cable, and almost as strong. I pinned her to the wall by turning the net into a cage, corner spikes biting deep into the wood. She thrashed her head back and forth until I feared she'd dash her own brains out. *Maybe that's what she wants. Go off to Tartarus with her family. To her way of thinkin' it's her only escape from this Maenad-chimera situation. From what I hear of the Hellene Underworld, that's a pretty desperate choice, though.* Just as I figured I'd have to stay with her until winter set in, Lampade went limp as a dead eel. When I removed Morphageus and changed it into its natural sword form, she flopped onto the straw and lay still. Quick as I could I tied her up tight with an old donkey harness so she couldn't harm herself or anybody else. She'd taken up enough of my time. Judging from the fierce racket outside, my services were needed elsewhere.

So many bodies and flame-bursts had struck the stable while I'd been inside it that I wondered how it remained standing. I got back out through the same window I'd used to get in. All careful-like I peeped around the corner to see how things stood with the thing that had once been Ino. Maybe when the fit passed she'd return, none the wiser. We just had to make sure not to kill the chimera, if that was even possible. For all I knew that'd be the end of the girl, too. That didn't look to be very likely, at least not any time soon. Three of Talos' six friends were dead or wishing they were. One had been thrown so hard against the barn that all of his bones had been crumbled. Another lay in a twisted heap, swollen like a balloon from the serpent-tail's venom. A third nursed horrible leg burns from a goat-fireball. Smoke boiled from a huge heap of manure and straw that had taken a stray flame shot.

But the other three men hadn't given up. While that might've been brave, it was also pointless, to my mind. Agile as they were, time was against them. They couldn't kill the monster. Their weapons only annoyed it. Any moment now it' would give up fighting on three fronts and either charge one of the fighters—real bad for him—or simply leap over them all and escape into the city—bad for everybody else. We all had to come up with a clever idea in a hurry.

As an experiment I reformed Morphageus into a long lance and jabbed at the chimera's hindquarters. My point bit a lot deeper than any of the Hellene weapons. Though I didn't draw blood, I managed to make the beast feel actual pain. It screeched, spun toward me, and licked at its backside. *Hmm. That was just a playful poke. If I go at it with some real enthusiasm I could maybe damage it. Or more likely, just make it mad as a hornet. It could also go at me with some real enthusiasm.*

"Don't bother," Jasper advised. "You're in Lusitania now and have to play by its rules. No weapon can pierce the hide of the chimera here."

"So it's heads it wins, tails I lose?"

"I didn't say that. You'll just have to think sideways, so to speak."

"If it gets loose into the city these poor Hellenes will be between two fires. They have enough to worry about with several brigades of undead loony women climbin' the walls."

The walls. That gave me an idea. Waving to Tyrell, I got him to land Alcibiades on the other side of the stable, away from the fight. I rubbed the horse's nose and told the Reb my idea. He laughed it off, at first, but then slowly nodded as he thought it over.

"Could work," he said. "Not too sure about the actual weight ratios, but Al's a sturdy fellow." He slapped a hand on his mount's neck, sending a cloud of dust flying.

"It's the fire we'll have to worry about," I told him. "The tail shouldn't give us much trouble, providin' I can keep that much distance between it and us."

"See that you do. I don't fancy having to explain to the Valkyries how their pride and joy here got snake-bit."

With that I made sure that Jasper understood what I wanted to do. He seemed to think it'd be loads of fun. I reminded him that if I caught a pants-load of fire he'd feel every bit of it, too. That dampened his desire for the enterprise, but off we went, nonetheless. Tyrell launched his winged horse back into the air, swooping over the top of the barn. I raced around the end of the building at the same time. For once, luck stayed with my side. The roaring chimera faced away from me. In an eye-blink I had my Morphageus net around the creature, a ten-foot cable with horse collar snaking out of the closed end. Al dove into it, snagging the whole package like a freight train grabbing the evening mail. Up the monster went, tied up like a Christmas package, belly-up. Since I hadn't let go of the line, I went with it. Though it took some hard work, I managed to climb up to my usual seat in front of Tyrell.

"Good so far," I said. "So long as his back is to the ground that goat-head can't shoot at us."

But it could spit at everything else. As we flew over Cumae, just above the red-tiled roofs, flame roared from our netted prey. Carts, vendors' stalls, awnings, trash piles...anything that could catch fire, did. Anybody not busy defending the city walls threw water or dirt on their burning property. Plenty of nasty looks and worse phraseology came our way. Al huffed from the effort of flapping through the hot air with such an immense burden. A couple of times I thought he'd have to give it up, but with some loving strokes and encouragement he managed to get us across town and back to the western wall.

Soldiers' jaws dropped so far it looked like they'd unhinged. Examining it from their point of view, I suppose it had to be unnerving. Pegasus overhead, dangling a fire-breathing lion, heading straight at them all. Not your everyday sight, even in Lusitania. The mob of armored men parted for me. *Hey! I feel like Moses.*

Jasper growled. "Yeah? Well, I feel like the bottom of the Pharaoh's chariot. Can we get this over with?"

I had to agree that it was now or never. Al's breathing was so labored I feared we wouldn't make it over the wall. With a last flurry of wing flaps he cleared the parapet and got us out above the throng of frenzied Maenads. Only twenty feet below, they leaped and clutched at us. Let me tell you, being in mid-air on a sinking horse, barely controlling a highly-irate chimera in a net, with ten thousand slobbering undead maniacs waiting to eat you, isn't something I'd recommend you try. *Just another day at work fer me and Jasper. Gosh, I'm tired.*

"Time to drop ballast!" Tyrell shouted, barely audible over the screaming fiends beneath us.

"Sure thing!" I yelled back. With a thought to Jasper he turned back into my trusty tin cup. The great bulk of the chimera tumbled earthward. Like any cat, he twisted around to land feet-first, his fall broken by a couple dozen outraged Maenads. Alcibiades shot up like a tree branch released from a snare line. We gained fifty feet of altitude and turned back to the Cumaean walls. When we'd cleared them and no longer had the monsters under us, I let out a breath I hadn't known I'd been holding.

The worn-out horse landed hard on the top of the wall, right next to Acastus' tower. I slid off and grabbed a water bucket. Al plunged his nose into it and sucked hard. Seeing him so taxed, I reminded myself to search my bottomless rucksack for something extra special for him. Soldiers crowded around us to stare at what they saw as a god-beast. At that moment, thinking about what Al had just managed to do, I wouldn't have given them any argument.

"Just in case you're in doubt," Jasper said, "I'm in need of a cigar, two stiff drinks, three fistfuls of chocolate, and a nap."

"Just in case **you're** in doubt," I countered, "the first half of that'd kill me where I stand."

The novelty of seeing a brother to Pegasus at hand vanished real quick. Everybody rushed to the far edge of the wall and gazed down. Many pointed and waved for their friends to come take a look, too. Curious as to what sort of show a Maenad-chimera contest might provide, I stuck my own snoot out and joined them all. We weren't disappointed. Mr. Barnum could've sold tickets and made a killing.

Except there was already a killing being made. At least, there would've been if either side had been able to die. Hemmed in by thousands of rotting animated corpses, the chimera couldn't go anyplace. It stayed right where we'd dropped it, those great lion's paws slashing to and fro while enormous sheets of orange flame gushed from its back. That thick scaly snake tail alternated between sinking its deadly fangs into unfeeling flesh and wrapping its coils around unbreathing throats. Disgusting chunks of Maenad flew into the air. Heads, arms, jaws, guts. You name it. Six-inch feline claws sliced up the Bacchantes like so much cheese. The monster's huge jaws bit down on skulls and shoulder joints. Still, no matter how many foes it dismembered, more came to take their place. And most of the fallen pieces also kept up the fight, unable to stop moving until thrust into deep running water. For their part, the undead women had no more effect on the chimera's hide than bronze sword blades had. Clutching fingers and foul teeth only made the creature fight harder, antagonized as if it had fallen into a hive of angry bees.

"War sure is a fine spectacle," Tyrell said from right next to me. He held Al's bridle. "Especially when you're several stories above it."

"Is this war?" I flinched as the chimera redoubled its efforts. It turned toward the city, focusing fangs, claws, and flame straight ahead, ignoring attacks from flank and rear. Its serpent tail concentrated on removing any entangling hands to the rear.

Acastus appeared on the other side of me. "I grant you, hoplite combat is more noble. There is no honor in this, only mere survival." He shook his head. "That is the girl Ino, is it not?" My silence served as his answer. "And I'd begun to believe her protests of innocence."

"Beggin' yer pardon," I said, "but I don't think she lied to us. I'll swear to any god you name that she don't know what happens when the trance takes her."

"Perhaps. But it is not relevant. Whether beast or child, that thing must be slain."

"How? Spears and sword don't hardly scratch it."

Tyrell interrupted, staring toward the south. "The devil-kitty may be the least of our problems."

We all turned to look in the direction of the great gate. While we'd been worried about the main body, a slightly smaller group of cackling Maenads had charged the entrance. Though its massive bolts held, the gate's wood proved soft enough for Bacchante claws to dig in. Thousands of decomposing madwomen climbed the doors. The Hellene guards couldn't knock them back fast enough. It was like trying to swat thousands of oncoming ants.

Cumae would soon be overwhelmed.

*A long thin hand reached out to grip the sword.
As soon as it did, Morphageus reshaped itself into
a bear trap and snapped tight onto the wrist.*

33 / Playing Possum

Despite the noisy, splashy spectacle below us, everybody's attention turned to the new threat. The word quickly spread that the south gate would be breached without more aid. Hundreds of soldiers grabbed spears and shields. Their sandaled feet made a noise like a distant rockslide. Soon our section of the wall was as bare as a Senator's conscience. Tyrell, Al, Acastus, and I remained, with a mere handful of others. But since there was nothing but smooth stone facing our Maenads, no good handholds, we felt pretty safe. *Well, as safe as you dare feel when confrontin' thousands of bloodthirsty flesh-eatin' cannibal women. Gee, I'm getting' awful sick of havin' to qualify everything I say and do.*

While we stood there, not sure which unbelievable form of mind-boggling imminent death to pay heed to, the Duke and Ernie arrived. The hound looked plumb tuckered out. I'd forgotten about him with all of the wacky goings-on. He guzzled water out of Al's bucket and stared at me like he was giving thought to hiking his leg on my foot. It occurred to me that he'd had to run across Cumae to this wall, then follow me all the way back to Acastus' house when I'd flown there to respond to Talos' assault, then turn around and chase me again when I'd returned with the chimera. This was one pooped pooch.

"Hey, yer grace," I said, stopping over to rub his ears, "sorry about all the travelin'. Things've gone a little outta control. Undead girlies, three-headed monsters, fire-breathin' goats...you know how it is."

That didn't mollify him. The basset hound stuck his nose up in the air, looking every inch the offended aristocrat. "It is too late," he sniffed in his outrageous Gaullic accent, "you are dead to me."

Jasper giggled. "Judgin' by our current predicament, I'd say just about everybody in sight is dead to him. Things keep goin' this way, pretty soon the livin' will be in mighty short supply."

"Maybe so, but I don't aim to shuffle off this mortal coil today," I said, squinting into the sinking sun. The blaze of afternoon light made it hard to see what was happening with the chimera. Shading my eyes by tugging down on the brim of my straw hat, I got a rude shock. Actually, more than one of them.

The embattled beast had made it to the city wall, despite all of the decomposing claws slashing at it. It hurled itself at the stone barrier again and again, actually knocking some chips from the face. Though we stood many feet above it, the strikes vibrated into our feet. Those great claws gouged more chunks out. I decided that Morphageus deserved more respect for protecting me from those vicious swipes. But scary as the monster's attack on our defenses was, it wasn't likely to bust through a pair of sturdy walls. No, it was the other unexpected sight that alarmed me.

A gray-robed figure stood on a barren hill directly across from me, waving a long staff. The same fellow who'd brought the windmills to life. And again his feet didn't touch the ground.

No sooner did I lay eyes on him than the Legacy Stone froze solid, hanging on my neck like a January icicle. You'd think that would've felt good, with the Lusitanian summer heat and all. But somehow knowing that the Maenads had a black magician master didn't much improve my mood. Now I knew for sure that I'd been tracked ever since I'd left the ship, or at least since landing in Iberion. Somebody or other was playing with me. Either that, or they had their own troubles with a third party I hadn't seen yet. That might explain why this stranger had only appeared twice. *Maybe I got a fairy godmother.*

My ruminating on my rotten luck ended when a blue-green bubble formed around the sorcerer. The instant that happened the Bacchantes went silent as an old tomb. They shuffled backward into a tight clump. Somehow their silence unnerved me more than their insane cackling had. As the stranger's staff moved in complicated arcs, all of the dead women raised their arms to the sky. A few dozen stepped forward into the open space next to the wall. Snarling and hissing, the chimera loped off toward the south gate, where plenty of battle noise could still be heard. If it wanted to get back into the city, those wooden doors were a more likely possibility.

"Who's that?" Tyrell asked.

"Yer guess is as good as mine," I said with a shrug. "Only seen him once before."

The Reb pulled out a pair of small binoculars from Al's saddlebag. That made his eyesight maybe half as good as mine. I could've spared him the trouble. Our mysterious friend kept the hood of his robe well down over his face. "What was he doing that time?"

"Turnin' windmills into feisty giant battle-monsters."

"Ah. The usual, then."

"Yep, just about. Ever seen his like?"

He gave up on the binoculars, as I knew he would. "Hard to say. One gray robe's pretty much like another. But the gesticulations he's making with his stick look a bit like Inner Council Merchantry mage stuff."

Oh, swell. Just what I need, some all-powerful friend of the Proprietor slingin' dark power at me. Ain't I got enough troubles already? "And in what possible way can that be anything but bad news fer us?"

"Oh, I doubt he's here to throw us a party. But he had a crack at you in Iberion and passed, correct?"

"Yeah, but—"

"Then maybe he has limited power. So far he hasn't attacked you directly, only with an intermediary."

That was worth considering. This fellow hadn't sent so much as an underwear-itch spell straight at me. It looked like his magick consisted of control spells, making others do his bidding. And he had yet to animate anything with a pulse. Maybe he couldn't. Jasper once told me that everything that lives has a weakness. This could be his. If true, I could stroll right up to him, nose-to-nose, and ask him what his business was.

"And if you do," said Jasper, "he might just spell your shoes to make you walk straight into the Proprietor's office. That'd be a Merchantry time-saver."

"Assumin' he's workin' fer the Proprietor," I thought back to him. "Fer all we know he's with one of them rebel outfits."

"In which case he probably wants to get his hands on you to use against the Merchantry leadership."

"Why don't he just ask then? Don't that put us on the same side, sort of?"

"If he learned his trade in the Scepter'd Isle, then doin' anything straightforward is foreign thinkin'. They all live to scheme and betray. Never lay their cards on the table. Information's like gold to 'em. Plus, ain't it more fun to control a few thousand walkin' dead than to sit down to a parley?"

I had to admit, if I could move Maenads around like dogs on a leash, that irritating bully Artie Radley would think twice about playing pranks on me at school. But at the moment I was the one on the receiving end. While I'd been conversing with Jasper the undead horde had begun another chanting circle like they'd done in the woods. One of their leaders had a thyrsus, too. Just as in the forest, they guzzled milk and honey from a sudden geyser in the earth, then began to claw at the ground. Only this time they had no tree to topple, only our wall.

"What good's that gonna do 'em?" asked Ernie, standing on the head of Alcibiades. "They gonna dig a tunnel under the wall? There's a river behind it, just waitin' to kill 'em for real."

"And another wall after that," I said. "Maybe their boss there has a plan I can't see."

The Maenads made good progress, with so much magick filling them. Between the power of Dionysus and the might of whatever the man in gray commanded, they dug a sizeable hole in only a few minutes. All of the remaining Hellenes on the west side of the defenses finally awoke to their danger. They called for reinforcements, then hustled over to drop boulders and spears on the attackers. That didn't slow the Bacchantes at all. Unless her hands were completely annihilated, each dead woman just kept scraping at the soil. Even a crushed skull or broken spine did nothing to interrupt the task.

Of course the wall collapsed. They'd dug the hole at a corner. A tower and thirty feet of stone barricade groaned, then began to plummet brick-by-brick. Flying dust obscured everything. When it settled we could see that Ernie had been right. Though a breach had been opened, rubble piled high, the Maenads faced many yards of deadly flowing water and a brand-new wall. Scores of the horrifying engineers lay beneath tons of limestone blocks, twitching with magickal life but unable to move. To me it all looked like so much busy work.

"Here comes the second wave," Tyrell pointed out, jerking his chin a little to our left.

The rest of the undead corps surged forward, that spine-tingling laughter commencing again. Like a raging river of rotting flesh, they scrambled over the heap of broken wall—and their pinned sisters—to fling themselves into the water. Of course each body that landed in the stream became just that, a body, now devoid of life for all time. But while a few floated with the current, enough followed to fill the channel. A terrible island of lifeless corpses grew higher and higher, like the bottom of Hades' hourglass. And still more came, climbing atop their deceased comrades. Now they were above the backed-up flow, high and dry. Water gushed through the gap in the wall to pour uselessly onto the ground in front. Sheer numbers had defeated our best ally. In no time at all they'd have a ladder made of Maenads, standing on each others' shoulders, arms linked. Those who still advanced upon the inner wall could climb up the 'living' bodies of the first Bacchantes and get atop the parapet. Though the guards did their best to pound them off with rocks and bronze weapons, too many Cumaeans had rushed to the south gate. Not enough remained to mount an effective defense.

"Can you fly out and knock 'em off?" I asked Tyrell.

"It'd be like waving at gnats on a manure pile," he said. "We'd have to stay there all day with so many enemies. I doubt that Al has the strength, after lugging that monster so far. And we'd run the risk of being overwhelmed ourselves and borne down into that sea of Maenads."

Ernie gave us a fierce nod from his horse perch. "Then there's only one thing for it." He aimed his knitting needle spear at the setting sun. "Their puppet master needs his strings cut."

I looked out over that ocean of fiends to the hill where the gray-garbed mage floated. "And just how do you propose we do that? He'll probably turn us into slugs as soon as we get anywheres close to him."

"Unlikely," Tyrell said. "It must require an immense amount of magick to control this man-eating rabble. And incredible concentration, or their dead minds would scatter the army in all directions. Our friend would have to release his hold on them to defend himself. Either way, the Maenads would lose their impetus."

Ernie added, "Plus, if he could transmogrify you, or anyone, why ain't he done it by now?"

An idea was bubbling in my noggin. Whatever we did, it had to be soon, or the monsters would be over the wall and all Hades would break loose. *Shoot, fer all I know, that's the city's fate. We might be piddlin' into the wind, as the boys at school say. But anything's better than standin' here watchin'. Time to act like a Stone Warden. That's why we're on this questy-thing, I reckon.*

"I was hopin' you'd reach that conclusion," Jasper said. "That magick-slinger's been on my agenda ever since we first laid eyes on him."

"Think we can handle him?" I had serious doubts that I could, especially as beat-up and worn-out as I felt.

"Remember what I keep tellin' you. Everything that lives—"

"—has a weakness. Yeah, yeah, yeah. But they usually don't conveniently advertise it like a medicine label. What might his be?"

"Arrogance, I'm guessin', like most Merchantry-trained mages. They all think their outhouses don't stink, if you catch my meanin'. So used to winnin' that they can't imagine losin'."

Tyrell had mounted Alcibiades and held out a rough hand to me. I grabbed it and let him yank me up onto the winged horse. "Here's hopin' you're right, boyo."

We swooped over the attacking Maenads on the Valkyrie horse's white-feathered wings, Ernie clinging to the forelock between Al's ears. As we covered the half-mile to the mage's hill, I laid out the tactics that I aimed to use. The tiny Marshal and the handsome Redeemer agreed that it could work, then made a couple of suggestions that I adopted as improvements. Jasper told me in my thoughts that I probably had enough magick to pull the thing off. 'Most certainly' would've been a more reassuring answer, but with Jasper you rarely got that. So I gulped a couple of times, got a firm grip on the tin cup, and tried to calm myself with some of Sha'ira's meditating tricks.

Dead at him we flew, so he couldn't mistake that he was under attack. I wanted the staff-wielding fellow to feel that he had no choice but to respond to us. Of course, you normally want to avoid telegraphing your intentions to a man who can bring windmills to life, but I didn't see a better choice. There was precious little time left for any clever flanking maneuvers. While we tried to sneak up on him, he'd still be enabling the Bacchantes to clear the wall and start snacking on Cumae's citizens. So straight at him it was, doing everything except waving a giant flag and blowing a bugle. Jasper suggested that he turn himself into both, but I vetoed it as likely to just distract me when I needed to concentrate on our already-risky scheme.

Most of the Maenads were in a tight crush near the hole in the wall, clambering up over one another to replace those the Hellene troops knocked down. Now we had nothing beneath us but Lusitanian dust and some thin shrubbery. Tyrell kept Al low. Because the ground rose toward our target hill, we came nearer and nearer to it. Altitude-wise, we flew at the same height as the sorcerer stood, if floating can count as standing. I let my whispered chanting do its work, flushing fear and doubt out of me. Nothing could remove all of it, of course. Since the Stone sped up my mind and let me see a slew of possibilities, I had visions of an awful lot of potential failures. *If this don't work, if he's smart enough to see through it, then we're about to see one brief and embarrassin' charge.*

Just as we'd dared to hope, the strain of burning through so much magick meant Gray Robe had to concentrate with every brain cell he possessed to control his undead battalions. Only when we'd flown to within a hundred yards did he react to our approach. Those ornate gyrations of his staff became a surprised flinch. He threw up his stick, which had swirly burned carvings along it that resembled tattoos, and aimed the point of it at us. When he did so he stopped floating. The mage sank onto the pebbly ground, landing heavily and skidding. For a moment I thought he'd fall. But he kept his footing, and also kept that staff aimed at us. Though I braced myself for some awful blast of dark magickal force that'd turn us all into katydids, nothing happened. Since he'd surrendered the initiative to us, I figured I'd take him up on his favor and carry out the rest of our plan. So I raised my tin cup and let Morphageus' recurved blade flash in the red sun.

Just as if we'd been rehearsing our play for weeks and this was opening night, Alcibiades came in low and hard, striking the top of the barren hill with what seemed to be too much speed. The golden Norn horse gave an award-winning performance, crashing into the ground and rolling forward. He tucked his wings to his flanks to protect them. Tyrell, Ernie, and me shot forward. Scattered in as many different directions, the three of us rolled like rag dolls, limbs tangled. Play-acting or not, it still hurt plenty. Those rocks and thorny bushes left all manner of bruises and cuts as I bounced along. In my head Jasper howled with indignant pain.

I lay still, giving my best impression of a girl knocked out cold. The sword lay beneath me, hilt poking out to entice our enemy. My heart pounded so loud I wondered that the mage couldn't hear it. Jasper whined so about our scrapes and bumps that I also wondered that the fellow didn't tell him to hush. Since I'd arranged my fall so I could face the stranger and Cumae, I cracked open one eye just enough to peep through my eyelashes. Across the valley, the Maenad horde had already begun to lose interest in scaling the wall. Soldiers shoved and beat those near the top until they fell onto the disgusting heap of their sisters. To the south, the gates held. *So far, so good.*

Sandaled feet appeared in front of me, blocking my view. The hem of the gray robe, which up close proved to be full of beautiful embroidery in subtle colors which only looked drab at a distance, fluttered not a yard away. That stick poked me a good one in the ribs. I remembered to groan like I was half-conscious. A long thin hand reached out to grip the sword. As soon as it did, Morphageus reshaped itself into a bear trap and snapped tight onto the wrist.

We'd caught ourselves a Merchantry sorcerer.

Weird constellations flashed by,
as did planets with vertical blue rings around them.
Multi-headed demons reached out for my face.
Choral screams from forlorn-looking
human faces deafened me.

34 / A Quick Trip Through the Obverse

A glass-shattering screech spiked my eardrums. I snapped my eyes open and looked up. Our prey had more than one reason to howl. Not only did he have a steel trap biting into his free arm, he also had four inches of warrior mouse chomping on the staff hand. Trained mage or not, the fellow yelped and let the long stick fall. Before it could hit the ground Tyrell had plucked it from the air. The Redeemer captain hopped back out of arm's reach. His LeMat hand-cannon caught the dying sunlight as he aimed it at the stranger. Just to make sure, Alcibiades sent the fellow sprawling to the dirt with a bat of his wing, then pinned him there with a front hoof.

"Hey!" Jasper said, his voice muffled for effect. "Can I let go now? This sweaty robe tastes like an old saddle blanket."

I jumped to my feet, the bear trap reshaping itself into a mirrored round shield, just in case the sorcerer intended to fling some desperate magick my way. His hands were already moving. But all he wanted was to attend to his wounds. He crossed his wrists and rubbed each injury with the opposite palm. Smothered gasps of effort and pain came from his mouth. Only now did I notice that our opponent wore a full-face mask of polished blue leather. Intricate exotic designs had been tooled into its surface. *How do you breathe in that thing, in this heat?* Now that I had time to look and listen with more care, I also saw something else of interest. Our prisoner had long hair, painted fingernails, and curves.

The mage was a woman.

Of course I should've known better than to be surprised by that. Shoot, my own mother was a Chauntline mage, and Sha'ira studied under her. But for some reason I just naturally figured that women would be too smart to fall for the Merchantry's seductive appeal. I expected the enemy's sorcerers to be crusty old guys with beaky noses, wrinkled cheeks, and chips on their shoulders. Women were supposed to be loving and on the side of right. *So much for yet another childish illusion. Next thing you know, I'll find out that President Lincoln is a demon.*

Ernie scampered along the hood and stood on her forehead. Before she could bat him away he'd tugged on the fancy mask and run off to Tyrell with it. Automatically she replaced it with her hands. But after maybe half a minute she gave that up and lowered them to stare at us without so much as a blink. Now that I could see her, I wondered what I'd been so afraid of. *Most of the Merchantry's power must come from bein' mysterious. She ain't much to look at.* Pasty, sweaty skin that looked like dough, brown eyes, hair the color of moldy hay, thin-lipped mouth, not a lot of chin. Probably about thirty-something years old. Only the triangle of tiny moles at her temple was in any way unusual. Could've been a farm wife anyplace in the States United. My respect for the Merchantry dwindled a little. Then I recalled how she'd controlled ten thousand of the walking dead and I took a step back. As Jasper had said, arrogance is a weakness.

"What gives?" I asked. "Who are you and why are you attacking Cumae?"

No answer. Just a dead stare into the sky past my shoulder.

"For that matter, why have you been following us?"

Still nothing. She set her jaw, stubborn as a log.

"And what do you want with this?" My shield melted into Morphageus, all its runes burning along the blade.

That got her attention. Though she still refused to speak, she looked at the magick sword like an addict gazes at an opium pipe. I swear her fingers actually twitched. It was plain as day that what she wanted more than anything else on this earth was to snatch the sword from me and...do what?

"You know that you can't use it," I said, ready to leap away if she went after me. "I mean, they did tell you that, whoever sent you? Anybody who tries to do magick with Morphageus but me dies...and not in a nice way." Actually, how it'd been explained to me was that 'their bones will turn to ash and their hollow skin will collapse onto the floor like an old gunny sack, while their liquefied internal organs ooze out of every orifice in a mass of blood.' *Maybe among the demons of the Obverse that'd be 'natural causes', but that counts as a bad end in my neck of the woods.*

Maybe she really hadn't known that it was lethal to the user. But what if she didn't plan to employ its power, just deliver it to somebody else for a big reward, or hide it so folks worse than her couldn't get it? Despite the doom-filled prophecy, I had no doubt that the Proprietor and his sorcerer cronies in London had a way to put Morphageus to use. Heck, if they could twist the entire world's history and culture into a snarled nightmare, channeling a single sword's energy shouldn't be too hard. No matter who she worked for, unless she was on her own, they couldn't be allowed to lay their mitts on it. As much as I wanted to be shed of Stone Warden duty and go back to being a normal kid, that wasn't the way to make it happen.

"Plus, you'd miss me," Jasper said. "Admit it. You'd pine away into the semblance of a sigh if I went away. All the other girls said so."

Other girls? There's a sprightly conversation for another day.

While I was ruminating, the mage woman took action. She bit Al on the leg that held her down. Strong Norn horse that he was, he still flinched. Before Al could recover and stomp on her again, she squirted out from under him and did a backward roll. As she popped up onto her sandals Tyrell leveled his gun and started to squeeze the trigger. I turned my sword into a boxing glove on a spring and shoved him in the chest. The shot went wide. We needed too many answers to be sending her off to sorcerers' heaven. Plus, I'd already been party to a lifetime of killing since this whole mess had begun. His pistol's .44 caliber boom did accomplish one thing, though. Her desperate grasp at the staff he held turned into an immediate retreat up the hill, though she managed to rip the mask out of Ernie's paws as she went. We all sprinted after her, me in the lead.

It turned out to be a brief pursuit. Six steps after she started she went down on both knees. At first I'd thought she'd twisted an ankle. But no, she'd deliberately stopped to touch the dry, chalky soil with both hands. *Why there? Just the same dirt as everyplace else.* Her hood fell back, revealing hair that floated in all directions on a pool of magickal energy swirling out of the earth. I heard her chanting words similar to those Ma had taught me on the *Kiss*. Daylight appeared beneath her as she levitated a couple of inches. The mage whipped her head up to glare at us with eyes that glowed with a fierce gold light, like an animal's at night. That brought us to a skidding stop. We'd all seen such a spectacle often enough to know that getting close likely wouldn't end well. Then I felt it, the true force that Pitcairn's stolen vessel could only simulate. What Ma had forbidden me to truck with.

We stood on a Chauntline.

Normal folks can't really detect them. Sure, they tend to feel better and more positive when near one, but they don't know why. But for those of us with the talent, or curse, stepping into a Chauntline is like riding a thundering locomotive down the steepest grade, not knowing if the brakes will fail. You feel like a tornado, but also like a house about to be hit by one. According to Ma the trick is to not try to resist the full power of Mother Earth. Instead, you should let it flow through you as if you're a wire for galvanic current. Since most people, trained or not, will seize up and panic, causing the energy to dam up inside them until they literally explode, I'd been banned from using them. Now I could see why. Though only a small one, maybe three times as powerful as the artificial line on our ship, it threatened to blow my arms, legs, and head off.

"Yee-hah!" yelled Jasper. I could almost see him swinging his hat in the air. "Ride 'em, cowgirl!"

I tried to back out of the field, but didn't know how. The whole life-force of the planet seemed to attract me toward the ground. *How do mages float with so much power tuggin' at 'em? Heck, how do they even breathe? This is miles and miles beyond anything I've done with my soul-store.* Taking a deep breath, I did the only thing my body would permit...I reached out and grabbed the woman's wrist. Maybe nothing would've happened if I hadn't had a mage for a mother, or if I hadn't worn the Legacy Stone. Most likely I'd have been left standing there, wondering where she'd disappeared to, a stupid look on my puzzled face. But because I conducted Chauntline force, when the sorceress vanished, so did I.

Strictly speaking, I only vanished from the point of view of my friends. As far as I was concerned, the rest of the world did the disappearing. For what seemed like an hour, but must've been a single heartbeat, I blasted through a strange world as if riding on the nose of a rifled Parrot shell. Weird constellations flashed by, as did planets with vertical blue rings around them. Multi-headed demons reached out for my face. Choral screams from forlorn-looking human faces deafened me. In reflex I mumbled the chant Ma had taught me, "Nhana pana yolnyu," over and over. Immediately all sound subsided to a gentle watery rushing. The unsettling sights became nothing more than vague shadows seen through violet gauze. Ahead I saw the top of the Cumaean wall, growing ever closer. *Huh?*

The real world smacked me in the nose—literally. I slid face-first along the rough floor of the outer wall, not twenty feet from where the soldiers defended the breach. My head pounded with the worst headache I'd ever felt. Sparkles flittered before my crossed eyes. Every inch of my skin itched something fierce.

"What the heck was that?!" Jasper yelled, not helping my peace of mind any. "And how do I get me some more of it?"

I shook my head to clear it, but that made my brain carom off the inside of my skull like a billiard ball. That nice Hellene lunch Lampade had served us came right back up. Somehow I managed to direct my shame over the wall and onto some Maenads, so it didn't feel a complete waste. The basset hound, left there when we'd gone after the mage, gave me a look of pure disgust. No more Chauntline energy buzzed through me. *Thank heaven fer small favors. Another two seconds of that and this quest business woulda come to a messy end.* My fellow traveler must've been an old hand at projecting herself across space, because she was already scampering down the wooden steps as if she'd arrived by first-class coach. Her fancy mask covered her face again. Groaning, I dragged myself over to the water bucket, plopped my head all the way into the slimy thing, and guzzled as much as I could hold. Then I came up with a sputtering gasp and stumbled after her, the Duke at my heels.

The few seconds I'd taken to drink had cost me. When I hit the dusty street below she'd vanished. My Stone grew warmer as she got farther from it. A mob of terrified women and children and shouting armed men swarmed all around, all beseeching the aid of one god or another. From their cries I gathered that both the south gate and the western breach would be lost causes in no time. Everybody fled away from the walls, toward the city center and the low Acropolis where the temples lay. I figured that the sorceress had to be doing the same, borne along by the wave of fearful folk. *And if them Maenads are about to pour in here, you'd best be doin' the same, girlie.* So I shoved my way along for a while, risking a trampling. After a minute or two I hit a logjam of bodies and decided to take the high road. Every muscle complaining, head about to explode like a barrel of powder, I climbed atop an abandoned cart. That didn't serve me well enough, so I jumped from that to a window and hauled myself up to the roof of a house. Its red clay tiles made for a slippery perch, but I held on long enough to spy what I expected to see.

"Madame," announced Jasper in a snooty Britannic accent, "your carriage awaits."

Alcibiades, silhouetted by the dying sun, swooped low over doomed Cumae. He still looked plenty tuckered-out from carrying the chimera. Tyrell had him zigzagging as they searched for me. I waved, but they didn't see me in all the chaos below them. So I raised Morphageus as a huge Confederate battle flag on a ten-foot pole. That sure did the trick. In no time I sat in front of the Redeemer, wriggling hound in my arms, as we flapped over the panicked mobs of Hellenes.

"What the bloody hell happened?" asked Ernie.

"You tell me," I said. "One second I had her by the arm, the next I was lyin' on the wall losin' my lunch."

The plump mouse laughed. "We saw that, all right. Fine aim, by the way. Two of them Maenads looked like they thought the wrath of Zeus had arrived."

"Corporeal projection," Tyrell explained. He still held the mage's staff. It made him look like a lance-bearing knight on a charger. "Very difficult magick. She took you through the Obverse like it was a turnpike, slipping you between worlds along the barrier. Makes for fast travel, but if done wrong it can trap you in limbo."

I shuddered, despite the July heat. "That explains the demons I saw, then. And the ordinary folks who reminded me of Dante's *Inferno*."

"Oh, do we get to see that, too?" Jasper wanted to know, his tone a little too gleeful. "You sure know how to show a fellow a good time on holiday."

I laughed and repeated what he'd said aloud, something I rarely did. "You call this a good time?" the Duke sniffed. "I had more pleasure rotting in the Bastille." He aimed his patrician snoot at Tyrell. "And thank you so much for putting me there, *mon capitaine*."

The Reb captain ignored him as he peered ahead, seeking our foe. Fires had broken out, probably from unattended kitchens or looting. You wouldn't think that a town of stone and tile would burn much, but Cumae proved that to be an error. Smoke hung over the city like a melancholic's gloomy mood. At our height, the wails of the populace sounded like a distant orchestra playing a somber dirge. Most of the mass of people pushed their way toward the Acropolis, not far from Lampade's home, resembling writhing snakes slithered along the narrow streets.

"She could be anyplace," Tyrell muttered, still clutching her captured staff. "Might even have projected out again."

"Not without a Chauntline, I'm bettin'," I said. "And it ain't likely there's another one inside the city. No, she's down there in that mess of folks. Set us down at Acastus' house. I want to see if Lampade and the kids are okay."

Since most of the distraught citizens had already passed the house, we had a clear landing spot next to the barn. The pile of manure and a few shrubs still burned, but the buildings hadn't caught fire yet. The bodies of Talos and the other chimera victims were gone. I set down the hound and dashed inside. It only took a minute to see that the place had been deserted. In the barn Lampade's bonds lay in a heap. Somebody had untied her. Her butchering knife was missing. That worried me some, but at least her children seemed to have escaped, too.

"Nobody here," I told my friends. Tyrell had dismounted, Ernie on his shoulder. The low-slung dog sniffed around idly. *I swear, he'd hunt fer food at the last Judgement. Probably chow down on some manna while the Apocalypse burned everything around him.* "Might've headed fer the high ground and the temples, like everybody else."

"That's a safe enough bet," Ernie said, pointing at the barn wall with his tiny spear. "Can yer read that? Me Marshal's coin translates speech, but ain't so good with writin'."

Next to the door, painted in what looked to be drying blood, somebody had written a single word: Athena.

"Says 'Athena'. Goddess of wisdom," I read aloud. "The opposite of Dionysus and his crazy emotions, if you ask me. Maybe Lampade or one of her servants is asking fer help in that direction." Something Ernie had said brought me up short. "Coin? You have a coin that translates fer you? Since when?"

"Since the day I put on me Marshal's spurs, duckie." The mouse tossed a coin so small I could barely see it. It landed in his open palm, a misshapen shining gold nugget. "All Marshals have 'em."

"It's magick, then?"

"You bet. Handed down ever since the foundin' of the Equity. An ancient Egyptian piece from Cleopatra's time. Does all manner of handy things, dependin' on what yer needs."

"Like what, besides translatin'?"

"That's its main job. But it also helps us cross borders and function in the new world created by the bleedin' Affluxion. Keeps us from gettin' disoriented by the Merchantry's spell. We don't have our memories played with like normal folks."

I frowned. "And where have you been keepin' it, since you

ain't got no clothes on?"

He cackled at that. "You don't want to know, missy."

He was right. I didn't. Besides, I had more to worry about than that. Because right then the Legacy Stone grew icy again...and the burning manure pile stood up, took on giant human form, and attacked us.

*Jasper giggled. "Time to do
glorious battle with the Outhouse Horror.
Instruct me on what tactics to employ.
I'm eager to follow your...ordures."*

35 / Manure on the Move

"This is gettin' deplorably predictable," complained Jasper. "What is it about you that attracts poop like moths to the flame?"

"Whaddya mean, me?" I countered, backpedaling away from the heap of smoking sewage, Morphageus in shield form. "This never happened till you showed up, buster."

"Are you implyin' that I might somehow be the cause of your persistent encounters with magickally-animated manure monsters? I take offense at the insinuation."

Tyrell and Alcibiades flapped themselves back to rooftop level. Ernie stayed on the ground and hopped aboard the Duke. "I ain't implyin' or insinuatin' nothin'. I'm flat-out statin' it."

"Pretty crappy attitude for a Stone Warden." My shield turned into a big cartoonish eye, gazing at my attacker in wonder and surprise. "Ooh, look, it's a lot bigger than the ones from the Washington Canal."

He sure had that right. Those had been about nine feet tall, lurching out of the sewage ditch at the behest of a platoon of Bullies. This one had to be a good fifteen feet of man-shaped burning muck. It had waste straw for hair and its eyes looked to be composed of clumps of stuff that didn't bear thinking about. The arms were unnaturally long and the legs were way too short for such a big form. And its fists rivaled beer barrels in size. Foul smoldering hunks of it dropped off as it lumbered toward us. Let me tell you, that stuff smells a lot worse when it's on fire. You don't want to be around one with a sensitive witched nose, that's for sure. *Here's hopin' he's as slow as them other ones were.*

No such luck. Though no greyhound, the poop-troll came at me with plenty of pep. Fairly nimble, too. We had to really scamper to avoid its first rush. The magick that gave it life came from the gray sorceress. I had no doubt about that. She had much more power and focus than the rag-tag band of disgraced mages in Washington had possessed. *Them little fellers was the militia. Merchantry hadn't taken me too seriously at the start. This here's the elite force, I'm bettin'.*

Duke *aarrooed* at the monster as he sidestepped away from its charge. Atop his back Ernie taunted the thing with some colorful Cockney expressions I'd have bet Jasper would soon be adding to his Dictionary of Shameful and Disgusting Expressions. Tyrell, circling just out of its reach, gave it a load of buckshot from the center barrel of his LeMat, but all that accomplished was to spray me with charred manure. *Oh, gee, thanks bunches fer that!* But bad as that had been, what followed was worse. The foul-smelling giant tore a hunk of gunk from its own body and flung it at me like a disgusting snowball from the Ninth Circle of Hell. I deflected it with my shield, but the stomach-churning meteor knocked me flat on my backside all the same.

Jasper giggled. "What next? Time to do glorious battle with the Outhouse Horror. Instruct me on what tactics to employ. I'm eager to follow your...ordures."

Ha-ha. Jiminy, don't he ever stop with the puns?

I didn't have time to worry about Jasper's sense of humor. Not only was this thing dangerous in itself, it was delaying us from helping the city. Any moment a tidal wave of Maenads would come rushing through Cumae. We needed to dispatch this icky, ploppy monster and get on to saving the city.

"Distract it!" I hollered to Tyrell. As he swooped into the creature's line of sight, I rolled away from a fatal foot-stomp and got Ernie's attention. "You fellers go find the puppeteer who's pullin' the strings. She can't be far away."

The hound waddled off with a final yowl, Ernie riding him like the oddest knight-errant in Lusitania. Another disgusting handful of fiery crud hissed past my head, exploding all over me when it splattered on the hard earth two feet away. Lucky for me Al had disturbed its aim. *Yuck! Why can't I ever do battle with anything normal and halfway clean? It's always slimy demons or decomposin' Maenads or walkin' manure piles. I swear, when they write the history of all of this they'll have to call it the Unendin' Quest to Scrub Off Unholy Muck.* I struggled to my feet, wondering how we were supposed to kill something that wasn't even alive.

"Maybe you can't actually kill it, but it can't chase you on one leg, can it?" said Jasper.

"Worth a try," I agreed. My will turned the shield into a medieval poleaxe with a ten-foot shaft. With all of my Stone-strength I slashed at the creature's left knee. The wide hooked blade sheared through the tree trunk of a limb as if it was only grass. My foe let out a gloppy rumble of complaint and tipped over. It windmilled its great long arms and crashed into the barn with a splat that shook the ground. I hooted in victory and waved my weapon over my straw-hatted head.

Too soon. I should've known that it wouldn't be so darned easy. My cheer died out quick as the severed leg wriggled and divided. Each piece shuddered, stretched, and grew arms. A head and feet soon followed. To my right the giant's missing leg also regenerated. Now I faced three poop monsters, the new ones just my height. Plenty spry, too. Soon I was ducking, rolling, and jumping to keep clear of them. Jasper hooted in my head and declared it to be great fun. At the same time more goo-bombs came my way, courtesy of the bigger beast. That couldn't last long. I had to come up with a better idea before what little luck I had left evaporated in the Lusitanian heat.

Tyrell guided Alcibiades down again to draw the giant's fire. That helped some. But the young twins kept up their assault, swinging ploppy fists at my head. I kept dodging. Fighting back wouldn't do me any good. Like as not I'd just break off a bunch of pieces and they'd come to double-life and surround me. No, I had to put some distance between me and these things, hoping that we'd find the mage and interrupt her spell. Returning

Morpliageus to shield form, I shoved at the nearest small pile of crap with all my might. It flew backward into its little brother, sending both rolling into a smoking heap about twenty feet away. *Perfect. Time fer one o' them retrograde advances.*

Zigzagging, in case any more goop got hurled at me, I crashed through the front door of the house. Stomping up the stairs, panting from effort, fear, and the climate, I tore through the gynaeceum. Like a terrified monkey I climbed out of the unshuttered window. Behind me I heard the sound of Lampade's lovely clean kitchen getting befouled by something horrible. I hoped I'd get a chance to apologize to her. Morphageus became a steel whip with a grappling hook at its end. With Jasper helping my aim I snapped it across the roof to latch onto a stout tile. Ten seconds later I'd hauled myself up the wall and onto the top of the house. Below I saw the first small poop monster reach try to climb out of the same window to follow me. Seeing it overbalance and fall onto the courtyard with a splat made my day just a little brighter.

From my somewhat secure perch twenty feet up I could see that disaster had fallen upon Cumae like a fell bird of prey. Fires burned unchallenged all over the city. Bodies of the small or unfortunate lay trampled by their panicked friends and neighbors, who all stampeded toward the Acropolis. Defeated and dejected soldiers, overwhelmed by ten thousand cackling Maenads, slogged from the wall to the west and south. When I squinted in that direction I could see that the crazed undead women had indeed forced their way into the town. Their spine-curdling laughter grew louder as they headed right for us. The only thing in our favor was that their number was so great that they got in each other's way and could only move at a crawl.

Behind me, the remaining poo-punk also crawled. The giant creature who'd spawned it had avoided Alcibiades and tossed it onto the roof. Now I was trapped up there with the stinky, smoky monstrosity. With Jasper's aid I turned Morphageus into a twelve-foot pair of tongs and grabbed the gooey brown thing. It proved to be as slippery and yielding as you'd expect sewage to be. Twice it nearly escaped and I had to re-clamp it. In my noggin Jasper kept up a non-stop, literally foul-mouthed, tirade about how bad it tasted. *I'll take yer word on that. Come on, Ernie, find that sorceress and interrupt her magick. This is gettin' ridiculous.*

When I just about lost my grip for the third time, I gave up waiting for help. Releasing it for a moment, I let the tongs reform into an enormous skillet. With a great big wind-up I bashed the noxious fiend off the roof. It splatted into its titanic parent and got re-absorbed, which was a tactic that hadn't occurred to me. After mentally promising Jasper a long soapy bath, I grapple-hooked back down to the ground, making sure to keep the house between me and Manure Monster, Sr. He tried to grab the Norn horse that harassed him. Nimble as a hummingbird, Al had no trouble avoiding his grasp. I whistled to Tyrell and pointed toward the Acropolis. He waved back, flew over, and picked me up.

Bad decision. Just as I got my backside settled in front of the

Reb, a manure ball the size of a haystack bowled us all over. Tyrell and his golden horse tumbled away from me. I sailed through the air and smacked hard into the side of the next house, all the wind knocked out of me. The giant had hurled his own head at us, lobbing it clear over the red-tiled roof. *What the heck? He's still on the other side of Acastus' house. How'd he manage that? Awful clever fer a brainless pile of muck.*

Maybe not so brainless. It struck me, so to speak, that the mage had to be close enough to see and control her puppet. Probably someplace nice and high, with a good field of vision. A look around showed me a couple of possibilities, like a statue of some unknown hero atop a big rock and, farther off, a clump of trees. If I could get Ernie and the hound to search over that way, maybe we'd get lucky. I had to hurry, though. The ground shook as the headless behemoth made its foul way around the house toward us. Not five paces away, the head that had taken us down started to shape itself into a mockery of humanity. Already it had legs and one long arm. Tyrell, off to my right, was busy inspecting Al for damage and didn't notice the danger.

I raised Morphageus to my lips as a shiny bugle and blew, careful to avoid kissing any lingering crud as I did so. My mounted companion, a Rebel Confederate cavalryman, had taught me lots of calls, just in case we needed to communicate. That sure came in handy now. I sounded 'Recall', hoping Ernie and the Duke were still close enough to hear and understand. The disgusting head had now transformed itself almost totally into a shape that could come after us. It blocked one end of the narrow street. In the other direction, the shadow of its parent loomed over me as it rounded the corner of the house. Smoke stung my eyes. Their awful stench made me want to puke. Every muscle in my overworked frame wanted to lie down and take a two-week nap. Things weren't looking too good. In desperation I blew my bugle again.

A long loud *aarroo* from the basset hound answered me. It came from the trees I'd spied as a potential hiding place for the sorceress. If they were already there, then she most likely wasn't. I pointed Morphageus as a huge steel arrow, indicating the colossal bronze statue. It seemed to have a hollow crowned head. Maybe our foe controlled her monsters from inside it. No place else looked to be as good a vantage point. A short dark streak shot out of the copse and sped toward the monument. Trusting that my allies could get the job done, I turned back to preserving my hide from imminent doom as the poop-fiends closed in.

"You know," mused Jasper, "it's at times like these that I wish somebody else had found me. A church-going old lady, perhaps. Or maybe a kindly teacher. Shoot, the way your life's been goin', I'd take a shoeless Confederate infantry private in a mud-filled rifle pit. The peace and quiet would do me good."

I ducked a swipe of the giant's hand. "What happened to that other Jasper, the one that liked to yell 'Yippee!' every time demons came after us?"

"He got a mouthful of manure, that's what happened. Worse than liver and onions."

Tyrell was aboard Alcibiades, who'd hidden his wings. They backed up next to me, against the wall of the house. Saber raised high, the Redeemer shouted, "Al bruised his shoulder. Might make for risky flying. Better not chance it yet." The great Valkyrie horse reared up as he spoke, then came down hard with both front hooves on the smaller monster.

"And you'd best not chance that sword, either," I told him. As another fatal foot stomp fell at me, I dashed forward into the narrow lane to avoid it. "Unless you want every chunk you shave off to become two of these nasty things."

"Don't I know it." He joined me on the other side of the street. The foe Al had kicked stood up again and staggered our way, still blocking escape. "But I just feel better waving it about in battle. Marshal Murat gave it to me at Jena."

We were getting hemmed in awful tight. Soon we'd have no more room to maneuver. I looked over at the big statue, but saw nothing happening. *This might be up to us.* Recalling what I'd done when rushed on the roof, I told Tyrell to ease to his left, turn Al, and get ready to kick. The smaller, quicker creature would get to us a moment before the giant. *Perfect.* With a wish I shaped Morphageus into the proper utensil and lay it flat on the dirt in front of me. *Here goes. Hope he's as dumb as he looks.*

It turned out he was exactly that dumb. Just as the six-foot-tall poop monster got within arm's reach of me, I heaved up on my giant kitchen spatula, tipping it to the right. Stinky-boy went that way, too, since he stood on it. Right on cue Alcibiades let fly a mighty kick with both rear haunches, sending the spatula head and its rider shooting directly into the belly of the headless giant. For a long moment he hung there, top half burrowed into the great brown steaming mass, stumpy legs kicking in vain. As we watched, those limbs disappeared like spaghetti being slurped up into a hungry mouth. With a sickly gurgle the enormous monster's head started to reappear atop its shoulders. *Yuck! Better not wait.*

"Run!" I hollered. "Make for that statue yonder!"

I smacked Al on his rump and told him not to wait for me. We'd cleared our escape route at the left end of the street. Alcibiades whinnied and galloped off, me close behind. The intersection lay maybe fifty yards ahead. Every bit of Stone-strength I had left went into my legs, pumping them as fast as my creaky bones would allow. Halfway there I risked a sideways peek back, then wished I hadn't. Our lumpy, lurching friend had off torn two burning handfuls of himself. He raised both in one hand and prepared to hurl them. In such a constricted space he was bound to flatten me with at least one. Not holding out much hope, I threw a Jasper-shield over my back and hunched down as I ran. *This is gonna hurt.*

But my prior planning paid off. Instead of me hollering in pain, it was somebody else's turn for once. From atop the statue, behind one dark empty eye socket, a girlish screech split the air. It sounded kind of funny, coming out of that brawny Hercules or whoever the monument represented. I didn't laugh, though, since I still expected a poop-pummeling. After holding my breath for a few seconds and finding myself un-bruised, I turned to face the crap-colossus. He'd ceased to be quite so colossal, actually. His restored head sunk into his torso, which melted and plopped into the hips, which twisted to send the whole disgusting arrangement avalanching onto the street. Sounded like a load of old wet shoes being poured out of a wagon bed. Two breaths later all that remained was a big pile of poo...and the smell. *Ain't enough magick in all Europa to get rid of it.*

"Yeah!" Jasper hollered. "Take that! You messed with the wrong magick sword, didn't you!"

"So you're claimin' credit fer all of my strategic plannin' and tactical brilliance?" I asked.

"We're an inseparable team, kiddo. Where would Napoleon have been without his Marshals, Elizabeth without her Raleigh, Alexander without Bucephalus—"

"Othello without Iago," I muttered.

"Hey! You wound me. I'm the one havin' to taste all of that poo, remember."

Worn out from all of the running, fighting, magick-slinging, and the constant expectation of being comprehensively dead, I just wanted to curl up in a ball and take a snooze. But we had to keep going. I forced my bare feet toward the statue, which still sent out squeals of rage and pain. Somebody's day had gone downhill and I hoped I knew who. *Can't be good fer your self-esteem to get licked by a fat mouse and a hound with four-inch legs.* Tyrell dismounted at the stone base of the monument, sword and pistol both at the ready, and stood guard. An occasional frantic citizen ran past us, but most seemed to have already fled to the far side of town, to the temples of the Acropolis.

A small shed at the base, which held an altar that smelled of incense, gave access to the top of the statue. Along the inside of one massive leg ran a circular wooden ladder. Sixty feet later I'd made it up to the hollow head. One sight of her showed why she'd made such a racket. Ernie had fanged her neck and one arm several times with his sharpened knitting needle spear. For good measure, His Grace the Duc du Ponteau had chomped on her ankle. Both my friends blocked the exit so she couldn't escape. The dangerous mage in gray sat in a corner, unable to walk or gesture. *Fine by me.*

I stared down at the bleeding woman, who looked back with suspicious calm. "So, just who are you, anyway? And why are so all-fired-up to cause me grief?"

She sneered, just like you expect from a proper villain. "Poor little put-upon Verity doesn't remember me. No surprise, really. You haven't seen me since the night you were born. I doubt your sainted mother has ever mentioned her sister's existence." The troublesome sorceress held out her unwounded hand. "Give us a kiss. I'm your Aunt Regan, honey."

*Charred skeletons mingled with their more-intact sisters,
managing to let out their mad laughter
even with no throats or lungs.
"So," asked Jasper, "what're you dressin' up
as for Halloween this year?"*

36 / Cumae Destroyed

I jumped back like she was a rattlesnake, slamming against the metal skin of the statue. My head spun. *What the heck is this? I ain't got no Aunt Regan. Ma's got no brothers or sisters at all that I ever heard tell of.* Getting hold of myself, I told the mage as much.

"Oh, Ellen, Ellen," she laughed, "still keeping your abomination in the dark about your doting family. How will the brat ever learn what she truly is?" Our wounded enemy sat up a bit, causing the Duke to growl. "Watch it, cur. I'm not so hurt I can't spell you into something that crawls on its belly and eats maggots."

"And I am not so much the Gaullic gentleman that I would forbear tearing your lying throat out," the proud hound retorted.

"Lying throat? How you must wish that were so. Why should I make up stories? The truth is ever so much more entertaining, particularly where this little monster is concerned."

I heard somebody climbing the steps. From his smell and

breathing I knew it was Tyrell. "I don't know that I care to be called a monster and an abomination, especially by somebody who witches the dead to try to kill me."

Genuine surprise filled her eyes. "Kill you? Why would I want to do that? I don't get my reward if I bring you in as a corpse."

"And what reward might you be expectin'?"

She paused, then gave me a big warm smile. "Your Mommy's head on a spike, dearie."

Everything turned red as I flung myself at her, Morphageus in sword form. She shrank back and spelled a faint sparkling blue energy shield in front of her. I froze, hanging in mid-air. But it wasn't her weak defense, the last gasp of her exhausted soul-store, that stopped me. A strong hand clutched the back of my overalls. Tyrell, just in time.

"Careful, now, Miss Verity," the Reb said. "Let's be thinking before we act."

I struggled a bit, but my flush of rage had already passed. He was right. We needed to get more intelligence from this witch. Nodding, I let out a long breath and relaxed. Morphageus became a tin cup, though I didn't let go of it. "All right, then. I reckon she can say her piece before we chuck her out the window,"

Still insultingly confident, my so-called Aunt Regan cocked her head. "Such a delightful child. How do you endure her, Redeemer?"

"Oh, it isn't so difficult," Tyrell replied. "I just have to defend her against scum like you every now and then, is all."

"My, my, don't you know how to charm a lady? Is that my staff?"

He did have hold of her carved stick. With a wrist snap he tucked it behind his back, out of reach. "A spoil of war. Perhaps they'll put it in the Equity Museum."

There's an Equity Museum? Oh, I gotta see that some day. Probably has the dog collar that the Emperor Hadrian gave to Romulus.

"If you can. We shall see. Perhaps you'll think better of me when you know more about your little traveling companion here." She grunted as she stood up, hopping on the one undamaged foot. "You have all placed your trust and the Stone in something more dangerous than me."

"Quit talkin' in riddles," I snapped. "You got somethin' to say, spit it out. Otherwise we're just gonna gag and hogtie you."

"Don't make threats you can't keep, niece."

Ernie ran up my body to stand atop my straw hat. "Have yer been payin' attention, mage? She's the one that brought yer down twice in one day. If anybody's talkin' too big fer her britches, it's you. Yer soul-store is about gone and there's no Chauntline here."

She snorted at him. "Ah, Ernie, is it? Still keeping up the Cockney pretense these days? Do your fellow Marshals know your full history? So many secrets for such a small group." The sorceress limped to her right until she stood between the open eyes of the giant statue. "True, there is no Chauntline here. And I am weak from controlling those smelly fellows without one.

But my resources aren't quite exhausted."

I tensed up, ready to defend against whatever new horror she planned to send our way. But the woman did nothing but blab some more.

"Quite the assembly of pathetic losers we have. A failed Bonapartist who thinks he can 'save' the Merchantry...a failed Gaullic Monarchist who now eats table scraps from the dirt...a failed Marshal who seeks redemption for his treacheries...and a soon-to-fail Stone Warden who cannot even save one little boy."

"Enough of this," I sighed. "Tie her good and tight. We gotta go."

"Finally, an accurate statement!" The woman clamped her mask back onto her face. "But, to be precise, it's me that has 'gotta go', as you so charmingly put it."

"Yer ain't goin' anywhere, witch," Ernie told her. "Except maybe to perdition when we roll yer down these steps."

"And now we're back to inaccuracy again," she said, rubbing her palms together. "I told you I still had resources. This structure, for example. It is a monument to Pentheus, torn to pieces by his own Maenad mother, when she was in the Dionysian frenzy. Fittingly, the Cumaeans built it atop the very rock where their ancient Hellene ancestors used to perform bloody human sacrifices. A place of great misery, this. And very useful, too."

Oh-oh. So that's why she's so cool and cocky.

"Watch out, y'all!" I cried. "This here's an ostium!"

I turned and shut my eyes tight as she clapped her hands.

Even so, the bright green flash seared my eyeballs. A yelp from the hound told me he hadn't reacted fast enough. A sharp smell like you'd get from a close lightning strike filled our noses. Blinking, I looked all over the small room, but I already knew what I'd see. Nothing. Our prisoner had used the Merchantry transporter to escape us.

"We really need to get us our own ostium tokens," said Jasper. "Sure beats hoofin' it everyplace."

"Yeah, and all it costs is yer soul," I reminded him.

Ernie rubbed his tiny peepers. "Blimey! Never stood in an ostium when it went off before. All I see are little black specks."

Tyrell said, "It will pass. The energy is harmless, but it does overwhelm the eyes."

The Duke sniffed at the empty space where Regan had been. "She is truly gone. That is either a great shame or a great relief."

"Both," I declared, heading back downstairs. "But at least now we're shed of her and can concentrate on the Maenads."

Though I did wonder why she hadn't yanked me through the ostium with her.

It turned out that they were easy to concentrate on. No sooner did we leave the small temple at the statue's base than we met a whole bunch of them, the vanguard of the invading horde. All of us mounted up on poor tired Alcibiades and outran the rotting monstrosities. By that time, every citizen who'd headed for the Acropolis had already got there and we had clear sailing. The hill where Cumae kept its important religious and public buildings was no great mountain, but it did have a certain steepness to it that got your attention. As beat as we all were, a molehill might've whipped us. *Good thing they carved steps here, or I might just bounce back down to the bottom.* I smiled when I saw that the complex had its own high wall, guarded with a triple row of hoplites and archers. *Well, that's somethin', anyhow. As good a spot fer a last stand as any.* Only trouble was, all the water flowed through the stream at the hill's foot. If we had to hole up for long, we'd get awful thirsty in a hurry.

Acastus had relocated there from the breached wall. Covered in soot, mud, and blood, the poor man looked as if he'd escaped Tartarus only ten minutes before. He ordered us to be admitted through the single stout gate. Like the rest of the Acropolis, it had been painted in every bright color you could name. Relief carvings covered every square inch, portraying all of the major gods and myths and probably most of the minor ones, too. On the bronze gate itself Athena and Dionysus faced off, one on each side. Wisdom and Frenzy at odds. It was anybody's guess who'd win the day. With the sun all gone now and slavering Bacchantes at the base of the hill, it was easy to bet on madness and doom.

"Where's Lampade?" I asked, afraid of the answer.

"In bonds at the Temple of Artemis," her bedraggled husband said. "Attended by her women. She is calm now, and wails for her children."

"They're safe?"

He nodded, looking back over his shoulder at a long thick-columned building. "As safe as anyone can be this day. The priests of Apollo guard them. They have to be prevented from rushing to rejoin her."

My eyes widened. "Even after she tried to skin 'em?"

"None of us can vouch for our own sanity in such circumstances. She lost command only for a dark moment." He sighed and shook his head. "If I had been there—"

I held up a grimy palm. "No, you wouldn't have wanted to see her like that. Bad enough that I had to."

His hand, just as filthy, cupped my cheek. "But grateful I am that you were present. I owe you a debt."

"Naw. Anybody else woulda done the same. Helpin' kids in trouble don't take no great analytical thinkin'. You just wade in and do it."

"Nevertheless, I shall repay you...if any of us lives to see the dawn."

We climbed the steps to the top of the wall. Tyrell, Ernie, and the Duke stayed below. Torches and great iron braziers began to blaze all around us. The doors boomed shut, a bolt as massive as that at the south gate securing them. Archers and spearmen lined the top of the wall, ready to knock off any Maenads who might scale it. Far below, where the stone steps began, a squad of burly men had knocked down the narrow bridge that crossed the stream. Now the undead mob had no easy access. Running water crossed our front and the hill was a sheer cliff of bare rock, over two hundred feet straight up, everyplace else. Back in the dim past the founders of Cumae had foreseen that invaders might come and had planned their Acropolis accordingly.

What they hadn't foreseen, though, had been ten thousand walking corpses, all bent on the annihilation of every living thing they encountered. Even without Regan's evil magick to impel them, the Maenads still had that destructive urge. Evidence of it was all too easy to see. Fires devoured three-quarters of the city. Most roofs had already collapsed, and many of the walls, too. The frenzied creatures responsible for it all smashed furniture, carts, and pottery. Wanton destruction seemed to excite them, to increase their mad joy. Shrieking, discolored monsters, mostly naked, chewed on chunks of unlucky citizens, horses, dogs, rats …anything unable to outrun them.

This felt like waiting for a loved one to breathe her last. Cumae let out its death-rattle as we watched.

All around me I could hear and feel the despair of the townspeople. Weeping from strong men, from hardened warriors, is a lot tougher to take than it is from women, somehow. Maybe because they all try so hard not to. In my world of 1862 misery, mourning, and funerals were so common they were almost an entertainment. Young children died of every little thing, old folks caught cold and got carried off, a carriages overturned and there' would be an empty chair at the dinner table that night. But watching the place you grew up in, raised your family in, went to school in, fell in love in…watching it get obliterated in front of you, that's a whole different thing. I sure hoped Washington wouldn't suffer the same fate soon, maybe at the hands of Tyrell's Confederate friends. Or just as bad, Mr. Lincoln's troops might sack Richmond like that. Leave it an empty, torched husk.

If a Hellene god is responsible fer this, then maybe folks here should start worshipin' somebody else.

The Maenads crowded right up to the edge of the water, but it was plenty wide and they didn't try to swarm across it this time. They just milled about, pressed together like sardines in a can, their cackling now mixed with a sort of weepy sighing. Creepy as they'd been before, the new sound only made it worse. My nostrils stung with the sharp odor of the flaming city. Sooty wood smell, carrying the sickly-sweet odor of burning human and animal flesh, plus the added joy of Bacchantes' putrefying carcasses. Some of them had been consumed by the fires, too. But that didn't stop them from moving. Charred skeletons mingled with their more-intact sisters, managing to let out their mad laughter even with no throats or lungs.

"So," asked Jasper, "what're you dressin' up as for Halloween this year?"

That made me snort a little, even in those circumstances. "I'm pretty sure we'll be stayin' home fer that particular night, thank you very much. Can you imagine how many real demons will be out then? Not to mention all of the other nasty buggers the Obverse and Merchantry hold? It'd be open season on poor little Verity."

"Yeah? And what do you call this?"

I stared out at the dark bloody nightmare that was Cumae's remains. "Hell, boyo. This is pure hell. And we're stuck in the middle of it with no exit in sight."

Figuring that I'd better investigate our resources before the enemy army found a way to come at us, I scooted back down the steps and poked my snoot into everything I could. A nice portly lady with a sad smile gave me a big hunk of bread and some olives. I munched on the meal as I strolled about. In the Temple of Artemis, decorated with hunting scenes, I found poor wretched Lampade, just as her husband had said. The strong lively woman I'd met when I'd first got to the city had vanished. Only her shell remained. She rocked and moaned, still bound hand and foot with leather thongs. Three priestesses, all about her age or older, sponged her fevered skin or whispered soothing words. Not wanting to undo any progress she might've made, I didn't let her catch sight of me. Instead I passed through the long building, squeezing around a knot of women who beseeched the image of the goddess for aid. A narrow back door let me out onto a plaza that led to the temple of her twin brother, Apollo.

This structure looked to be a mirror of the other, which only made sense. Where his sister's place had been painted with bows, arrows, and dogs pursuing stags, Apollo's frieze had lyres, laurel, and suns. But he had bows, too, being the god of archery. Since he was also the god of health and beauty, I wondered if it offended him to have so many disgusting undead creatures assaulting his hill. Their god seemed the polar opposite of Apollo. *Bet they don't exactly kiss and hug at family reunions on Mount Olympus.* For that matter, it probably didn't make Artemis happy, either. The deer was her sacred animal.

Dionysus' suppliant women had been chowing down on plenty of them lately. I doubted that he'd asked her permission.

Both of Acastus' sons huddled beneath Apollo's altar, tended by a pair of handsome young priests. The boys' eyes were bloodshot with crying, but other than that they appeared to be in fair shape. Strong kids, like their parents. Just as with Lampade, I avoided the kids in hopes of keeping them calm. That proved easy to do, because the place was packed with even more frantic worshippers than in Artemis' temple. They came near to trampling me as they strained toward the lovely thirty-foot-high statue. Before I got stomped into the marble floor I snuck out a side exit to see what else might be nearby.

Next door sat Ares' temple. At least I figured that was his, judging by the mob of soldiers in front of it, all waiting to get in. From what I knew of Hellene mythology, I wanted nothing to do with that fellow. So I gave the whole place a wide berth and turned to my right. I found myself in front of a taller, wider building than all the rest. Athena's. *What is it with Hellene gods and the letter A?* Its relief sculptures and paintings were of looms, swords, olive trees, and owls. In school we'd learned that she was the goddess of wisdom, but also of battle strategy and craftiness. That was why she supported the sneaky thinker Odysseus. She also was the goddess of justice. *Here's another deity who just has to be miffed at Dionysus' arrogance.*

And that's how I got my bright idea, gazing up at the Temple of Athena. Maybe she helped me out, maybe I just needed inspiration. Either way, I hatched a doozy of a plan.

"Yeah...well, I have noticed that whenever you show up,
people lose their cities, lives, and illusions."
"Oh, so this whole miserable Stone Warden questy-thing is
suddenly all my fault? I distinctly recall sittin' in that dark
chamber beggin' you to go away and leave me be, but no—"

37 / How To Confound a God

Now the trouble with hatching anything, plans included, is that you never know exactly what that chick will look like. So I naturally expected to produce one great big ugly duckling before the night was over. Whether it might turn out to be a swan or a snapping turtle was anybody's guess. But when you're out of any other options, gambling starts to look real sweet. I shared my idea with the rest of my crew. They'd been discretely following me.

"Madness," Tyrell said.

"Lunacy," agreed Ernie. He spun one little finger around his ear.

"Derange´," added the Duke in Gaullic, itching his ear with a rear foot.

Alcibiades shook his head and rolled his eyes. I swear.

"Complete and utter folly," Jasper pronounced, turning himself into a tiny court jester's head. "Not that I'm necessarily against it on that account. Sounds like more fun than a drunken sleigh ride down the Matterhorn." Then he sent me a crystal-clear image of that very thing, from the point of view of a participant. Made me so dizzy I had to grab Al's tail to stay standing.

No, I didn't ask when he'd ever been on one of those. He dearly wanted me to, though. I could tell. His unseen pout when I ignored him filled my brain.

"Swell," I grinned. "Then it's right consistent with everything else we've been doin' lately. Let's get crackin'."

I assigned each of them a task in the Grand Scheme to Save Our Miserable Hides. Once they'd scattered to carry out their roles, I climbed the steep steps of Athena's temple to do my part. Of all the pieces of the plan, mine was the chanciest...and the most essential. If I couldn't swing my end of things, nothing my friends did would matter much. In the other temples I'd paid careful attention to the rituals and requirements of the altar. Once or twice I'd even asked a priest or a suppliant a question, just to get things clear in my head. That was why my first action was to slink into a storeroom, block the door with a bench, and climb into my enchanted rucksack. In there I stripped down to my bruised and freckled essence. With soap and water I scrubbed myself raw. When my skin fairly glowed with cleanliness and friction I hunted up a Lusitanian girl's garment of white wool. After pulling it on and brushing my short red hair so that I looked as presentable as the hand of man could make me, I crawled out of the bag. *Here goes nothin'.*

Lots of terrified folks mobbed the altar. I had to wait a good half hour for my turn, even though the priestesses ran three people at a time up to the flower-strewn ledge. That turned out to be for the best. It gave me a chance to see how everybody else made their offering and spoke to the goddess. When I got called up I felt fairly sure I knew what to do. A wreath of olive leaves adorned my noggin. Pouring oil on my head and hands for purity, I washed my sins away so as not to defile the sacred presence. Spitting cleansed my mouth of any wrong words. Then I stepped to the flame and sprinkled some barley into it, head bowed. In my right hand I held the required sacrifice.

With a big deep breath I raised my arms and chin up to the enormous alabaster and gold effigy of the great goddess. Looming above me was a statue of a strong, handsome woman, helmet tipped back on her head, an owl perched on one shoulder. The gleaming thing, painted in colors so real it looked ready to wink at me, stood taller than Ford's Athenaeum. Only then did it strike me that my theatre had been named after the being I spoke to now.

"Hear me, *Glaukopis*, Bright-Eyed One; *Promachos*, She Who Fights in Front; *Athena Polias*, Protector of the City. I come as soul-child of the mighty and clever Odysseus. His *metis* animates me, gives me purpose. I, too, am a shield-maiden, guardian of justice. Search my heart and you shall see the truth of my words."

I'll allow I'm not religious by nature. You won't find me in church of a Sunday. More likely you'll find me lounging on the bank of the Potomac with a fishing pole in my hand. It never occurred to me to pray for anything before. And it might not have happened there in Cumae, either, if I hadn't seen the evidence with my own eyes that in Lusitania gods truly existed. They might have been a bunch of spoiled, power-mad, arrogant children; they might not have been actual deities, maybe just mages with little self-restraint; they might have been more trouble than they were worth, most of the time. But by golly, I had to admit that they were real. So I bit my lip and made my case to Athena.

"I desire redemption for Cumae and its people. I seek the refuge of your Aegis for the innocent, the honorable, and the brave. I ask the protection of your sword, to guard against the unholy and defiled ones who approach your sacred temple. But most of all, I implore the judgement of all Olympians against Dionysus, who treads upon everything that you hold dear. The hinds of Artemis fall before his maddened minions. They destroy the health of the devout, and bring ugliness instead of beauty, neither of which should Apollo tolerate. Their souls are forfeit to Hades, which is the rightful way of things, yet he is denied what is his by their undead state. And their very existence is an affront to your wisdom and justice. This god of passion has overstepped his allotted bounds, Lady, and I appeal to you to give him naught but what he deserves at your hands, and at the hands of your mighty and pitiless Father, wielder of the thunderbolt."

With that I offered my sacrifice, tearing off a hunk of it and consigning it to the flames. Then I lay the rest of my most prized possession on the altar and stepped back to stare at it as if I could command it to speak to Athena all by itself.

My straw hat, the one I'd worn through every skirmish, battle, and magickal encounter since Richmond. Giving it up felt like a scalping. I couldn't have been more naked if I'd shucked my Hellene gown and stood there in the buff.

Nothing happened, of course. At least, not right that instant. I hadn't really expected it to. Maybe in some old-time romance the statue would've come to life, strode out of the building, and commenced to slaying Maenads. It would've laid waste to them by the hundreds, obliterating the undead horde in five minutes of unstoppable divine carnage. Apollo would've dispatched them with his godly arrows. Artemis would've unleashed her hounds to rip them all apart. But this was real life, sort of, and things never come about so perfect.

"Maybe Athena helps them that help themselves," Jasper suggested.

"Wouldn't doubt it," I said as I backed away from the altar.

"So, should we get to work doin' that very thing?"

"Gee, it's like you can read my mind."

"I do card tricks, too. And feats of prestidigitation that will amaze one and all. Only five cents admission. Come one, come all."

I snatched up my rucksack and skipped out the front entrance and down the steps. To the west Cumae glowed red with all the fury of a simmering volcano. The seething mass of Maenads still crowded against the river moat, crying and laughing. *Looks they're waitin' fer somethin'. Reinforcements? Not likely. A signal, maybe? Or the arrival of their general? Whatever it is, it ain't gonna raise nobody's spirits on this side of the wall, that's fer sure.*

The hound waddled up to me, a sausage hanging from his jowls. Aboard his long back, Ernie munched on a grape the size of his whole furry head. He'd gone native and donned a bronze thimble as a helmet. A woman's round brooch served as his shield. "All's in readiness, commander," the tiny Marshal told me. At least, I think that's what he said. Most of it got lost in gushy fruity chompings.

"Swell," I said. "What about Tyrell and Al?"

"They flew off like you told 'em. Haven't seen 'em since."

"That Reb's got more lives than a roomful of cats. I ain't too worried. He'd better hurry up, is all."

The Duke gulped down his meal and ran his impressive pink tongue all over his big nose. Jasper declared that a neat trick and suggested I try it. "I can attest to his survival skills, having tried my hand at besting them on more than one occasion."

I raised an eyebrow at that as we moved toward the gate. "Yeah? You'll have to fill me in on the particulars of your past associations with the Cap'n. Oughta make fer a great yarn."

"If by that you mean a fascinating tale of adventure and intrigue," the stumpy, floppy dog said, "I shall not gainsay you, young one. Let it suffice to say that he ruined more than one of my good silk shirts with that wicked smallsword blade of his."

Acastus met us at the base of the wall in full bronze armor, the black horsehair crest of his gleaming helmet waving in the slight breeze. That wind brought us the wrenching scent of his city's fiery death. I hadn't thought his weathered face could show more pain than it already did, after all he'd been through. But that awful smell hollowed out his eyes just a bit more deeply. His brother, standing beside him and also dressed for battle, looked every bit as wretched. Pelias frowned at Ernie, mounted on the hound like some mythic hero. Our stout-hearted mouse saluted him with his tiny needle-spear. The sturdy Hellene shook his head and looked back to me.

"Callisto, you have more courage than speech may express," Pelias said. "But it is wisdom that we need now."

"Which is why I just begged Athena for aid," I told him, putting on my best grammar so as not to confuse the strangers around us. "Let us hope she decides to grant it." I raised my gaze to Acastus. "Did Cadmus manage to tell you what to do?"

Lampade's man nodded, but his uncertainty was clear. " Your brother speaks strangely. It took a good while for him to express your need. But the god-horse finally grew impatient and wrote it all out in the dust."

Huh? Al speaks Hellene? Since when?

"He did?" I hoped my expression didn't show too much shock. This was the first I'd ever heard of Alcibiades understanding anything besides apples and nose rubs. "Uh, excellent. All is ready, then?"

"It shall be, soon. Though I cannot honestly claim to understand your intention. But your cleverness would confound

Hermes and I will not argue against it."

"And your men? They all know the part that they must play?"

"They do. I told them that the gods had given us a sign and unflinching obedience to their will is our only hope."

Jasper whistled in my head. "Gee, no pressure on old Verity there. No, siree. Looks like you're a regular Delphic oracle, huh?"

"Maybe," I said to him. "Or just some creepy harbinger of doom, like poor Ino."

"Yeah...well, I have noticed that whenever you show up, people lose their cities, lives, and illusions."

"Oh, so this whole miserable Stone Warden questy-thing is suddenly all my fault? I distinctly recall sittin' in that dark chamber beggin' you to go away and leave me be, but no—"

A series of horns blared above us, from atop the wall. More soldiers clattered up the steps. Just as many took their places in a deep formation behind the gate, spears and shields ready to repel anything that might get through. Women screamed, grabbed their kids, and hustled away toward whatever protection the buildings might offer. Down beside my foot, the Duke growled as if he planned to take on every Maenad all by his lonesome. *This is it, I guess. Them ugly hags must be makin' their move. Hope I made all the right decisions to frustrate 'em. This'll be a mighty short battle, otherwise.*

Acastus and his brother joined their comrades atop the wall. I waited until they'd made it halfway up, then scooted with the Duke and Ernie in the opposite direction, towards the rear cliff.

Nothing could get up that way, but getting down would be simple. All you had to do was jump. Two hundred feet later you'd land, for better or for worse. The ground rose the closer we got to the edge. Once we'd nearly made it there I turned to stare back down at the valley. From our new vantage point we had a clear view over the top edge of the defensive wall. What we saw didn't ease the dread we all felt.

The Maenads had crossed the stream.

Unlike the wall breach, they hadn't needed to sacrifice any of their own to do it. All they'd required was rubble from the town they'd just wrecked. Cracked stone blocks, broken doors, shattered wagons, even the corpses of those they'd butchered had been hurled into the stream at a dozen points. Thousands of the undead monsters had already made it across and were lurching up the hill. Maybe a third still waited on the other side. As soon as the way was clear they'd be surging up at us, too. Beyond them, Cumae's bones smoldered, the fires that had consumed it beginning to die out from lack of fresh fuel. The whole landscape looked like a vast graveyard come to horrible life, just waiting for Hades to leave Tartarus and claim it.

Which was just what I counted on.

Making that happen, though, would take a whole lot of luck. And I'd already pushed so much of it that my arms were about to fall off. My only hope was that I'd also used up all of my bad fortune for one lifetime and that things would finally break my way. Just as that thought flitted through my busy mind, Morphageus flowed out of its cup form and became a big cartoony hand. It crossed its first two fingers, and the next two. Then it impossibly crossed the pairs in a way that a real hand never could've...at least, not without some noisy and painful bone-busting.

"Just doin' my part to increase your luck," Jasper explained. The goofy mitt untangled its plump digits, ran up my arm like a lizard, and rapped hard on my noggin.

"Ow!" I hollered, grabbing it and holding it away from me as if it stunk.

"Knock on wood!" he sang, cheerful as an undertaker at a smallpox epidemic. "Can't be too careful where providence is concerned. He formed a giant pair of scissors. "Find me a rabbit. We need a big old foot for the cause."

"Ick! No! You leave the poor bunnies alone."

"What if it's an undead Maenad rabbit with nasty big pointy teeth and a vicious streak a mile wide?" The scissors became a meat cleaver. "Can I chop it up then?"

"Ain't likely to bring us much luck in them circumstances."

"Hmm. Got a point there. Guess we'll have to settle for what can manage on our own. Did I tell you your plan is cuckoo? "

"You and half the population of Lusitania. If you got a better idea, I'm all ears."

"All ears?" He turned into a goofy-looking rabbit. "Now you're back to the bunnies again. Make up your mind."

That was all the witty sword banter I could handle. We had to get going. In a few minutes, the crazed Bacchantes would smash into the wall and the last battle for Cumae would commence. No telling how long the defenses would hold. Near as I could figure, the undead had the living survivors of the city outnumbered ten-to-one. Only that stone barrier and the cliffs I stood on barred their slimy way. We had precious little time to get our reinforcements in place.

"So," Ernie said, spitting a grape seed over the edge into the deep black void, "are we here to take in the view? Because I have to tell yer, I've seen better vistas lookin' down a privy."

"Make a habit of that, do you?" the Duke sniffed.

"In my line of work it pays to be cautious. Ask Miss Verity here about what sort of vile things can come up from beneath an outhouse."

That made me shudder a little as I recalled being trapped in the jakes behind my house in Washington, only an hour or two after finding Morphageus. Bullies had brought to life something gloppy and mean in the bottom of the privy. I'd had to seal the hole with a Jasper shield and squeal for help. "I've taken to peepin' down there myself on occasion, that's all I know."

The basset hound shook his big head, making his long ears sway. "Mon Dieu, you make me long for the civilized hygienic amenities of my beloved Gaullic chateau."

Ernie snorted. "Gettin' tiresome squattin' on yer haunches in the dirt, Yer Grace?"

"You have no conception of my shame, Monsieur Mouse."

I shushed them with a wave. Squinting out over the northern wall, rather than down at nothing, I saw what I'd been waiting and hoping for. Distant sparks began speckling the brushy plain.

As we watched, they began to magickally shape themselves into fiery letters twenty feet high. In Britannic, not Hellene: VERITY.

"Are you stakin' a claim to some real estate?" Jasper asked. "I'd advise against it. The gossip is that mortgage values are plummetin' in Cumae."

"I expect there's more of their spies here
than there are dogs and cats."
*"They probably **are** the dogs and cats,"*
Jasper pointed out.

38 / Damn Zombies!

I ignored Jasper's comments and kept my eye on the burning letters. Once the tail of the Y had blazed into life, ending in an arrow pointing at the Acropolis, a spark drifted upward, like a bit of burning paper floating on the breeze. The orange ember bobbed toward us. Soon it grew large, stopped its aimless course, and shot arrow-straight in our direction. When it got within hollering distance its indistinct shape firmed into just what I'd expected: Tyrell, astride Alcibiades, towing an irate chimera.

"If this were a propaganda painting," the hound said with a low laugh, "I would say it represents the Britannic lion, tamed by the Gaullic man-of-war."

Ernie poked the dog's ear with his tiny foot. "Careful there, Yer Grace. We ain't all snail-chompers here, yer know."

"You say 'snail-chomper' as if it is a bad thing, Monsieur. Have you ever tried it? Such a delightful India rubber texture. C'est magnifique!"

I noticed that Duke's Gaullic words weren't all translating as smooth as before. Ernie's phony Cockney accent seemed thicker, too. *Uh-oh. The spell might be wearin' off. We've sure been burnin' through a lotta magick and that's a fact. One more reason to wrap things up and get outta Lusitania.*

Alcibiades wobbled through the night air with his load and set it down just at the edge of the cliff. Tyrell whipped off the loop of rope that had held it by its serpent-tail. I braced myself, Morphageus shield up, for a blast of flame. Nothing happened. The goat's head belched a couple of weak puffs of orange light, but they only traveled an arm's length from its jaws. At the front end, its lion face sagged as if exhausted. Way back at the rear, the adder-tail drooped on the rocky ground. A lot of the fight had left the monster since we'd seen it last. *Fine by me. I got enough to worry about without fendin' off poor Ino, too.*

"I can't believe you made it work," I said to Tyrell. "Where'd you find her?"

He wiped his sweaty face with a CSA bandana. "Northwest corner of the wall, surrounded by close to five hundred torched and broken Bacchantes. Despite the damage, they all still tried to crawl back in after her. She'd plumb exhausted herself trying to slay the unslayable. More battalions of the things were advancing. I feared she'd nearly reached the end of her fire reserves, so we plucked her out of that predicament. Somehow she recognized us as friends and let us do it. While we flew over to the northern fields Al spoke to her in Hellenic. Don't ask, I didn't know he could, either. He certainly doesn't put himself out speaking Britannic to me. Must have got through to her, because she spat those flames right on cue as we flew your name-pattern."

"And that's supposed to accomplish what, exactly?" Ernie wanted to know.

"Lead our friends to us, if they're up there lookin'," I explained. "Surely by now they've called in every bird in Europa to find us."

The Duke snorted. "As has the Merchantry, I'll wager."

I made a sour face. "Look around! Y'all think they don't know we're here by now? Nothin' this bad happens without them bein' in it up to their eyebrows. Shoot, there's a dadburned ostium downtown! I expect there's more of their spies here than there are dogs and cats."

"They probably **are** the dogs and cats," Jasper pointed out.

"Good point," I thought back.

Ernie used his spear to scratch a spot the hound was having a hard time reaching. "So now we just hope the cavalry arrives before the Maenads do?"

I stepped to the panting chimera, carefully touching its enormous paw. "Nope. We need to manufacture our own luck, like always." The three-headed monster opened one yellow feline eye to look at me. "Ino, you in there? I'm guessin' you're due to change back, ain't you? That's how come you could understand Alcibiades. Yer humanity's takin' over again. Am I right?"

A rumble like a threatening volcano vibrated me all over. For a second it scared me, until I realized it was just...purring. The lion's head nodded.

"Swell! Do we have some time before that happens? Time to use you? The Cumaeans need some help. I reckon that don't carry much weight with you, and can't say as I blame you none. But what helps them will help us...and you, when all's said and done."

Another nod.

"Okay, then. Here's our plan."

Five minutes later we made a grand parade past the Temple of Ares, where the mighty soldiers of Lusitania just about wet themselves when they saw me riding the fearsome chimera. When they grabbed their spears and jumped into a threatening formation, I just patted the goat's head in front of me and grinned. Al whinnied from just behind me, and the Duke aarrooed at the end of our line. Bronze lance heads and jaws dropped. I waved for them all to grab their shields and get behind us. Almost to a man they did, jamming crested helmets onto their noggins. Others who'd been praying for deliverance at the other temples saw that and joined the throng. *Guess they're all tired of cowerin' in corners and just needed a nudge in the right direction. Glad Tyrell thought of this. Mighty handy to have an experienced soldier to rely on.* Soon we arrived at the gate, trailed by hundreds of fighting men who'd found their courage again.

"What is this?" Acastus demanded from atop the wall. "What god makes this happen?"

I squinted up at him. "Uh, all of 'em, I hope. All but one. I got it on good authority that Dionysus has started a family feud he can't finish. They've given me power over the dreaded chimera, as proof that I'm favored of the Olympians."

"Boy, talk about tellin' a whopper," Jasper said.

"I'll allow it's a stretcher," I admitted, "but it could happen. I've done all I can to make it happen, anyhow."

Acastus considered my words for a moment, then nodded. He'd seen so much of the impossible where I was concerned, it didn't take much to convince him. "Who can doubt it? But I hope they come soon, because the foe is upon us, little one."

I hopped off Ino's back and rushed up top to stand beside Acastus. Sure enough, the mass of Maenads had oozed up the hill to within bowshot of the wall. Arrows stuck out of them like hedgehog quills, but of course that was just a waste of ammunition. We'd need a lot more than that to save ourselves. Measures had been taken, but whether they'd be enough to slow down the assault until our prayed-for deliverance came was anybody's guess.

Boy, this better work. "Everything's ready, like I asked? Smashers above and pumpers below? The channel's been cut?"

"We only await your order to begin."

"Well, then...I guess you better get to it."

Acastus waved a finger at an officer farther to our right. He repeated the gesture to his trumpeter, who let fly a pair of long, clear notes. Below us, six sturdy hoplites stood at the base of the wall, armed with great wooden mallets instead of swords. *Guess they drew the short straws today*. All at once they raised their hammers and struck a single flat spot on the ground. Instantly they recovered and smashed at the place again. Four more times they did so, the hollow booms echoing down into the valley. With the last swing the stone cover of the well broke open. They dropped their tools and dashed for the gate as a terrific water spout gushed from the hole they'd made. It became a fearsome wave from the pressure of a hundred soldiers, all pumping furiously from the ancient well-room below Poseidon's temple. The apparatus there was normally used only sporadically, to fill cisterns with the river water needed for normal Acropolis operations. But this was no ordinary day, and eight dozen strong men pounded on those handles as if they could drown out the fires of the Underworld. That alone wouldn't have helped us much, but hundreds of their fellows had been sent out earlier to reshape the approach to the Acropolis wall, the narrow route that was the only way to get to us. Banks had been raised on both sides. These were high enough that as the water poured into it and flowed toward the Maenads, the monsters soon found themselves in a trap.

The undead ladies were trapped in a newly-made river, the one thing that could return them to true death.

Sucked straight from the same stream that fed the city's moat, the water rose to a depth of maybe three feet, but that was enough for our purpose. Maenads sighed and dropped like wet towels as the flood touched them. Hundreds fell dead before most of the army even knew what was happening. All along the top of the wall the Cumaean troops cheered till I feared the stones might crumble. As word spread down below to the anxious civilians cowering in the rest of the Acropolis, the triumphant noise shook the ground as if Poseidon, god of earthquakes, had gotten mad at the world. Mothers hugged their children, sure that they'd all see the next sunrise.

But we might've started the victory party too soon. Our trap had been a little more successful than we'd counted on. So many Bacchantes collapsed into the water that in less than a minute their rotting corpses had dammed the thing up. The barrier of bodies forced the flow back toward the wall. Some water spilled over the banks and down the hill, but most of it had no place to go. A small lake formed in front of the great gate. Soon the stones on our side grew damp as the pumps forced more water up. After a minute or two the back pressure created a waterfall through the joints of the doors.

"It's at times like these," said Jasper, "that one wishes one had access to...oh, I don't know. Maybe a nice raft?"

Acastus ordered the pumps to stop, before we flooded the whole sacred space. That ended some of the gushing into our side. Out front, the pond kept the remaining Maenads from getting at us, but just barely. Some few thousand still stood, howling and cackling at us. Many even climbed the huge heap of their dead sisters so they could threaten us from closer in. To add to the bad news, more refuse from the demolished city was being passed overhead to make another causeway and enable the monsters to reach us. Tables, wagon beds, doors, even chunks of roof and wall, danced across the top of the mob. It looked like an ant colony transferring its treasures to a new home.

"The mage ain't controllin' 'em anymore," I muttered. "So how come they're actin' so smart and organized? Don't act as crazed and chaotic as when we met 'em in the woods."

I jumped as Ernie flipped my ear with both paws. He'd snuck a ride on me without my noticing. *Are my Stone-senses gettin' weak, too, like my translatin'?* "Great minds think alike, missy. That very concern was ticklin' my brain, too. This is an army, not a mob."

"So where's their general? How are the orders gettin' passed? Don't see no officers or sergeants. No obvious chain of command."

"Well, they **are** magically-animated corpses, dearie. No reason to suppose their telegraph needs wires."

"Hmm. Guess so. But we can't sit here and puzzle it out. That logjam has to go, and quick."

After telling Acastus what I was about to do, and getting his permission and assistance, I rushed back down to the chimera. Ino licked herself like the giant kitty she was. The goat head munched on a rusty old breastplate. As quick as I could I laid things out for her and the rest of my friends. It didn't take long, since it was chiefly the same plan we'd agreed on earlier. Tyrell had worried about just such a situation as this, having seen something similar in Austria in 1807. Though dying to know, I hadn't asked for details.

"Pity we have no powder," the Reb mused. "A few barrels of that would blast through that obstruction in no time and that's a fact."

The Duke let out a doggie laugh. "Permit me to observe that we had a small warehouse full of gunpowder back in Iberion, just across the border, but someone insisted in blowing it all up."

That earned an eye roll from me. "Well, excuse me, Yer All-Knowin Excellency, fer not anticipatin' that I'd need to explode a couple thousand freshly-dead zombie women."

"Truly, you barbaric Americans have a talent for living in the moment, as they say, rather than planning for contingencies."

"This from the same bunch of fellers who didn't see the Gaullic Revolution comin' till yer heads were on pikes? Please! Don't make me whack you on the snoot with a rolled-up newspaper."

My tin cup turned into a steely copy of the *New York Herald*. "Ooh! Let me, let me!" chortled Jasper. "Bad dog! Bad! Bad! No biscuits for you tonight."

While I tried not to laugh through my nose, Alcibiades rose into the red-black sky. Tyrell saluted me. "Luck be with you, Miss Verity!" he called out over the noise of the Cumaean soldiers, who were slapping their swords against their shields. All over the Acropolis people made noise with whatever they could find that would make a bang. Feet stomped on wooden steps, fists pounded on doors, spoons rattled against pots. And along with that rhythmic racket came a matching chant that confused me at first, until I recalled my own alias. "Cal-lis-to!

Cal-lis-to! Cal-lis-to!"

"Hey!" Jasper yelled, though he didn't really need to. "You're famous, like Alexander the Great, like Napoleon, like...me." The newspaper turned into a big first prize ribbon.

"Heck, we ain't done nothin' yet. Let's see if they're still cheerin' twenty minutes from now. They'll be pickin' up our scattered bones, more likely."

The huge bronze-shod doors groaned open. We got drenched as water spilled over the troop-dug earth barrier in front of the entrance. A lot of water had sunk into the dry soil, so the flood didn't last long. I hauled myself up onto the chimera's back and got a firm grip on my tin cup. Ino bounded into the shallow lake. Since she was at least six feet tall at the shoulder it didn't amount to much of a problem for her. Being mostly cat, though, she shuddered and complained at getting wet. Ahead of us the refuse-bridge advanced at a steady pace, built on a stomach-churning foundation of dead bodies. It occurred to me that most of them were likely the daughters, wives, and mothers of the local citizens. That made what we were about to do just that much more awful.

My monstrous mount sploshed through the half-fathom-deep water, her immense haunches propelling us with increasing speed. We'd need plenty of momentum to succeed. *I just hope I don't upchuck when we do it.* While thinking that, I held up the cup in front of me and willed it to change form. The odd scent of brimstone and lily stung my nose, as usual with Jasper's magick. Metal reshaped itself, flowing from my hand like quicksilver. It moved down over the chimera's broad feline head. In three seconds we waded behind a giant locomotive's cowcatcher, anchored against the beast's formidable shoulders and chest. I added a sort of float on the bottom, like a boat hull, to let us glide through the water more easily. In another ten seconds we smashed into the makeshift bridge to Jasper screaming, "Yee-hah!" in my head.

His shout couldn't compete with the jarring noise of wood and tile shattering, and the unearthly screeches of a few thousand outraged Maenads. I hunched down behind the re-made Morphageus. Hunks of debris flew past my aching ears. So much stuff hit the water that I got as wet as if swimming in the Potomac. Bacchantes tumbled into the water and lay still, like fallen leaves. *At least they're clear of Dionysus, anyway.* A few launched themselves at me from high atop the pile of junk. Ino's serpent-tail latched onto these with needle teeth and plucked them from the chimera's flank. The goat head incinerated a few more in mid-air. After maybe half a minute of terrible confusion we'd forced our way through the bridge material and struck the really disgusting part.

With a *whumph* the cowcatcher smacked into the pile of corpses. Immediately we bogged down, pressing against the semi-yielding dead flesh. They felt like mud-filled sandbags, except that these had once been little girls bouncing on their fathers' knees, mamas kissing their babies, grandma's cooking family dinners. I scrunched my eyes so tight I feared that they'd bleed, not daring to risk catching sight of their accusing faces.

But my too-active imagination betrayed me, showing my mind's eye the damage that the Jasper-blade did to now-human flesh.

"They can't feel it, you know," Jasper reminded me. "They're with their families in the Lusitanian Underworld."

From what I've heard of Hades, that don't reassure me none. "Yeah, yeah," I said aloud through gritted teeth, "tell that to my stomach. It's about to come outta my mouth."

"You're tellin' me. This feelin'-whatever-Verity-feels business isn't all it's cracked up to be."

Circumstances helped to take my mind off of the gut-wrenching images. As water flowed into the new channel we were boring through the corpse-dam, more Maenads died a true death. Their secure perch collapsed and they flopped into the stream. That created a brand-new blockage, of course, but not nearly as watertight as the first one. To widen the gap and keep the deadly fluid flowing, I waved a hand toward the sky. Alcibiades swooped down like a hunting falcon. A rope hung below him, fastened tight to Tyrell's McClellan saddle. At its other end the Redeemer had tied a farmer's plow. It snagged limp bodies in a way that still makes me cringe to think of it. In no time the entire right side of the barrier had been reopened. Seeing that success, I turned the chimera to my left and broke up the other side. Ino roared and batted the loose corpses away while also protecting me with flame and fang.

The Maenads who weren't dispatched by the fresh flow hissed and scuttled back into the burning town. At the bottom of the hill the cascade, free of our channel, spread out so much that it lost its magickal effect as its depth decreased. Maybe three thousand of the undead creatures remained, still a good-sized combat brigade in the Army of the Potomac back home. *Nothin' you'd wanna tangle with if you got any choice in the matter.* They all bunched up at the edge of the wrecked city, backlit by embers and orange smoke. Most of them huddled around a slight boyish figure in a green and purple robe. The skin of a leopard covered his shoulders. Dark oiled ringlets framed a pale pretty face. He wore a laurel wreath in that luxurious hair, and one slender hand held a short staff covered in writhing crimson flowers, topped by a pine cone. A thyrsus.

Their general had arrived on the battlefield. This was the fellow who been controlling them so effectively. He raised his other hand and lowered a bunch of ripe grapes to his feminine lips.

Dionysus.

*The blade became a blur as the strong arm of the actor-priest
plunged it toward my heart. I grunted as I made one last
great effort to escape. Nothing doing. This was it.
My great quest was about to end in a dadburned dream,
of all places. Sorry, Tommy. Sorry, Ma. Sorry, world.*

39 / Verity's Religious Experience

"Boy, he looks sort of...girlie," Jasper said. "Maybe you can take some lessons from him."

"And maybe I can toss my magick sword down a mineshaft," I whispered in my mind.

He made a pouty voice. "Gee, you try to offer a little constructive criticism..."

"Sshh! Ain't nothin' constructive gonna happen here. He's fixin' to get real de-structive real quick, I expect."

We stood maybe a hundred feet from the front line of Maenads. *Too close, if you ask me.* But as disgusting and dangerous as the rotting monsters were, they paled beside their commander. Nothing he said or did seemed particularly threatening. Truth be told, Dionysus looked like a spoiled too-pretty rich boy who might attend St. Usher's private school in Washington. *Dress him in one of their monkey suit uniforms and he'd fit right in there. Of course, it's a secret Merchantry headquarters, so maybe I ain't bein' fair.* Though he had no fangs or a forked tail, he just gave out a feeling of dread that made me go weak in the knees.

The god took a deep breath through his nose as if he was a hound checking a scent trail. To be more accurate, it looked like he was testing a new vintage from an obscure winery. I'd seen the puffed-up swells at Ford's do that at cast parties. Dionysus twitched his nose. Then he half-swallowed and swirled something around in his mouth. Making a face, he spit into the muddy desolation between us and cocked his head. Those huge green eyes stared at me without blinking.

"You don't belong here," he said. His voice felt like the low notes on a harp. "You're wrong."

My own voice came out a lot fainter than I'd hoped. "Funny, I was just about to tell you the same thing."

"Such sweet arrogance." He stroked the head of the Maenad nearest him. She had a broken neck and one corner of her mouth was so torn that I could see all of her yellowed teeth on that side. "And so misguided. How can you say we do not belong? This is our world, our land. Not yours."

I shrank Morphageus from cowcatcher form into a tall Hellene shield. Its outer surface I made into a crystal mirror so he could see not only his own beautiful self and his icky girlfriends, but the ruined city behind him. "Take a good look. Who treats his own land so? Who treats his own people as prey?"

"Funny you should mention that word. If they had prayed more I might have preyed less."

Three thousand Bacchantes just about killed themselves laughing at that, so to speak. Believe me, that's not a sound you ever want to hear. Their god giggled like a schoolgirl, proud of his own wit. I felt like I was at the world's creepiest slumber party. Any minute the Maenads would start pillow-fighting.

I swept that image into a back corner of my mind, where Jasper would have loads of fun with it, no doubt. "Glad I could provide you with some amusement, but that don't answer my question. You think bein' a god gives you the right to do anything you want? Shoot, you're just like the bully-boys back home, stompin' on bugs and punchin' little girls to make themselves feel tough. So you got a lotta power. Fine. But that's just like havin' a loaded musket. Plenty of responsibility comes with all of that force."

"Oooh! Look at you, all feisty. What do you know of power, child?"

"I didn't know nothin' about it till a few weeks ago. Till this got forced on me."

With that I released Morphageus into its natural sword form, recurved blade catching the light of the burning town. The ancient runes along it blazed with an even fiercer gleam. For the first time I noticed that the vegetation curling around its crossbar was a grapevine. *Hmmm, that's quite the coincidence.*

"Ah, the mortal has a shiny toy! It can cut things. How precious." Dionysus raised his thyrsus. "My purview is agriculture, human. And wine. And drama. I am responsible for life itself. All that breathes here would die without me. Crops would fail, lambs would die, mothers would miscarry. I am the Epiphany, He Who Comes. Through me man may see the True

Mystery. You think I am just a troublemaker who brings good times to his worshippers? How shallow is your thinking. With wine, with tragedy, with ecstatic frenzy each man may leave his body and journey outside himself, to mate with the Cosmos and join that which frightens even the Olympians."

"Okay, that was impressive," Jasper admitted. "Can't let him see you sweat, though. Return his serve."

I did my best, though I expected to get jumped by his sorority sisters at any moment. "Frighten the Olympians? How do you expect to frighten a kitten in that get-up? You might want to decide whether you're a boy or a girl, fer starters."

Jasper sighed. "Oh, that really hurt him. Look at him bleed. He's staggerin' from the force of your mighty blow."

"You first," Dionysus replied with a smirk. "All I see before me is a woman-child who prefers a boy-child's garb." Two fingers waved and my Hellenic clothes became my usual overalls and hat. "You live in shorn hair and male apparel. Is that the norm in your world? I rather think not."

"Nyah-nyah-nyah-nyah **nyah**-nyah!" Jasper squealed. "I'm rubber, you're glue. Insults bounce off me and stick to you. This guy's good."

I ignored them both. "And this is yer epiphany? Yer big revelation to humanity? 'Kiss my feet or I bring the cannibal zombies to town?' Sounds pretty immature to me."

"What would you know of maturity? I was born thousands of years ago. My father is Zeus Immortal. Naiads reared me to manhood. You have seen how many summers? Eleven?"

"Twelve!" I snapped.

"Touchy-touchy," Jasper chided.

Dionysus let out a chilly laugh. "Oh, twelve. Pardon me. That makes all the difference."

"Don't act dumb. You know that maturity ain't about how old somebody is. Shucks, back home we have men in their fifties and sixties who started a civil war over nothin' but stiff-necked pride. Over who'd get the right to hold power over a race of folks that don't neither side really care about much. Just an excuse to kick up a fuss and show folks how tough they are. I may only be twelve, but I know how stupid that is. So don't try that 'you're just a kid' business with me."

"I concede your point, then. You are wise beyond your years. What of it? The fact remains that you understand nothing about this world or these people. You have no inkling about my importance here. Let me show you."

He flicked his thyrsus at me before I could react. Even my Stone-aided reflexes couldn't put up a defense quick enough. A green sun overwhelmed my sight. Heat flooded every cell in my body. My pulse pounded in my ears, but other than that I lost all feeling and sense. I floated without a body. Time had no meaning. Try as I might, I couldn't talk to Jasper or make use of any magick. Eventually the grassy-light faded into a vision of stars and planets. Now it felt like I was flying through outer space, as if riding on a cannonball fired from some enormous gun.

I grew dizzy from all of the bright spinning stuff that zipped past me. Our Moon, the brilliant Sun, cratered Mercury, clouded Venus, red Mars, giant striped Jupiter, lovely ringed Saturn, pale Uranus, and rich blue Neptune. That was all of the planets in our solar system. A small icy rock whizzed by later on, but what it was I had no idea. After that I looked around to see what else might be in view. My belly heaved at the sight. Swirling whirlpools of stars, vast exploding suns, multi-colored nebulae, comets and meteors galore. Everywhere my focus went I found some new marvel.

Okay, god-boy, you've made yer point. Verity feels like a freckle on a grain of beach sand now, thank you very much...

Faster than I'd gone out, I got yanked back. Every point of light became a blinding white line as I fell back to earth. *Planet Earth. What a dull name. Never thought about it before. They didn't have any nifty spare god names they could've used? At least it's home. Safe. Harmless. Well, mostly harmless, given my recent experiences.*

I spun my disembodied self around to face the beautiful blue and white ball that hurtled toward me. Though I knew I already stood on it and wasn't really about to crash into the Lusitanian ground, I still tried to scrunch up into a ball to minimize my damage. That was a waste of time, and not just because it was pure illusion. My point-of-view swooped me into a lush field in a valley, skimming over the ripe wheat at maybe ten feet up. Warm sun cooked my skin. A hawk glided alongside me for a moment, before banking away to scoop up a mouse. *Ouch! Good thing Ernie ain't watchin' this.* Off to my left a flock of sheep grazed. Songbirds hopped along branches. A team of women picked olives in a grove, laughing and singing as they worked.

Just as I began to enjoy the new, more leisurely, situation, Dionysus kicked me over a cliff. It felt that way, anyhow. Visions flooded my brain with unbelievable speed, like I was flipping through pages in Matthew Brady's catalog. Each lasted a gazillionth of a second, growing more and more disturbing. Scythes cut down grain stalks. Wheels of cheese aged in storerooms. Foals wobble-walked on spindly legs. Lambs suckled. Wine flowed like spring water. Goats mated. Then pigs. Then every darn thing with a pulse was going at it, making babies right and left, the images piling on top of one another till I couldn't keep them straight.

Young animals and humans came out of the womb dead, misshapen, deformed in horrible ways. Mothers of every description wailed in mourning. More wine splashed into more cups. Mobs of folks staggered, drunk and stupid. Clothes got shucked. Limbs intertwined in ways I'm pretty sure Ma didn't want me to contemplate. Punches thrown, pottery smashed, swords drawn. Men howled like wolves to the moon as they guzzled from big wine jugs. The moon assumed a lurid face and howled right back. All that wine made my eyes cross and head spin as I were drunk myself. Naked people crawled on all fours through the woods, snatching up small creatures and devouring them alive. Packs of them brought down a wild boar and tore it apart with their bare hands. A dark-robed figure raised its arms up high.

As I followed that particular vision the others vanished and I found myself in a stone theatre built into a hillside. The robed form wore a distorted linen mask with a wood frame. False hair streamed down to the padded shoulders. High thick-soled boots made the fellow unnaturally tall. All around were other individuals, though they had on simpler and matching outfits. They chanted in a language my spell wouldn't translate. As one unit they performed a shuffling dance to the weird music of a lyre, drum, and double-flute. While the music grew louder and faster the formation waved its hands, then clapped them in unison, repeating the pattern and closing in on a marble altar built into the center of the stage. It might have all been a glorious spectacle, worthy of Ford's Athenaeum and John Wilkes Booth, except for one teeny problem.

I'm the one lyin' on the altar, staring up at the knife in the big feller's fist.

Though I had no restraints on me, I couldn't move. Much as I wanted to roll off that slab and escape the plunging blade, I had no willpower. Nothing happened. And somehow I knew that I'd been trapped, that this was an illusion with teeth. If that knife caught me, I'd end up well and truly dead. Looking around for help, I saw thousands of folks in Hellenic duds, sitting on benches in the audience. They stamped their feet in time with the music, urging the sacrifice to commence. Men had disturbingly excited looks on their bearded faces. Mothers held up their little babies so they could see the bloodletting. Old folks waved their walking sticks with enthusiasm. Every seat was full.

Look on the bright side, Verity. You're goin' out to a full house.

The blade became a blur as the strong arm of the actor-priest plunged it toward my heart. I grunted as I made one last great effort to escape. Nothing doing. This was it. My great quest was about to end in a dadburned dream, of all places. *Sorry, Tommy. Sorry, Ma. Sorry, world.*

Six inches away from me the knife stopped dead. The crowd let out a disappointed moan at my salvation. *Gee, thanks, folks. My apologies fer wreckin' y'all's entertainment. Refunds available at the door. Thanks fer yer business. Please stop by again.*

To be strictly accurate, the sacrificial weapon didn't stop all by its own self. It had help. Another blade had snuck in between it and my delicate bosom, a blade I recognized. Curved and elegant, I'd seen it in action plenty of times, dispatching demons and dueling with Shades. An Arabe scimitar, gripped by a slender tattooed hand.

"Careful, little one," Sha'ira said with as much of a smile as she ever displayed, "the dreams of the gods are no playground."

"Huh?" I replied in my clever and articulate way.

"I have little time to explain. Your signal was spied by a pelican. We will be in Cumae within the hour. You must hold on until then."

I shoved the fellow and his pig-sticker away from me and at up. Somehow Sha'ira's intervention had fouled up Dionysus' spell. "How the heck did you manage to find me here?"

She tossed her head, making her shining mass of black hair

fly. "I am a Dreamweaver, am I not? Naia sniffed you out like a fine bloodhound."

"That's right, you are. I'd been wonderin' whether you'd ever get me a message this way. Sure glad it happened now. Thank her fer me, will you?"

"Do so yourself, Stone Warden. In an hour."

"Okey-dokey. So you're shed of the Merchantry ships, then?"

"For now. But they are persistent. There is no telling what is happening back on the sea. We have stopped in a cave just long enough for me to chant this message. I must leave my trance now so we may get our party back into the air."

"You're flyin'?"

"We are. Special aid has come our way. Look for us in the northern sky. Now you must break your own trance. The god is beginning to suspect. Farewell."

Her embroidered green and gold robe billowed as she turned and vanished. One second she stood beside me, the next she was gone, like a soap bubble breaking. Taking her at her word, I struggled to my feet atop the altar. Like the most pompous actor ever to hold a stage, I gave the now-silent audience a bow with an absurd series of flourishes, stuck out my tongue for a delightfully juicy raspberry, and shook my head hard.

The death-smoke of doomed Cumae stung my lungs as I gasped and returned to the conscious world. Every muscle felt as tight as a piano wire. I forced myself to relax and focus on my surroundings. That was made extra-difficult by a high-pitched boy's voice in my head.

"Whee-doggies!" Jasper sang, as if he'd just dived from a cliff into shallow water. "You should sell tickets to that ride, girlie! Supernovae and free love! We can call it 'Life, the Universe, and Everything!' I'm tellin' you, with the right promotion and some color posters—"

Dionysus and his disgusting brides hadn't moved. Apparently my trip across the cosmos had only taken a few heartbeats. "Well played, mortal," he said, a bit miffed. "Let us do this the old-fashioned way, then." With a flick of his finger the Maenads all shrieked and rushed at me.

*The fiery runes along its blade must've been
immune to the translation spell.
"Anybody know what these say?" I asked.
"Post no bills," Ernie suggested.
"If found, please deposit in the nearest
mailbox," Jasper offered.
"Postage guaranteed."*

40 / Hades' Ladies

Lucky for me I had friends in high places, because my mind was still befuddled from the fever-dream and Sha'ira's interference. Even though the zombie women were about as slow as napping donkeys, my legs didn't work much better than theirs. I swung Morphageus as a two-handed medieval great sword while trying to stumble backwards. That lopped off a couple of heads, but it didn't stop the main group. Shoot, it didn't even stop the ones I beheaded. They kept on staggering after me, fumbling along the muddy ground trying to locate me. For an instant I considered trying to ride the chimera back the way I'd come, but Ino was having just as much trouble as I was. All of us were trying to move uphill, slipping on the slimy ash-filled mud. If it hadn't been so darned dangerous I'm sure it would've been hilarious. Jasper sure seemed to think so. He giggled so much I was glad he couldn't lose control and wet on himself.

Tired of sliding all over the place, I willed him into spiked boots for my bare feet. The long sword flowed down my body like molten lead, forming clumsy overshoes that dug into the treacherous surface with long teeth. That let me pull away from the pursuing monsters a little, but the soil was so unstable that pretty soon all I was managing to do was chew up the mud with my fancy feet. In no time I'd lost my lead again. Just as several cold dead hands fastened on my legs, a hunk of metal swung past my face. It nearly took off my nose. While I was wondering what the heck it'd been, the thing returned from the other direction. This time I recognized it as a Hellenic plow. And something plump and fuzzy rode on it.

"Grab hold, missy!" Ernie commanded, his tiny tricorn worn at a jaunty angle. "We don't have all night to wait for you, you know. Let's go! Chop, chop!"

He didn't have to tell me twice. With a wish my Morphageus boots became wicked-sharp hedge clippers. They sliced off three or four of the strongest hands that gripped me, then grew cute little feet and ran back up my leg to hang at my belt as a tin cup again. At the same time I clutched the plow blade with both hands, clinging to it where Tyrell's rope attached. I shot forward and upward with a lurch. In a few seconds we were free of the Maenads, flying beneath Alcibiades at a height of about twenty feet.

"Whoo!" Jasper hollered. "You should add this to your amusement ride, too! The greenbacks'll roll in like a tidal wave."

His business plans weren't at the front of my thoughts right then. All I knew was that I hadn't relished passing through the heaps of fresh corpses the water had created. I particularly hadn't wanted to encounter the bodies we'd torn apart with the cowcatcher. *There's one blessin', anyhow.* We twisted to and fro under the winged horse, heading back up the hill toward the Acropolis. Ernie excused himself and scurried down my back to pry off a severed Bacchante hand that still held onto my overalls. He'd just managed to make it drop away, all the while complaining about its foul ooze, when our usual luck returned.

The knot came untied and we plummeted back to earth.

I'll allow that I was none too happy. And I'll admit to sending some pretty salty sentences Tyrell's way, cursing his knot-tying skills and suggesting that he should've joined the Confederate navy instead of the cavalry. He might've learned to tie a better bowline if he had. There wasn't a lot of time for that, as we hit the grimy ground in a hurry. The wind left me with a *whoof* and I started to roll back toward the hungry girlfriends of Dionysus. Jasper plucked a picture from my panicky mind and a small steel anchor grew from the tin cup, attached to my belt with a thin chain. It bit into the mud and stopped me with a great yank. Ernie kept on going like a furry little bowling ball. His profanity was a lot more creative than mine. *Whaddya bet Jasper's takin' notes on that?*

I reached around for a handhold. What I found was an actual hand. It was the same one Ernie had jettisoned. *Like a bad penny, you are.* Making a face, I hurled it at the oncoming Maenad horde. Well, I tried to. It hung on to my wrist like I'd clung to that plow. *Are you kiddin' me?* With a growl and an eye roll I shook the thing like it was flypaper I couldn't get rid of. No dice. Those vile rotting fingers still held on, knuckle bones poking through the peeling skin. So I grit my teeth and stepped on the hand with my bare foot, trying to get shed of it that way. All that accomplished was to transfer it from my wrist to my ankle.

"You know," Jasper said, "I suggest that when you write your *Great and Glorious Annals of the Stone Warden's Quest to Save the World from the Shackles of the Merchantry Tyranny*, you might want to leave this part out."

"That's the first thing you've said tonight that makes a lick of sense," I told him. "Now help me out here. The nasties are almost upon us."

I reached back and found a small but sturdy rock. One thing about Lusitania, there was no shortage of those. Secure from sliding back downhill, I let the anchor dissolve into a long trident that we called a frog-gig. It took a couple of tries, because the hand kept wriggling. Piercing my own foot struck me as counter-productive. Once the barbed tines were jabbed firmly into the awful thing, I jerked back to get it free of my ankle. Then I flipped my wrist and changed Morphageus' shape again. The undead hand tumbled straight up into the night air. Just as it reached the top of its arc, I swung my new steel tennis racket and served the tenacious member back to its zombie friends.

"Good show!" Ernie cried, appearing next to me from the gloom. "I do believe it bounced off the top of a Maenad's head. One point for our side."

"Gonna take a lot more than that to win this here match," I said, squirming back to sit on the stone. I reformed Morphageus into its natural sword shape and stood up. The fiery runes along its blade must've been immune to the translation spell, or else Jasper was just being a snot. I still couldn't read them.

"Anybody know what these say?" I asked, hopping uphill from rock to rock to avoid sliding down into the oncoming battalions of monsters.

"Post no bills," Ernie suggested.

"If found, please deposit in the nearest mailbox," Jasper offered. "Postage guaranteed."

"Hold this sword by the other end, fool," the tiny Marshal countered with a mousy snort.

"The management accepts no liability for misuse of this product," Jasper giggled.

Things were getting pretty darned silly, considering we were in imminent danger of annihilation by flesh-eating zombies. "Never mind," I sighed. "I choose to believe it's a cheery exhortation for the doomed Stone Warden to keep her chin up high as she's eaten by the hellish foe."

"Actually, that's not as far off as you might think," Jasper told me.

"Good to know." We'd arrived at the edge of the new lake, which had subsided to a glorified little pond now that the pumps were no longer active. What water was left pooled just in front of the wall, where the ground was flat. Bodies floated in it like driftwood after a storm. I considered wading like mad and hoping we got to the gate before the Bacchantes ran us down. There was no sign of Tyrell or Al. *Looks like our aerial rescue might have to wait. Maybe Al's too tired. He's been flyin' all night. Luggin' chimeras has to take a lot out of you.*

Thought of the chimera made me wonder what had happened to Ino. She'd been with us when I'd been hauled into the sky. But now she was as absent as the Redeemer and his wonder-horse. The Maenads were only a hundred yards away now. If she'd stayed where we'd been they'd have overrun her. Either that had happened or she'd run off down the side of the hill. I heard no commotion indicating that a fight was taking place amidst the mass of Maenads. So maybe she'd escaped to the flank. Standing on a boulder, I peered into the dark, searching down the hill with my witched eyes for some sign of the beast.

A sound of flapping wings made me whirl around to greet Tyrell. But it wasn't the Reb captain. Instead it was just about the worst thing I could've conjured up. My heart sank when I saw who'd arrived.

Eight Furies, with daggers...crouching in the muck between me and the safety of the gate.

"They ain't any prettier here than they were on the deck of the *Kiss*," Ernie said.

I felt my shoulders sag. "Don't suppose it's been an hour since we talked to Dionysus?"

"Nowhere near that? Why?"

"Oh, just hopin' that my luck might change, that's all. Silly me."

I wanted to plop down in the ooze and blubber. No matter what I did, it never turned out all right. *Lost my only friend in the world. And Pa. Purt near lost Ma. Have to look over my shoulder every minute of the day fer fear some ungodly monster's creepin' up on me. Each and every time I manage to survive one scrap, another one starts right up. No time to rest, no time to take stock. Now that I think of it, when's the last time I had any food or sleep?*

"Tired," I sighed with a shake of my head. "Bone tired. Twelve year-old girls oughta be home studyin' grammar, not whackin' demons and zombies."

After taking a deep breath of the foul ash-filled Cumaean air, I squared off to the Maenads and the Furies, turning sideways so I could keep an eye on each group. We were as good as dead, of course. That went without saying. No miraculous air rescue was coming. Even if I fought my way to the wall, there were no Lusitanians to open the gate. Where were they all, anyhow? The place was deserted. Not a single sentry on duty. Did they skedaddle through some secret tunnel? Did they leave us hanging out to dry? *That'd be just peachy. No Tyrell, no Al, no Ino, no Sha'ira. Just me and Ernie.*

"What am I, chopped liver?" Jasper wanted to know.

"A liver chopper, more likely," I told him. "Say, when they rip me into shreds and eat my innards, what happens to you?"

"I get reassigned as a spatula in a Hungarian restaurant."

"Really?"

"No, not really! Jiminy, you're gullible."

"My apologies. It's been a long day, what with the zombies, chimeras, flamin' poop monsters, and findin' out my aunt's a black sorceress and all. Not as sharp as I might like to be."

Jasper became a hoplite lance. "That's okay. I'll be sharp for you." He reformed into a mace with dozens of wicked spikes. "Here, make some pointed remarks to the foe."

That made me snicker. "Foe? I'd need fo'ty-fo' times as many weapons to get my point across."

"Ooh! Ain't we punny in the face of imminent extermination."

He sure wasn't joking about the imminent extermination. Though they'd slowed coming up the hill, just as inconvenienced by the slick mud as the rest of us, the Maenad horde had now struggled to within a hundred feet. On the other side, the loathsome Furies flexed their leathery wings and crept closer. I glanced about with more hope than expectation. No timely arrows or cavalry sallies came from Fortress Acropolis. No wand-waving white mages appeared in a puff of smoke to fight at my side. No shining Olympian gods arrived on clouds like I'd requested. Heck, I'd have been happy if Pitcairn's seagull squadron had flown in to poop on somebody. But, no.

I turned to face the Furies, because they were closer and because there were fewer of them. And also because, hideous as they were, they still weren't as yucky as all of those zombies. Some of the Maenads had stopped on the way up the hill to tear a few tasty morsels from their late lamented sisters. Mostly the soft gooshy bits. Since my belly was none too settled anyhow, I chose to stare down Hades' ladies. They stared right back, which is an experience I don't recommend to you. Made me feel like I was a gopher and they were fiendish falcons. As if that weren't bad enough, they screeched and hurled themselves at me, wings spread wide, talons out.

That hideous sound overwhelmed my sensitive ears. I dove into the slime, a Jasper-made turtle shell protecting my fearful self. Muck covered every inch of me. *Gonna be some powerful laundrin' happenin' if I survive this night. Shoot, I'm gonna need a wire-brush scrub with lye soap even in the afterlife.* While down there I saw Ernie, not two inches from my snoot. Mud, blood, and disgusting bodily fluids coated every whisker and hair on him, too. We shared a look that seemed to say "Nice to have known you" and tensed up, waiting for oblivion to arrive.

It never did, at least not for us. Those Furies flew straight over the top of us and pitched into the Maenads. *Huh?* Sure, the undead women had the benefit of numbers, but it did them precious little good. The winged creatures were savvy, battle-trained, and quick. Organized, too. They fought in teams, never staying still for more than an eye blink. No sooner did a Bacchante latch on to one of them than her partner hacked the offending hand off with her long knife, or wrenched the thing's head around backward, or hovered above and booted the enemy a good ten feet away. Whenever things got too hot, they flapped up out of range, looking for a new chance to inflict harm. Pretty soon they'd created a heap of writhing, still-animated Maenad parts and forced the main body of zombies back about ten yards.

"You know, I have to admit that if you'd given me fat odds

that I'd see this happen tonight," said Ernie, peeking under the lip of our shield, "I would've turned down the bet."

"Me, too," I agreed. "What gives?"

"Who knows? This is a bloody hard place to make predictions."

Our answer came soon enough. While the Maenads cackled and regrouped, the flying abominations flew back a little ways and landed. The slippery slope seemed to have no effect on their footing or balance. Facing one another in two lines of three, they reached down to the ground with their fearsome clawed hands and dug in. With a low tearing noise the earth came loose. As if peeling back an old carpet, the monsters walked backward, the surface rolling up. Revealed beneath was a red-orange glow and great roiling clouds of steam. Tempted as I was to crawl up to the rent and look in, I stayed put. *No sense pushin' my luck any more than I've already done.* Good thing, too. Not three heartbeats later the Furies threw themselves high into the air. Just as they did so a black river exploded out of the long gash. It roared like a freight train passing and thundered down the hill.

I almost pitied those poor Maenads…almost.

That turned out to be no ordinary water. The color and thickness of molasses, but with such a stench of brimstone as Jasper could only weakly aspire to, it caught the hissing Bacchantes flat-footed. Half of them got inundated right off. Some horrid magick turned them into bleached skeletons the moment they got drenched. Most of the rest scampered sideways and got clear. But that didn't mean they were safe. On each flank Furies landed and repeated their maneuver, bringing forth two more dark streams. All of the Maenads fled downhill then, with that disturbing uneven walk-crawl of theirs. Unluckily for them, the Furies could fly faster. A fourth river, streaming across the bottom of the hill, soon cut them off. In the time it took for me to scramble to my feet, put Ernie on one shoulder, and return Morphageus to cup form, almost every rotting hunk of corpse-flesh had become a pale bunch of bones. While we watched they all sank beneath the surface of the four rivers and vanished.

Quiet, of a sort. No cackling, screaming, screeching, or hissing. Just the rush of all that miraculous water. I started to feel calm, as if I might actually live to see Ma again.

"What's the record for impossible happenings in one day?" Ernie asked, trying to rub some of the filth from his face. "Ain't we just about there?"

"I reckon so," I said. "And the last few minutes, especially, are gonna be awful hard to top."

A high male voice piped up from just behind us. "Oh, just you wait, mortal child."

I jumped so high that I almost left my overalls where I'd just been. Twisting around to face the other way, tin cup now a fiery Morphageus, I saw that Dionysus stood in the lake. Actually, that's not quite right. He stood **on** it, as if the water was rock-solid.

"My chorus may have left the stage, but the lead actor still has his part to play," he went on. "But is it a comedy or a tragedy we present this evening? To be honest, I've lost track in all of this excitement."

Jasper reshaped himself into the well-known masks of the theatre. The tragic one grew a little hand and thumbed its nose at the god; the comic one stuck out a cartoony tongue and made a very rude sound. Then they both merged and changed into bare butt cheeks. I laughed out loud. *Couldn't have done that better myself.*

Dionysus smiled, believe it or not. The slim boyish figure had something across his shoulder, like a big sack. He shrugged it down into his arms and held it out to me. It was Ino, in her human shape again. She hung limp and pale. Her open eyes stared blankly into the dark sky.

"Tragedy, I think," said the god of Frenzy.

Owls. A squadron of enormous gray owls,
all wearing Hoplite helmets.

41 / Family Feud

I had two immediate impulses, neither of them good. First off, I wanted to just flop down and bawl like a pathetic infant. Second, I wanted to rush Dionysus and test his immortality with a Morphagean battle axe. Whichever I chose had big drawbacks. Blubbering would just get me sneered at. Fighting would probably get me sneered at, then dead, then sneered at some more. It was clear that this so-called god expected me to try one or the other. Instead, I did neither.

"Ah, you've slain a child," I said, as smooth and uppity as I could manage under the circumstances. "Such a worthy feat for the god of life." Once at Ford's a traveling troupe had performed *Faust.* The fellow playing Mephistopheles had used such a manner, oily and unflappable. I called upon every ounce of my acting ability to imitate him.

"Take care," he shot back. "Try my patience too often and I'll use you to begin restocking my Maenads."

"I would expect you to say something like that. Apparently you have particular difficulty being challenged by girls. Why might that be, I wonder? Difficulty with mommy, perhaps? Did poor little Dion not get enough love in the cradle?"

"I warn you—"

"Or too much love of the wrong kind, perhaps? Reared by all those naiads. Women everywhere you look, fussing over you. No father figure around, old Zeus bein' the love-em-and-leave-'em sort of fellow."

His pretty mouth turned up. "And aren't you the one to talk? Verity Sauveur, giving lessons on proper parenting. Where was **your** sainted father, then? Hmm?"

Ah...so that's the way he's gonna play it. Guess I'll keep my mouth shut and let him bloviate. Maybe I'll learn somethin'.

When I just stared back at him like I had all the answers, he batted his girly eyes and went on. "Did he bounce you on his knee? Read you bedtime stories? Take you on Sunday carriage rides in the park? I fancy not, since he wasn't there, was he? Disappeared the night you were born, that's the party line at your house."

Party line? As in 'a story concocted to keep Verity in the dark'? That don't sound good.

"Let me see if I can accurately describe your mother's behavior on this issue. She never mentions him at all. There are no pictures or mementos of him anywhere, not even in storage. None of your friends or relations tells you about him, either. In fact, you don't even know his name, do you? It could be 'Zeus' for all you know." Dionysus snorted. "Wouldn't it be hilarious if we were siblings? Not as far-fetched as it sounds, the way he spreads the family seed. Plows more furrows than all the farmers who ever lived, that one. A wonder he gets any other work done, rutting like a satyr every five minutes..."

He paused, jaw set in anger. With a deep breath he cleared from his mind whatever image had brought him up short. My idea of letting him run on seemed to be working. His own family troubles were doing more damage than anything I might try. *Still, he's got a point. Ma's attitude sounds mighty suspicious, the way he puts it.*

"Don't let him rummage around in your head," Jasper advised. "He'll plant poisonous weeds there. Shoot, you don't let me visit every corner of it and I'm your bestest buddy."

The mere thought of Jasper skipping merrily through my private thoughts made me shiver. "Don't know as I'd go that far," I told him, eyes on Ino's unmoving form. Near as I could tell with my Stone-senses, she still breathed. But it was shallow as an actor's morals. Running around as a homicidal chimera and then shape-shifting back as a god's prisoner couldn't be easy on one's system.

Dionysus recovered his wits and went on. "Well, that's neither here nor there, since you most assuredly are not my sister. Your precious papa isn't on Olympus. Oh, no. He's somewhere much more interesting, isn't he? He went back home that night you came into the world. Home to his true family and friends. Perhaps on his own account, perhaps with some...strong encouragement from those he'd abandoned to run off with your mama." He paused, like the god of actors he was. "You really don't know? Can't even guess? But I was told that you were preternaturally intelligent for a child." A heavy sigh left him and he shook his curled head. "Such a disappointment, when we get our hopes up and our heroes turn out to have feet of clay. Ah, well, such is life. Your father, little one, is in—"

What he was going to say got interrupted, to my towering frustration. As much as I hadn't wanted to, I'd held my breath and hung on his every word, so eager was I for any clue about Pa. But I'd have to wait a while longer. Because his final words got drowned out by thunder. At least that's what I first thought it was. A long rumbling boom whacked my sensitive ears. Dionysus raised his face to the night sky with a frown. That told me he had nothing to do with it. I did the same. No clouds were in sight, so it couldn't have been thunder. Natural thunder anyway. Given my circumstances I wouldn't have placed any bets on what might be possible or not in Lusitania.

Anyhow, it went on for too long to be storm sounds. My second guess might've been artillery, if we'd been back home. No shells landed, though, so that wasn't it. In fact, nothing that entered my confused mind was anywhere close to what it turned out to be.

Owls. A squadron of enormous gray owls, all wearing Hoplite helmets.

When I say enormous, I don't just mean abnormally big. These birds weren't merely your 'wow, I declare, that's a king-sized bird' kind of large. No, they were immense. My house was smaller than their leader. The dust kicked up by the beating of their wings created a sandstorm around us. I shut my eyes and formed Morphageus into a fine-meshed screen mask so I could see and breathe. When I opened my peepers again the great owls were landing all around me, making a semicircle that faced the fortress. As the cloud of dirt began to settle I removed the mask, returned it to tin cup form, and nodded to the one in front. Wings folded, he stood a good fifteen feet tall. After blinking his wagon wheel-sized eyes at me, he lowered his head to the ground. At first I thought he was bowing to me for some reason and I started to return the favor. But as my head began to go down I spotted the real reason for his action. He wanted to make it easy for his passenger to slide off his back.

Wearing a short white man's robe, a shining bronze breastplate, and a rich green cape, that rider turned out to be a Hellene girl about my age. Under one arm she clutched a helmet similar to those sitting on the owls' heads. The other hand gripped a long battle spear. Her black hair hung long and straight. Just as dark were her eyes, which looked to be the model for those in every owl's face. Though they were the color of polished coal, they also gave out a sort of glow. Things being how they were, I felt sure I knew who she was.

"Looks like prayers do get answered here," I said with a nod and a grin.

Athena returned my nod, but not the grin. She settled for a tight smile instead. "Only the sincere ones." Her head moved in that self-assured jerky way that owls move theirs. "I chose this form to make our meeting easier for you. The glory of my true appearance would slay you, of course."

Of course. I hear the same comment from Jasper on a daily basis.

"And where is my foolish, arrogant half-brother?" she asked, eyes scanning the terrain in front of us.

I turned to look. Dionysus had fled, taking poor Ino with him.

"Uh...he was here only a minute ago," I muttered.

"I swear," Jasper snickered, "you'd misplace your rear end if it wasn't attached."

After sending him a mental picture of a tin cup being tossed into a cesspool, I said, "There's a certain annoyin' magick sword about to get misplaced, if you follow my meanin'."

"No matter," Athena shrugged. "The twins will hunt him down. Artemis can track the scent of a shadow's thought, and Apollo's bow can shoot around a tree trunk."

Hmm. Glad they're on our side. "Dionysus won't just dematerialize and pop up someplace else a few hundred leagues away?"

"Unlikely." She checked the strap on her tall sandals and headed up the hill. "His power is that of the root and stem, of the creeping vine and budding leaf. He has much might, but it is the slow sort that comes from the ancient earth."

I nodded. That made sense. A tree takes its sweet time growing, but once it does you sure have a tough time uprooting the darned thing. "Then we want to find him and hogtie him before he has a chance to harness his earth energy?"

"Precisely. He'll be more difficult to discipline if he manages to secure the chthonic power of Gaia. Then even Poseidon's command of the earthquake may not be enough to bring him down."

"Can he do that anyplace he happens to stand? Or does he need a particular sacred spot?"

The goddess glanced sideways at me. "For a mortal you ask probing questions that strike to the heart of the matter. Yes, Dionysus does need a holy site. For though he may tap the bosom of Gaia at any point, there are few places where the power he requires to defeat massed Olympians may be found."

"And I'm guessin' that one of 'em is on the Acropolis."

"Why would you guess that?"

I pointed my cup at the approaching wall. "Because two minutes ago that door was shut tight."

Sure enough, the great gate that Acastus and his troops had sealed with their very lives hung open a good six feet. Still no humans showed themselves. *Where is everybody? They have to be in there. I know fer a fact they didn't come rushin' past me.*

"My guess is that they're throwin' you a party for bein' so gosh-darned spunky," Jasper offered. "Maybe they're hidin' inside, ready to jump out and yell 'Surprise!' I can taste the cake and punch already." With that he turned himself into a pointed party hat and hopped onto my head. It must've looked pretty silly, perched on my beat-up rusty noggin. Athena spotted it and raised one eyebrow.

"I don't have earth magick," I explained. "Mine comes on all sudden-like...mostly when I don't want it to." I snatched the cone from my noggin, but it turned into a party horn. In typical

Jaspery fashion, it made a very rude noise when it tooted.

Being the goddess of wisdom, Athena stayed well above Jasper's sense of humor and ignored him. She eased ahead of me and lowered her spear. With its bronze point she flicked the enormous door open as if it had the mass of a dry leaf. Since I knew for a fact that each portal weighed around two tons, I whistled in appreciation and let her take the lead. Just to be on the safe side, though, I let Morphageus take true sword form.

Inside the fortress we found emptiness and quiet. Not a soul in sight. Spears stood stacked like uncovered Injun teepees. Helmets sat in neat rows as if they were gleaming crops in a garden. Swords grew out of the earth, points stabbed into the ground. Fires burned untended. All of the frantic terrified bustling that had attended the Maenad assault had vanished. *Did some god gather 'em all up and spirit 'em to safety?*

"No, we did not take them," Athena said, in answer to my unspoken question.

Swell. Now I got two eavesdroppers inside my noggin.

"Relax," the girl-goddess said with a hint of a smile. "It's not eavesdropping when I do it. I'm supposed to be all-knowing, remember?"

I sort of smiled back and concentrated on shutting every mental hatch and door I could locate. While I worked on that we moved farther into the Acropolis compound. Cemetery silence settled onto us like a woolen shawl. It lay so thick and spooky that I feared the Cumaeans had given up in despair and taken their own lives. With that worried thought I looked at Athena for her opinion. She shook her head, reassuring me that that particular dread was unfounded. Relaxing a bit, I stretched out my Stone-senses and searched for the Hellenes. Though I knew that my escort probably could hear an ant dancing in the next county, it made me feel better to think I was contributing to the search.

We both froze and turned our heads to the left at the same moment. *Okay, maybe my senses are better than I thought.* In the largest temple—Athena's own—a crowd sent up a whispered chant, a prayer. Those who couldn't fit inside knelt on the paving stones all around the huge pillared structure. Warrior, sage, maid, crone, and child all held hands, differences forgotten in the need to send one voice to the heavens. Now I understood why so many Olympians had arrived on this dusty, burning patch of ground. I'd flattered myself that it had been my prayer alone that had brought Athena and her siblings.

"As I said," she told me, "we answer the sincere ones. And do not think that yours was of no value. It awakened me to the crisis here. And this great communal orison proved that you had just cause to call for our aid."

She took a deep breath through her strong Hellenic nose, as if savoring the prayer's scent. I'd read that the gods actually lived on the odor of prayer and sacrifice, that it served as the source of their power. Seeing Athena take in the suppliants' chant and grow a bit brighter, I could believe it to be true. The goddess detoured around her temple, leaving the Lusitanians to continue their mass entreaty. I followed two steps behind as we threaded our way through the other gods' temples and came out upon the high barren area next to the northern cliff.

Somehow my name still burned in the valley beyond the Acropolis. That had to be some sort of magick, because any fuel available down there had to have been consumed long ago. But I didn't have much time to ponder the mystical science of fire, because we'd come up on something a lot more urgent.

Dionysus was about to sacrifice Ino to the earth goddess, to Gaia.

My long-suffering friend floated maybe four feet off the ground, bobbing as if on the surface of a pond. Just as when I'd last seen her, Ino was senseless, unmoving. Standing beside her, the feminine man-god had thrown back his leopard skin cape. He clutched a wicked curved knife in both hands. A pulsing chant in a language my spell couldn't or wouldn't translate flowed from his pretty mouth. It built in volume and intensity. Any moment the awful knife would spill Ino's maiden blood onto the thirsty ground and Dionysus would seal his bargain with Gaia. Then we'd all have some serious trouble on our hands.

Next to me, Athena had jammed her horse-crested helmet onto her head. While I stood flat-footed worrying about our predicament, she was taking action. Her arm flashed forward like a falcon in a dive, launching her spear straight at her renegade half-brother with the speed of a cannon shot.

It missed.

To my utter astonishment the gleaming bronze tip passed

between his shoulder and his jaw, slicing off a lock of curled and oiled hair. The goddess of battle, warrior-princess of wisdom and war, had failed. Dionysus watched the spear sail off into darkness behind him. His luscious upper lip curled as he turned back to us with a low chuckle. He pointed his sacrificial blade at Athena, posing like the actors who worshipped him.

"Good evening, sister. I expected you eventually, of course, just not quite this soon. No matter. It seems you're losing your touch. I remember when you could have skewered a falling star with your dread lance. Just more proof that the world order is shifting in my direction."

Athena stayed calm, showing no sign of distress at her failure to stop Ino's slaughter. "You congratulate yourself prematurely, as always. So full of yourself you could survive on the savor of your own self-love. I wasn't trying to hit you, only make you pause and gloat. It makes you a better...target."

Dionysus only had time to begin a frown. In the next breath the knife disappeared from his grip, knocked away by an arrow from the darkness to our left. An eye-blink later another feathered shaft grew from his wrist. The god of Frenzy emulated his minions and howled in rage and pain. *Good to know he can be hurt, at least by godly weapons.* New arrows notched on their bowstrings, a matched set of the loveliest young people I'd ever laid eyes on strode into view. Artemis and Apollo, no doubt. I recovered my own wits and changed Morphageus into a steely lasso, tossed it around Ino's foot, and pulled her out of danger.

"Speaking of premature self-congratulation," Dionysus

snapped, glaring at his pitiless family members, "perhaps you should have followed your own advice."

With that he raised his wrist and slammed the protruding arrow point into his own throat. Blood gushed onto the ground, causing steam to rise. Then he spiked his thyrsus onto the same spot. And laughed.

Apollo made me all churny inside.
I wanted to lay a big wet one
on those lovely Hellenic lips of his.
Artemis whacked her brother upside his handsome head.
His spell faded as he turned to scowl at her.
"What is it with the men in this family?" she growled.
"Can't you leave the earthly girls alone for five minutes?"

42 / Thyrsus' Child

I guessed it was a laugh, anyhow. Hard to tell with an arrow in the throat. Maybe it was just rhythmic gurgling. Whatever it might've been, Apollo and Artemis weren't amused. Their bowstrings twanged in unison. Silvery arrows streaked toward his bare bosom.

And hit nothing.

My jaw fell so far I almost bruised my toes. Two identical shots from the most renowned bow-wielders of antiquity, from maybe twenty feet away, struck only air. *When's the last time that happened? 8,000 B.C, during a windstorm and earthquake?* To be fair, their target hadn't stayed put. In fact, their target hadn't even held its shape. In the split-second it took for the arrows to reach him, Dionysus had dissolved into a tall stalk of supple green wheat. The light evening breeze swayed the plant just enough to make the bolts fly past. Either that, or the sentient stem moved all by itself. Seeing how things stood, the twin gods yanked matching bronze short swords from their shapely hips and threatened to thresh the god of agriculture.

"Looks like they're goin' against the grain," Jasper snickered. "**Stalk**ing their prey."

Except that by the time their slashes reached him, he'd shifted again. The earth's power, gained through his blood sacrifice, let him perform miracles he hadn't seemed able to before. Instead of a sturdy hunk of living wheat, the blades met a cloud of yellow swirling dust. Apollo messed up his pretty face with a frown and a pout. He whipped his weapon through the mist in frantic circles, accomplishing nothing.

"What foolish game is he playing?" he cried. "What is this funny smoke?"

"Not smoke," Artemis told him with a little smile. "It is pollen you battle so bravely."

"Pollen? What can he hope to gain by that?" He kept waving his sword through the stuff. I swear the breeze laughed at him.

Athena echoed that faint sound, but out loud and heartily. "Entertainment, if nothing else. He mocks you with every stroke."

"Wheat...then pollen," I said, thinking hard. "So he's usin' Gaia's earth magick to boost his own power, but only along the lines of his godly attributes?"

A loud bell rang. Jasper had changed form and was clanging away in my hand. When I looked down, wondering what he might be up to, he reshaped again and became a big blue ribbon like you'd win for Best Pecan Pie at the county fair.

"And we have a winner!" he blared in my head. "First prize in

Combat Cogitation goes to the funny-lookin' kid in the muddy overalls." He changed a third time, into a shiny silver dollar. "Here, go buy yourself a pair of shoes."

"I like goin' barefoot, thank you very much," I reminded him. With a wish I remade the dollar into a wooden nickel. "Here's what I think of yer advice, boyo."

"Fine. When you stub a toe on a bleached skull or some such nasty thing, don't come cryin' to Uncle Jasper."

I was getting another one of those raised-eyebrow looks from Athena. She must've thought reading my mind was a decidedly mixed blessing. "You are correct again," she said, accepting her spear as an owl returned it from where it had landed. "It would seem that he has achieved great but limited might for a brief time. We must engage him on those terms."

At a nod from her the squadron of great owls beat their wings while remaining on the ground. The stiff gale they produced dispersed the pollen, preventing Dionysus from coming back together into a more solid form. That would keep him busy for a few moments, but we'd need a brighter idea pretty soon. While I waited for somebody more divine—like, say, the goddess of wisdom—to have a spark of genius, I waved at Apollo.

"Say, ain't you in charge of medicine and the like?" I asked him.

He seemed to notice me for the first time. Though his chosen form wasn't as young as Athena's, he still didn't look a day over eighteen. And he hadn't cheated himself in the looks department, either. Tall, sturdy, with curly black hair and eyes that looked right through you—maybe literally, for all I knew—the god resembled Michelangelo's *David* statue, except with more clothes on. I felt thankful for that, for a lot of reasons. Heat ran all through me, and it had nothing to do with it being July, know what I mean? Tomboy though I was, I was still a girl. Woo-eee!

"I am," he nodded. His voice had low music in it and I started to flush a little more. *Careful, Verity. Remember his reputation. He didn't do poor Cassandra no good and that's a fact.*

"Well, yer no-good brother has hexed my friend here." I pointed down to Ino, lying pale and still on the ground beside me.

"And you would like me to heal her?"

"If you'd be so kind."

"And what would the young mortal offer in return for such a gift?" He shook his lovely locks and gave me the same look I'd seen on stage when John Wilkes Booth had charmed some ingénue in a romantic play. That 'god's gift to women' stare was extra-appropriate, considering who was giving it. Every other time I'd been exposed to it I'd wanted to gag and scrub myself with lye soap. But Apollo made me all churny inside. I wanted to lay a big wet one on those lovely Hellenic lips of his. In fact, I wanted to—

Artemis whacked her brother upside his handsome head. His spell faded as he turned to scowl at her. "What is it with the men in this family?" she growled. "Can't you leave the earthly girls alone for five minutes? And this one is only twelve!"

Apollo came over all sheepish, a look I didn't buy for a moment. He shrugged. "What can I say? I am my father's son. But she is right, of course. Another time, perhaps. When you are older and wiser."

"Any wiser and she'll be wearing my armor," Athena snorted.

Jasper spoke up in my noggin. "That was close. You'll never know how relieved I am that you didn't smooch him."

"Why? What's it to you?" I thought back.

"Because I feel everything you feel, remember? There's limits, you know."

"Boy, you're gonna really be unhappy when this whole puberty thing hits, ain't you?"

"Don't remind me. I shudder in horror at the thought."

While we'd been having that icky exchange, Apollo had laid his slender hands on Ino's brow. Just as when Romulus had healed my blisters in Virginia, blue-white firefly lights danced around the point of contact. They flew up to the god's head, encircling it like a laurel wreath. As they sunk in, he blinked a couple of times as the evil spell got absorbed and neutralized. Ino gasped and took a huge breath. Her eyes shot open and she clutched the dirt beneath her. I knelt and grabbed one of her clammy hands while she got her bearings.

Apollo winked at me and blew a kiss. I felt like throwing a rock at his perfect nose. *Boys…*

Waking out of a trance where you've just been a three-headed fire-breathing monster, to find yourself surrounded by three Hellenic gods and two dozen giant owls, all flapping their wings at a pollen cloud, can't be a body's first choice. Poor Ino shrieked and tried to scoot away. I held on tight and said some reassuring things in as soft a voice as I could. Looking back, the sight of yours truly probably scared her as much as all the rest of it. Covered in soot, blood, mud, sundry yucky Maenad body parts, not to mention the scrapes, bruises, cuts, and everything else, I didn't inspire confidence.

After a minute or so she calmed down enough to recognize me. We had a hard time making ourselves heard over the thrum of so many enormous owl wings. Since that hadn't been the case when talking to the gods, they all must've been speaking in my head, not my ears. So once she begun breathing in a normal way and stopped trying to run away, I hugged her tight and hollered that everything was okay and she could go home soon.

Verity Sauveur, world-class professional liar.

The stalemate with Dionysus ended right then. That cloud of golden pollen hadn't been able to fight the steady wind put out by the owls. But neither had the gods thought of any way to use their temporary advantage. Now that I'd restored Ino and repulsed Apollo's advances, I could spare some brain cells for our predicament. With a nudge from Jasper I saw a way to capture the taunting Dionysus. Athena read my mind, as did the twins. They all gave me tiny nods of understanding and encouragement. So I stood up and lunged at the dancing specks of dust. At the same time the owls stopped beating their wings and everything went dead silent. No sound could be heard except the whoosh of my tin cup, now eight feet across, slamming down on top of the swirling pollen.

Correction: there was another sound. Dionysus' cackling laughter.

The cup, nearly weightless—which was how Morphageus always felt—slapped right onto him. My divine comrades cheered as the trap fell. But since the wind that had kept him scattered had ceased, he could respond in the blink of an eye. We all raced up to capture Dionysus, but as I raised the oversized cup, rich red wine flowed downhill in finger-like rivulets. I considered seeing if I could transform Morphageus into a giant towel, but decided that was just too improbable. Anyhow, the god of wine gave me no time to try that. No sooner did we all turn to pursue the fluid than it sank into the dry ground like fresh rain.

"Where did he go?" Athena cried, head whipping in all directions. At a wave from her the owls all took to the air, staying low and spreading out in every direction. Their sharp predators' eyes would spot anything bigger than a bug, even in the dark.

"Absorbed into Gaia's bosom," Artemis said. She scooped up a handful of earth and let it pour out of her splayed fingers.

Apollo stamped his foot as if he were Poseidon shaking the ground. "He can't stay there. What's he up to now?"

Acastus and his warriors jogged up to us from Athena's temple. Now that their communal prayer had been answered, the citizens were free to help. *Mortals aiding the gods. Welcome to wacky Lusitania.* I dissolved Morphageus back into its sword form and saluted the Cumaeans.

"Honor to you all," I said, meaning every word. "Your piety has brought relief and hope."

I found myself talking to the tops of their heads. Everybody had dropped to their knees as soon as they'd spotted the gods. Despite looking human, and so young, it was plain to them all that Apollo, Artemis, and Athena weren't your average trio of improbably gorgeous young folks. Maybe it was the giant owls circling overhead. More likely it was the faint glow each gave off in the murk, like St. Elmo's Fire.

"Rise," Athena said in a mild voice. "We need strong arms, not weak knees."

Acastus' head lifted up a smidge. Peeping at me through his eyebrows, he sought reassurance that they wouldn't be blasted by Olympian thunderbolts. I gave him a thumbs-up and a grin. He rose, gesturing to his fellows to do the same. They stood at attention, in a tight formation, spears at their sides.

"Command us!" Acastus said.

Artemis took him at his word. "Dionysus has taken wine form and sunk into the earth. We need to find him."

Following their captain's lead, the soldiers fanned out and began prodding the ground with their lances. I had no idea what that could accomplish. Were they going to tickle Gaia into expelling Dionysus? Stabbing for wine was unlikely to produce results, to my mind. *Oh, well. Idle hands are the devil's playground, I guess. At least they'll feel useful.*

While the humans jabbed at Mother Earth, the gods seemed to withdraw into themselves. Apollo sat cross-legged, speaking in some unknown language while stinky steam came up from the ground between his knees. Artemis held her bow above her head while turning in a slow circle, mumbling to herself. Athena used the butt of her spear to draw figures in the dust. Not knowing what all that was about, I consulted my reference librarian about Dionysus.

"If I'm right, and Athena there seems to agree," I said to Jasper, "then Dionysus has a limited number of choices. What are his areas of influence? What is he known for? Some we learned in school: wine, drama, agriculture. Anything else?"

"Plenty, and most of it you didn't learn in school because Miz Finch preferred to avoid prosecution for corrupting America's youth," Jasper answered. "Lots of naked running around and increasing the flock. Get my meanin'?"

Knowing Jasper, I could well imagine. As a one-time farm kid I was aware that agriculture was more than just planting grain. It involved animals getting frisky and 'becoming one'. Somehow, though, I didn't think that was what Jasper meant. More likely he was talking about the human version of that, where all of that Dionysian passion seemed to lead. I'd heard that the ancient dramatic festivals, especially the comedy parts, were so obscene that they didn't bear thinking about.

"Yeah, yeah, yeah," I said. "Your mind's in the gutter, as usual. Actually, a gutter would come in handy right now. We could channel Dionysus in his wine form and pour him into a couple of amphorae. But give me something I can use, apart from your fevered gushy dreams."

"There's talk of a cult of souls, and communing with both the living and the dead."

"That explains his undead Maenads, which I never heard tell of in any mythology book."

"He wears a leopard skin, or a fox skin."

"Uh-huh. I saw the leopard. What else?"

"Let's see…bulls, snakes, centaurs, satyrs. He's got more variety than a traveling minstrel show." Jasper paused for effect. I knew he had more.

"And…?"

"He's a resurrected god. Like Osiris."

"Meanin'?"

"Meaning he's not likely to stay dead, even if one of your god-buddies manages to dispatch him."

"Why, ain't that just peachy? What's our option fer stoppin' him, then? Find a way to trap him and have the gods stow him someplace?"

"Well, you are in Cumae."

I got that one right quick. "And Cumae sits on a gate to the Underworld."

"God or no god, being a guest of Hades is bound to be no picnic. We've already seen him deal with those Maenads like nobody's business."

"Here's hoping you're right. Something's up."

Apollo had waved his strange smoke away and stood up. My thoughts went in 42 different directions before settling on just one. Something about that whole scene had tickled my brain. I'd just recalled that he was the god of prophecy, and of the Delphic Oracle. The priestess in Delphi would inhale vapors from underground vents and make predictions in her trance. Was that what Mr. Charm had been doing? Trying to predict Dionysus' next move? That might've been so, because he was jabbering orders to his twin sister, who stood there and took them. Artemis resumed her circling chant, this time sending a flaming arrow far off the hill into the forest, an impossible two miles away. While that was happening, Apollo spoke to Athena, who clapped her hands and laughed. *Okay, I'm glad somebody's havin' fun tonight.* She brought an owl out of the sky to land beside her. It listened carefully as she gave it instructions, referring to the diagrams she'd drawn in the dirt and to her half-brother. When she'd finished it bowed and sprang into the air again. In no time all of the great birds had vanished.

"Do the gods have a plan?" asked Ino in a faint voice. I'd forgotten she was beside me.

"Sure looks like it. Hope it's a good one, because this Dionysus feller is one tricky cuss."

"You have no idea. It will take all of the gods to snare him, now that he has joined with Gaia."

I scrunched up my face as I considered something. "But don't other gods have a claim on the earth goddess, too? Poseidon controls earthquakes, and Demeter the harvest. Mightn't they help out?"

"Possibly. But my prayers to Poseidon have not borne fruit this night. As for Demeter, there is bad blood between her and

Hades."

"Over Persephone?" *See, Miz Finch, I was payin' attention last year!*

"Yes. Since Hades has already struck at Dionysus, consuming his Bacchantes, Demeter might well spurn us, just to spite him."

I spat on the ground, then thought that might have been an unwise choice. *Oh, well...* "Seems to me the gods need to grow up and act like adults. Biggest bunch of spoiled brats I ever did see. Then I thought that saying that with Athena reading my thoughts was also an unwise choice. *Oh, well...*

"They sound like my kind of folks," Jasper said with a giggle.

"True," Ino replied to me, unable to hear the Pompous Sword of Doom. "All power and no one to make them behave."

I laughed out loud, making her frown in confusion. "Oh, yeah," I thought to Jasper. "They sure are yer kinda folks."

"Ah," he sighed. "Abuse."

"Yes."

He sighed, low and miserable. "I think you ought to know that I'm feelin' very depressed."

"From one little insult? You're gettin' awful thin-skinned lately, bucko."

"Oh, it's not from your pathetic attempt at witty banter."

"From what, then?"

Morphageus became a big arrow-shaped signpost that read 'This way to the latest disaster.' I turned to follow it with my eyes. What I saw made me feel as melancholy as President Lincoln reading dispatches from General McClellan.

Thick ivy vines snaked up from the ground where each soldier stood. They wrapped around each man in less time than it takes to tell it, covering him in leafy death. The soldiers' muffled screams stabbed clear through me. But what was worse was what happened next. Before Artemis or Apollo could begin to chop at the vegetation, it turned brown and rotted away. And where once sturdy Cumaean warriors had stood, now something more horrid and threatening faced us.

Horned men with hoofed goat legs, pointed ears...and disgusting lifeless eyes.

Undead satyrs. A hundred of them.

*"You know, we don't consult mortals on everything we do…
even those of you with godly powers."
"You hear that?" Jasper said. "Godly powers. Just what I've
been tryin' to get through to you. I should start a church.
Now what should my worshippers wear on holy days?
Would orange and green hoop skirts be too tacky?"*

43 / Satyr-Day's Child

"You know, I'm startin' to get a little tired of this whole undead business," Jasper sighed. "Makes you long for the good old days when we only had to fight hordes of demons."

I backed away from the new menace, toward the cliff. "Dionysus is gettin' in a bit of a rut. Ain't showin' a lot of imagination fer the god of drama."

"Speakin' of imagination…" The decomposing satyrs began advancing on us, still in the Cumaeans soldiers' neat formation.

"Yeah, yeah, yeah. I need some, and quick. Any suggestions?"

"Can't pitch in and start loppin' off heads, any more than you did with the chimera. Deep-down they're still your friendly local townsfolk."

The local townsfolk didn't seem any too friendly at that moment. Anything but, with their yellow fangs and staggering gaits. "Don't I know it." We were nearing the drop-off at the top of the Acropolis. Nowhere else to retreat to, except two hundred feet down. Not a great problem for my divine associates. They looked as cool as if they were off on a picnic. *I wonder if they've given a single thought as to what I'm supposed to do now. Ain't holdin' my breath in expectation of them lowerin' me down on a cloud, that's fer sure. Wonder where them owls all got to?*

I peeked over the edge. At the bottom of the cliff was an irregular ring of fire, like the rim of a small volcano. The entrance to the Underworld, I guessed. A strong stink of brimstone stung my nose. Unlike with Jasper's magick, no sweet lily smell accompanied it. Fantasies of devils with pitchforks filled my head. *Hmm. Wonder if I can pull that bat-wing trick with Morphageus like we did with the Hellfiend Legion in Virginia? Might be able to glide to safe ground beyond that fire pit.*

Uh-huh. And maybe I could spit in the moon's eye while I was at it.

While I'd been daydreaming about miraculous escapes, the satyrs had moved to within thirty feet of us and stopped. I'd expected them to just rush us over the cliff and be done with it. Dionysus had decided to play with us first. Though that was sort of a welcome development, from a not-immediately-dead standpoint, what happened next was anything but.

One of them spoke to me. In Acastus' voice.

"Callisto," he said, hoarse and pained. "Why have you come here? Why do you interfere with this world?"

Zombie goat-men had been bad enough. The speech made it much worse, somehow. At least the Maenads had only cackled while trying to eat us.

I shook my head to clear the voice of my friend from my ears. It was plain to me who was really talking. "You perform well, god of the drama. Excellent casting. Every tragic cycle is accompanied by a satyr play." As I said those words, something I'd read in an old book about Greek theatre started stinging my brain. Along with that was Athena's confirming that Dionysus was limited by his own attributes. Could it really be that easy? If so, we wouldn't have to harm any of our transformed friends.

"And you make an excellent coryphaeus," I went on. "Someone has to lead the chorus, to keep it in unison."

The Acastus-satyr bowed. I noticed that he, along with the rest of the monsters, was tipsy. I could smell the wine on all of their breaths. It just about knocked me over the cliff all by itself. *What's that mean? Has Gaia's extra power pushed him beyond the limits of his control?*

"I am choragus, as well," he rumbled. "Sponsor and patron of this production. I shall claim the prize at the play's end."

"Only if you win," I chided. "Don't claim your wreath too soon. And who are the judges for this festival? Who is qualified to determine a winner?"

He was really weaving in drunkenness now. "Dare I say...the Olympians themselves?"

"Careful, greatest of actors. Beware the curse of hubris."

"You do well to warn me of excess pride, barbarian child. But is it hubris in this case to believe that only my fellow gods may judge me?"

I had to admit that he had a point there. But this was no time to say so. Not when my plan depended on keeping up appearances. "Your logic is as faultless as your acting. The decision has, in fact, been rendered."

Turning to Athena, I made sure that she could read my thoughts. With a nod she assured me that she knew what I was up to. The twins smiled and stepped forward to keep our little scene going. All three gods assumed grave expressions suitable for the ultimate theatre critics. Knowing several of those pompous fellows back home in Washington, I snickered inside. *Yep, they'd sure love this. Drama Critic As God. Not a one of 'em would think it absurd.*

When I turned back to the intoxicated satyr, I held a silver laurel wreath in both hands, as high as I could get it. His big yellow eyes widened. "Come, choragus. You have reached the pinnacle of success. Your fellow citizens fully recognize your achievement."

The goat hooves clopped on the rocky ground. He staggered forward to present his shaggy head to be crowned. With as much reverent seriousness as I could muster I set the metal wreath on his noggin, balancing it on his short horns.

"Blech!" Jasper spat. "He smells awful!"

"Sshh!" I thought at him. "Don't ruin this. He might be in my head."

If Dionysus was reading my mind, he showed no sign of it. He wavered and clutched at the wreath to keep it in place. Behind him the chorus of drunken satyrs went into a funny skipping dance, made all the more hilarious by their being rotting zombies. *Yep, Lusitania is the height of hilarity. Too bad there ain't no real critics about. I can hear 'em now. 'Laugh? I thought I'd die.'*

"Your worth is known!" I announced. "All assembled here have judged your performance and wish to reward it accordingly."

With that the silver laurel wreath sprouted more leaves and more stems, flowing down from his skull to wrap around the hairy swaying form like garlands on a Christmas tree. Only these decorations were as strong as steel ship's cables and as tight as mummy bandages. Try as he might, the satyr couldn't break free. When he realized what had happened, Dionysus sobered up real quick. Acastus' voice faded and was replaced by the god's own, angry and defiant.

"Clever girl!" he hissed. "Your mama must be proud."

"Leave my ma outta this," I snapped back. "You got enough troubles without gettin' me madder than I already am."

"Oh, look at me tremble in fear of the outlander." The goat-man turned his head to his dancing minions. "Kill them all! Throw them into Tartarus!"

Comedy turned back into tragedy in the snap of a finger. His chorus stopped dancing and gave us murderous glares. The beasts growled and galloped straight at us, intent on bowling us over the cliff. It might've worked, too, except that in his hurry to be clever Dionysus had neglected to recall one of the most important things about satyrs. That thing I'd recalled reading about.

They're cowards.

Athena raised her bronze spear. Artemis notched an arrow and Apollo drew his sword. All three gods sent out a deafening battle cry that threatened to tear a gash in the night sky. When they took two steps toward the satyrs all hundred of the monsters shrieked like little girls, turned tail—literally—and scampered off down the hill toward the temples. In ten seconds they'd vanished amongst the temples and other buildings.

"Ah, well," sighed Dionysus, "you send a satyr to do a god's job..."

I grabbed a loose end of the Jasper-wreath, turning it into a bullwhip. It was time to turn my prisoner over to his siblings. What they chose to do with him made no difference to me, so long as I got out of Lusitania and met up with my friends. With no little glee I yanked it as hard as I could, spinning him like a top. He turned on his axis so fast he became a blur. When he didn't stop I started to get worried. *Okay, now what's he up to?*

Dionysus looked like a broomstick on a lathe, turning at a dozen revolutions per second. Apollo got tired of waiting for him to stop and reached out a hand to interrupt the spinning. It worked, too. The misbehaving god interrupted his motion and returned to his normal effeminate male form, thyrsus in hand. But he still wavered, unsteady on his feet. Not from drink, though.

"Oooh!" he giggled. "That makes a fellow dizzy!"

We should've stayed on our guard. Distracted by his ridiculousness, even the gods were thrown off for a second. That was all he needed. While Apollo paused, hand on his half-brother's slender arm, the leopard skin cape resting on Dionysus' shoulders came to life, filled out, and leapt upon the arresting god. The spotted beast snarled and clawed at Apollo, who hacked at it with his sword. Before Artemis could let her arrow fly the thyrsus became a hissing snake that twined around the bow, making it unusable. Athena thrust her spear at Dionysus. If he'd kept his human form she might've hit him, but the point ended up too high to strike the small fox he became. By the time she withdrew the lance and prepared a second blow the fox had dashed after the fleeing satyrs.

"Go!" she commanded me. "Don't let him get into the temples!"

I turned Morphageus into a bracelet and sprinted after the little animal. Athena stayed behind to help her brother and sister deal with their attackers. With every Stone-sense I had I kept tabs on the sleek fox. If Dionysus got out of sight he could change into who-knew-what and we'd be in even more trouble. My legs felt like they'd been filled with lead shot. *Need to sleep fer a week. And how much magick can I have left?*

"Oh, you're good for a little while longer," Jasper said. "This is so much fun I get a charge out of just bein' alive."

"You ain't alive," I reminded him.

"Hey! No cause for insults, young lady. Where are your manners?"

"Must've left 'em in my other britches."

Luck was with us. Though the satyrs had disappeared into the maze of buildings in the main part of the Acropolis, the fox couldn't. His way was blocked by the rest of the Cumaeans, who'd gathered up their courage and started up the hill toward us. There were so many of them that they made a solid wall of people five rows deep. The fox ran back and forth, searching for a way through. Stymied, Dionysus slowed, then backed away from the crowd and toward me. I skidded to a stop and turned the bracelet into a shield, ready for anything.

That anything turned out to be the biggest, blackest bull I'd ever laid eyes on.

Sure, we'd had a bull on our Maryland farm. But he'd been a normal-sized fellow, and a sweetie-pie, too, except when you got between him and his latest girlfriend. This monster had to be three times as big, with wicked horns a good eight feet across. His eyes gleamed red in the darkness, and steam blew out of his flaring nostrils. When he pawed the ground in rage I could feel the tremor in my teeth.

Jasper snickered. "This makes sense, considerin' all of the bull Dionysus has been spoutin' this evenin'."

I made the mistake of joining him in laughing at his little joke. The next thing I knew I'd landed thirty feet up the hill, with more bruises and scrapes to add to my growing Lusitanian collection. *Ow! Jeepers! That'll learn you to pay attention the next time there's a god-monster chargin' at you.* That was all the self-disgust I had time for. Faster than a locomotive, and just about as solid, the bull kept after me. No sooner did I scramble to my feet than he hit me again. This time I spun with the blow like

Sha'ira had taught me. Those dreadful horns scraped along the shield and the creature thundered past. As he did so Jasper became a big fist that thumbed my nose at Dionysus.

"You keep doin' that and he might start to get mad," I quipped. Taking stock of my aching frame, I decided that nothing was broken yet. *Score one fer our side.*

"Keepin' him mad is the plan, girlie," Jasper informed me. "His mischief is limited as long as he's in this form. Plus, it keeps him from plowing into those citizens."

"Good point. Let's keep him busy till the gods get down here. Then they can lasso him and end this." I flung myself to one side as the bull charged again. The horns just missed my shoulder.

"Keep tellin' yourself that. For gods they're not all that impressive so far."

"I'll allow that it looks that way. But I also expect that in this world the outcome has already been decided by Fate."

"You think so? What about the Affluxion?"

"What about it?"

"For better or worse this world is designed to be a Maenad playground. The Merchantry spell makes that happen. You've already interfered with that. So where's your fate in all of that?"

I turned Morphageus into a big spring and bounded over the next assault like some overdressed Minoan bull-leaper. "How do you know I ain't Dionysus' fate?"

"Ooh, you know I like it when you get all philosophical."

The great black bull shook his head and turned to face me again. Despite his form, I could still see Dionysus in the thing.

He was less than happy. The odd foreign girl had upset his night out with the girls. And every time I frustrated one of his attacks it just tightened his clock spring a little bit more. Soon he'd snap. Whether that would result in him going away or destroying all of Lusitania was anybody's guess.

Let's find out.

Knowing that it would drive him crazy with anger, I formed Jasper into a crimson bullfighter's cape. Assuming the standard haughty pose, which I'd seen in a painting once, I waved it at him as a tease. Locked in his bull shape, Dionysus automatically pawed the dust and rushed at the red fabric. A mini-earthquake trembled the earth as the monstrous animal approached. I left the cape there and the bull smashed into it nose-first.

Only the back side of the cape was an anvil, anchored ten feet into the ground.

Dionysus tumbled end-over-end and lay still, huffing and snorting.

"Bet you two bits that really, really hurt," Jasper said.

I had to agree. It made me wince, enemy or not. While we watched the bull shake its enormous head and start to rise, I felt a warm presence beside me. Athena raised he eyebrow as a token of appreciation for my animal-taming skills.

"At last," she murmured. "Just as Apollo foresaw."

Apollo predicted this? How about lettin' a girl in on stuff like that?

She read the thought, of course. "You know, we don't consult mortals on everything we do...even those of you with godly powers."

"You hear that?" Jasper said. "Godly powers. Just what I've been tryin' to get through to you from the beginnin'. I should start a church. Now what should my worshippers wear on holy days? Would orange and green hoop skirts be too tacky?"

I shoved his annoying voice to the back of my mind, because Artemis and Apollo had arrived. All three gods wore smug looks. Something was up and it miffed me to not be part of it. *Welcome to bein' on the bottom rung of the Ladder of the Eternal Verities, I guess.* While I was pondering my place in the universe, the bull got back up on all four feet and was staring at us.

"I can do this all night," he said in a cool tone. "I am one with Gaia now. So long as I cling to her bosom, you Olympians shall not overcome me."

"My thought, precisely," Athena agreed. She turned to Artemis. "Sister, are your companions arrived?"

"They are," replied the goddess of the hunt. As she spoke a new chorus sounded. Not of satyrs this time, but of hounds. Her hounds. The pack that never lost track of its quarry and which always brought it down. Dozens of dogs, mostly giant, scruffy, wolfhound-looking things, poured through a sudden gap in the wall of citizens and raced toward the bull. Dionysus roared and tried to fight, but there were too many of them. Though he flung several away with his horns and kicked many more, the odds were against him. And once they'd latched onto him with their teeth he was committed to his bull shape and couldn't transform into something else. With dogs clinging to him like barnacles to a ship, he panicked and galloped away from the yelping pack, the Cumaeans, and the gods.

Right over the cliff.

I squealed and raced after them, hoping to save some of the poor doggies. But by the time I arrived at the edge all but one had fallen over with the bull and were plummeting toward the volcanic mouth of Tartarus. Distraught, I hugged the one remaining mutt and blubbered about the ones we'd lost.

It turned out that I needn't have worried. When you have the gods on your side in Lusitania, you're on the winning team. Athena's squadron of giant owls had been circling over the fiery pit, waiting for just this moment, foreseen by Apollo, god of the oracle. They snatched up the dogs in their huge talons, one with each foot. Not a pooch was lost. But somehow there just weren't enough birds left to spare to rescue the tumbling bull. Blasted by a surprise bolt of Olympian lightning—a parting gift from his daddy—Dionysus disappeared into the orange crater with a string of spectacular curses.

"Such language!" Ernie said, right in my ear.

"You'd think a god would show some better breeding than that," added the Duke with a Gaullic sniff.

I sniffed, too. Twice. The first one was to get a whiff of the dirty-socks smell of basset hound, just to reassure myself that I wasn't dreaming. The second was to keep my nose from dripping too much as I blubbered at being reunited with my buddies.

"Careful, now," said Ernie. "You'll embarrass us in front of the troops."

Sure enough, the soldiers had resumed human form with the departure of Dionysus and were climbing the hill toward us. Cheering citizens followed them, Ino in the lead. Owls began landing all around us to set down Artemis' baying dogs. And mixed in amongst them were Alcibiades, bearing Tyrell and Sha'ira, and Romulus, borne by two strange white owls that weren't part of Athena's formation. Beside them glided the Dread Pirate Roberta.

I laughed and cried at the same time. *Now this how all my battles should end.*

"Try not to be too dim-witted, missy."
"Well, pardon me fer livin', Mr. Snotty.
We ain't all omniscient magick swords who've
been around fer thousands of years, you know."
*"No, it only **seems** like I've been around you for that long."*

44 / She's Got Some Gaulle
Thursday, July 11, 703 B.C.

My memory's kind of fuzzy on details after that. Like usual, burning through so much magick on little food and less sleep knocked me out. But between my hazy rememberings and the stories told by Tyrell and the others, I managed to get a good picture of what happened that night and the day after.

"No sign of your gods," Tyrell said. "Looked all over. Saw nobody matching your description of them. Must have made themselves scarce once the need for them had ended."

"Well, they probably have a mighty heavy workload. Other things needed doin', I expect."

"You keeled over like a ship with no ballast," Roberta told me. "We found you huggin' that ridiculous-lookin' hound there, fast asleep."

The Duke took offense at that and let her have a barrage of insults in rapid-fire Gaullic. Luckily, it was just barks and howls to her. Though I only caught a smidge of it, I wanted to take a scrub brush to my brain. *Yep, my translation powers are just about gone.*

"Somebody wanna explain what happened to y'all after I left the *Kiss*?" I asked.

"We didn't have no clear idea what happened to you, chile," Romulus rumbled when I woke up the next afternoon. "Dat undersea ironclad come, we all braced ourselves to get rammed, and poof! You was nowheres to be found."

"Tweren't any part of my plan for that day, believe me," I told him. "Sure gets them alarm bells a-ringin' when a merman hauls you over the side into the open ocean in the middle of the night."

Jasper piped up. "I always said you were wet behind the ears. Gives me a certain feeling of self-satisfaction to know that I was right."

"Yipee," I said to him, "that makes maybe three times you've been right since I've known you."

"Really? Well, here's number four: Verity Sauveur is a cranky brat when she gets out of bed after a long night of god-whuppin'.'"

I pitched into the eggs and cheese that Acastus' girls had just made for me. Lampade lay in her room, a bit recovered from her mental breakdown but still unable to see her kids. They blubbered quite a bit about that, despite nearly getting their throats cut by their own mama. Though there was a guard on her door, in case she went berserk again, Acastus claimed it probably wasn't needed. His beloved wife felt so mortified by her behavior that she chose to lock herself away.

Sha'ira looked up from a corner of the gynaeceum, where she sat cross-legged on the floor sharpening her curved dagger. "You truly swam all the way to Iberion underwater?"

After burping and swallowing some hydromel, I told the full story of the undersea battle, the trip to the coast, and my travels disguised as an Iberion maiden. That last part proved to be real entertaining to the Arabe Dreamwriter and Lady Roberta. The pirate queen perched in the window, the scarlet and blue plumage of her cursed parrot form gleaming in the summer sun. She'd been the one to guide them all to Cumae, after Tyrell's signal had been spotted by the pelican patrol.

"I gotta admit, I'd pay a chest of Merchantry booty to spy you playin' the Arabe ingénue. Tried my hand at somethin' like that myself once. See, we'd infiltrated this Venetian bawdy house used by enemy agents—"

Ernie interrupted her before she got to any of the more tender details. Jasper huffed his frustration into my noggin, but I pushed him away. "These Hellenes sure know their cheese. What's this one called?" He held up a square inch cube over his head with both paws.

The Duke slurped it up with his long basset tongue, much to the mouse's indignation. "I call it an hors d'oeuvre. Merci boucoups, mon petit marechal."

After tossing Ernie another piece to mollify him, I told everybody about Castle Carrasco and the horrifying goings-on there. Tyrell, leaning back with his hat down over his eyes, seemed to think that getting saddled with the Duke counted as part of the horror. That set off a ruckus between the two of them that almost restarted the Gaullic Revolution. When we'd calmed them down some I took my story up to where I escaped the castle and dashed into Lusitania.

"Muskets?" Romulus said with a frown. "And kegs of powder? In Iberion? You sure about dat?"

"Sure as I am of my own name," I told him. "Stood right there in that storeroom and counted enough rifles to outfit a battalion. And the powder made a mighty spectacular sight when I blew it up. Like a dozen Fourth of July's."

Sha'ira's whetstone ceased its screechy slide. "That is disturbing. Before now the Merchantry has tended to rely on only local methods to exert control, for fear of upsetting the natural course of events."

"Well, somebody sure wasn't worried none about that in Castle Carrasco."

"Nor in Cumae," Tyrell said, pushing his hat back and sitting up. "While we were flying over the city last night as it burned I counted a couple of explosions that couldn't be accounted for by any Hellenic means. So this morning I rode over to those spots with Acastus. Sure enough, two barns showed clear signs of gunpowder scorching. You could still smell it in the air."

"Maybe that's where them Furies who came after the *Kiss* got their muskets," I suggested.

"Could be," Romulus nodded. "Thing is...why?"

"Maybe Merchantry, maybe one of their dissatisfied offshoots," Tyrell offered.

Roberta peered down at us through her spectacles. "That'll take some considerin', shipmates. The Equity needs to send some spies about to hunt for any sign of weapons caches or transports. Ask at the docks. Sailors is a nosy bunch of swabs. Somebody's bound to have seen somethin' suspicious-like."

"I'll get a message out within the hour on one of the gulls," Ernie said.

"You didn't have no trouble crossin' into Iberion or Lusitania, then?" Romulus wanted to know.

I shook my head and spread butter on a hunk of bread. "Uh-uh. Should I have?"

"No. The Stone lets you do dat without the Affluxion spell catchin' hold on you. I just wanted to make sure it's workin'."

"Normal folks without strong magick can't cross like you did," Tyrell explained. "Either the spell gives them a good reason to change their minds or it seizes them and creates a fantasy that they journeyed to the next land when they never did. Only at a few rare points are there gaps in the enchantment that permit easier travel. Those are well-guarded by Merchantry agents who man the ships, coaches, trains, what have you. They control each traveler's experience as far as they're able."

"Well, all I know is I passed through the border barrier without noticin' anything odd, except that nobody from Castle Carrasco followed me. That'd explain why."

While I kept filling my face with every bit of food I could lay my mitts on, including a small cup of thinned wine (to Jasper's immense joy and the replenishing of my magick), I continued catching my friends up on my adventures in Maenad-Land. Drowning zombies, taming chimeras, chasing off the crazy lady sorcerer, going nose-to-nose with the god of madness. All of it. The general feeling seemed to be that Verity had more luck than any hundred girls her age. They got no argument from me. I just about had to pinch myself to make sure that my miraculous survival wasn't a cruel Merchantry vision.

"Outta idle curiosity," I said, all innocent, "which of you knew I had a black arts mage fer an aunt?"

You could've cut the embarrassed silence with the proverbial knife. After a couple of unnecessary coughs and plenty of pointless looks in every direction except mine, I had my answer. Just about everybody in the room knew about Regan and none of them had seen their way clear to mentioning her to me. *Thanks a lot. Same as Ma not tellin' me that Pa's alive. Treatin' me like a kid. Ain't I earned more than that?*

After a long and painful minute Romulus spoke up. "Like I said befo', when you asked about yo' daddy. Weren't my place to say. Yo' mama swore us to silence. Said it'd be a danger to you. Said she'd let you know what was needed, when it was needed."

"If it ain't needed now, when will it be?" I snapped. "Jeepers Gawd Almighty, I been chased from one end of this ruined world to the other by gods, monsters, bounty hunters, and the undead. My only friend's rottin' in a London dungeon fer darin' to stick by me. Fought fer my life against all manner of death-dealin' demons and mercenary soldiers. I've had to grow all the way up in just a few days. When's it time fer the so-called adults to start trustin' me with simple facts?"

"The squid's got a point," Roberta admitted. "If knowledge is power, then maybe her cartridge box needs fillin'."

"Maybe so, but that's still Ellen's decision, not ours," Ernie said. "I've bloody-well seen what she does to demons when her dander's up. I ain't about to get on her bad side."

That seemed to be the group's last word on the subject. Prodding and pleading got me nowhere. I vowed that me and Ma were going to have it out when I got back to the ship. *This stumblin' around blind has gotta stop. One of these days I'm gonna really miss some pertinent fact that gets me transmogrified into a centipede or somethin' just as yucky.*

"Aw, you'd look so darned cute," Jasper cooed. "All those adorable little legs wigglin' about."

"Till some ill-mannered boy squashed me flat," I said. "You feel everything I do. How would you like them apples?"

With nothing left to discuss on that front, I kept stuffing my face and let the others fill me in on what had been happening on their end while I'd been fumbling around rural Europa. Had it really only been three days since I'd left the ship? It felt like three months in a torture chamber, as far as my bones were concerned. Everything hurt...joints, muscles, skin. *I swear, even my freckles need liniment.* Each little movement to reach for an olive or chew a grape made me wince. The only good thing about it was that Jasper was in the same boat, as he didn't tire of telling me.

"Is there any unbruised, unscraped, uncut, unbeaten part of your integument? I'm havin' a real hard time concentratin' on this grub for all of the misery. Hey, maybe we can find a gullible

 Jasper's Foul Tongue

citizen to take your pain with a healin' spell," he suggested. "Romulus had no qualms about volunteerin' to take your foot blisters in Virginia. There oughta be at least one grateful Cumaean hereabouts who'll do the same for you today, in exchange for riddin' 'em of the Dionysian zombie menace."

"If you think I'm gonna manipulate some grievin' Lusitanian into acceptin' my aches and pains, you're even more obnoxious than I thought you was. They're all buryin' their loved ones, fer Pete's sake."

"Don't come over all persnickety. It was just a suggestion. Sheesh!"

Jasper slunk off to wherever he went to when he pouted. I could now pay attention to the group explanation of what had occurred on the *Penelope's Kiss* and how they'd all managed to find me in the nick of time. Though nobody could say for certain, the strange underwater craft that had tried to ram our frigate might've been a Redeemer ship. Tyrell claimed to have heard rumors for years about some renegade tycoon who'd paid for the best engineers on Earth to make him such a vessel. The Coterie Redempteur had managed to convince him of the worthiness of their cause (I thought reforming the Honourable Merchantry from within was a fool's errand, but no one listened to my opinion). If this was true, then the attack on the ship might've actually been a rescue attempt.

What made that seem more likely was what happened the next day. A trio of the Proprietor's ships, disguised as ordinary Gaullic pirate-hunting steam-privateers, blocked the *Kiss'* path north. Though a real 'avast, me hearties' pirate (he preferred the term 'sailor of fortune'), Pitcairn found himself engaged in honest work, for once. When he tried to point this out via signals to his foes, they struck their false colors, raised the red and gold Merchantry flag, and fired on him. Time was of the essence and a protracted engagement would have only played into their hands. Salmos' comrades had just informed Pitcairn of my situation and the need to get to Gaulle. Our original plan still held, me not being dead and all. So the *Kiss* took all advantage the wind could afford them, aided by mermen fouling enemy rudders and General Gracchus' Legion of rats chewing apart vital lines on enemy sails. Bob's pelicans even dropped melons down the Merchantry smokestacks to even the odds.

For most of the next couple of days and nights the quartet of ships maneuvered with amazing skill, to hear my friends tell it. 'Four fine boxers in one ring' was how Romulus described the episode. Morning, noon, and night the game went on. No sooner would one captain outguess his opposite number and threaten to end the thing than a grand surprise would upset the cunning calculations. Finally, though, sheer numbers and a lack of wind were about to close the trap in the Merchantry's favor. At that point, when the situation seemed most dire, Pitcairn loosed the final coup. I was as surprised as the enemy commander must have been.

"Fire sprites?" I sputtered. "What in tarnation are they? And where did he get 'em?"

"They're just what they sound like," Jasper sighed. "Try not to be too dim-witted, missy."

"Well, pardon me fer livin', Mr. Snotty. We ain't all omniscient magick swords who've been around fer thousands of years, you know."

"No, it only **seems** like I've been around you for that long."

Ernie did the explaining. "They're tiny blokes, pixie-like. Pitcairn keeps 'em handy for tight spots. See, what they consider great sport is to ride cannonballs."

I turned up my mouth at that. "Yer joshin'."

"I swear I ain't. They climb into the cannon, straddle the shot like it's a racehorse, and laugh like lunatics when the powder ignites. Yer can't harm 'em with explosions. That's why they're fire sprites."

"That's all well and good, but how does that serve Pitcairn?"

"Simple. In exchange for such fine entertainment, each sprite agrees to guide his cannonball directly onto the target his gunner selects."

"So that's why Mr. Nickleby never seems to miss a shot? He has fairies steer his lead?"

"I swear on me mother's life. Only, don't call 'em fairies to their faces. They'll scorch your eyebrows for the insult. And stay off the gundeck for an hour after a battle. Shot-riding makes the wee buggers more than a little bit intoxicated. Pandemonium ensues, let me tell you. Woo!"

He still didn't have me convinced. "How come I ain't never laid eyes on one in all the time that I've been on the ship?"

"They're the size of small moths, for starters. In fact, I'll you've probably seen 'em and thought they were just little bugs." I recalled the orange sparks I saw coming back to the ship against the wind the night I arrived on the *Kiss*. "And they tend to avoid folks, savin' for them's they choose to befriend. Each gunner has one or two with him. They sleep in his hair."

"Ick!"

"Don't be judgmental, missy! They keep the lice and fleas down to a tolerable level."

I made a sour face. "You just put me off my food."

"Speak for yourself, Freckled Fiend," Jasper said. "I'm famished. Keep packin' it in if you want to restore all that magick you burned through last night. And I better get an after-dinner smoke outta you, too."

I slurped some more hydromel and motioned for everybody to finish the story. Three sprite-guided shots blew up a boiler on one enemy vessel, shattered the mainmast on another, and beheaded the commander of the third. After that Pitcairn had no more trouble with them. They slunk away to lick their wounds and, no doubt, concoct a plausible explanation as to how three steamships managed to lose to a single wind-powered frigate. *Don't relish 'em havin' to do that. Their Merchantry bosses ain't known fer their Christian charity in the face of failure. By now them crews're probably a mess of cockroaches in a Marseilles sewer.*

While the chase had gone on, Sha'ira had tried Dreamwriting a message to me. It'd proved to be easier said than done. Dreamwriting required a precise ritual, bloodletting, fire, and a soul-pen that wasn't seasick. With all of the sudden changes of direction, rough seas, and general unease, she hadn't been able to do so till late on the third day. That'd been when she'd intervened in my impending sacrifice at the hands of Dionysus. Merely thanking her for that had seemed inadequate. She'd shrugged off my clumsy attempt at it, saying that after so many years of being a Shade with the assassins Guild, saving lives was reward enough. Then she'd gone off with Romulus to help the Cumaean citizens with putting out fires and searching for survivors. They'd only just returned.

So the upshot of it all was that the *Penelope's Kiss* now lay in a hidden Equity anchorage just north of Bayonne, waiting for us. With Merchantry patrols littering the Atlantic like spent Minie balls after a battle, she couldn't linger there. The plan was to get us back there as soon as the sun set. Flying across Lusitania would take all night, even on owl-mages. And we had to set down for rest stops as seldom as possible. Sure, we'd shed ourselves of Dionysus and his personal Maenad horde, but there were plenty more of the undead women. Ino told us that they infected the entire Lusitanian countryside. Even though they didn't hunt in packs of ten thousand, it didn't take many to wreck your day. It'd be a sad state of affairs to defeat an entire army of Bacchantes just to get chomped on by a lone straggler in the woods a hundred miles off. And as far as threats went, we still had no clue as to who had sent the Furies, or why. An aerial ambush was a possibility we couldn't afford to ignore.

I spent the time between my meal and dusk setting things

right between Ino and Acastus. Most of the Cumaeans still wanted to lynch her, just to make certain they had no future chimera infestations. Once I'd explained that she was a harbinger of disaster, not the cause, and that Athena had told me that the gods wanted her in one piece (yep, I lied through my teeth), they shrugged and let her alone. It was crystal-clear, though, that they wanted her gone. We agreed to fly her out of Cumae and back to her home village. That'd give me a traveling buddy for the first half of the night. She sure looked like she could use a friend. The poor kid had been through a lot in her short life and it didn't look like Poseidon planned to ease up on her none.

Lampade had to be reunited with her beloved children, of course. That I couldn't quite arrange, with her trying to butcher them and all. Husbands take a dim view of that, no matter the reason. But I explained to Acastus that the gods of wisdom, healing, and childbirth had all answered my prayers—our prayers, actually—and I felt certain that Lampade's madness had more to do with the god of delirium than anything else. With him gone and them looking out for his family, things would be all right.

After that I flopped under a tree on the Acropolis and smoked my pipe. Nasty a habit as it was, Jasper's magick got renewed by it quicker than nearly anything else. Most likely because it made me gag. Sore, tired, with my brain aching from all the horrific things I'd seen, and done, since leaving my ship, I wasn't much good to anybody for a while. My friends left me alone and spent the three hours till sundown acting as a special aid unit for Cumae. Alcibiades and Tyrell flew over the destroyed city, helping spot those still living but undiscovered. They also carried food, water, and bandages to where it was needed, since most of the narrow streets were blocked by wreckage. Romulus used his brawn to move beams and boulders so the clean-up crews could get started. Tiny Ernie squeezed into places nobody else could get into, finding buried folks missed by the airborne eyes but not by the Duke's wonder-nose. With the local Maenads sucked down into Tartarus, help arrived from neighboring towns.

"Looks like things will be okay," I said to Jasper, who sat beside me in the form of a rag doll with a corncob pipe in its mouth. "Not perfect by a darned sight, with so many loved ones dead, but better than the total annihilation we all expected."

"Small comfort to most of these families," he told me. "Speaking of family troubles, what do you plan on sayin' to your ma?"

Good question. I'll spend the whole trip north ponderin' that very thing.

And I did just that, all the way to Gaulle, clinging to the back of a giant owl while trying to hold polite conversation with Ino.

"I ain't rightly sure what metal they forged you from.
You might have a bit o' iron,
but most of it is somethin' else entirely."
"Whips and snails and puppy-dog tails?"

45 / Unlocking the Letter
Friday, July 12, 1804

Compared to my previous three days in Europa, the night-flight to the Gaullic coast was as placid as a church social, if you don't count my war-torn mind. All the pipe smoking in the world couldn't have soothed that. In addition to my impending set-to with Ma I had to come to terms with all that had happened since washing up on the coast of Iberion. The Legacy Stone always had a calming effect on my nerves. That had sure come in handy to keep me sane and thinking straight in the tight spots I kept getting into. Good thing it did, because even with that benefit the shock of it all just about knocked me off of my owl.

About halfway across Lusitania, high up where the cool breezes tickled my bare toes, the memories smacked me upside the head like a solid shot from a 12-pound Napoleon. *Furies swarming the Kiss. The undersea skirmish. Living windmills assailing us. Carrasco butchering his guests in that Great Hall. Rotting Maenad women devouring human flesh. Traveling between our world and the Obverse. Ino in chimera form nearly killing us all. Lampade almost slaying her own children. Feeling foul Dionysus controlling my mind. Watching the unoffending city of Cumae burn.*

I commenced to gasping and trembling as if I'd contracted malaria. In fact, I might have slid from the great bird and tumbled to the ground if Ino hadn't been there. She bear-hugged me, her knees clamping hard against the owl's flank. Her soft voice shushed me and said it'd be okay. Believing her was no easy feat. Ever since I'd found Morphageus beneath Ford's Athenaeum toward the end of June I'd done little else but run from or fight things that had no right existing.

Dearth demons with mouths full of fangs. Bullies, seemingly just innocent little kids till they witched you with a spell and made you their puppet. Zombie Rebel soldiers. Staves that fired Pluto's Bane and set you afire from the inside-out. And poop monsters. Poop monsters, for crying out loud! This sure wasn't the first time I'd broken down from the shock of my experiences. Heck, I'd blubbered like a colicky baby just from hearing Jasper in my noggin the first time. But somehow this felt worse.

Maybe because I keep survivin' and gettin' closer to the Scepter'd Isle. That final showdown with the Proprietor and his elite Merchantry mages will likely be the last thing me and Tommy ever do on this Earth. Shoot, the mere thought of that'd make a marble statue cry.

"You lament the past and dread what is to come," Ino whispered, barely audible over the rush of air and the thump of beating wings.

"What, now you can read my mind, too?" I sniffed. "My noodle must be a big fat open book to anybody who happens along."

"It's not that. I have much experience with that state of mind, is all. Ever since falling under Poseidon's dominion, yesterday brings nightmares and tomorrow brings terror. Such have the Fates decreed for me. It is neither good nor bad. It merely...is."

"So this is what fate has in store fer me, then? And I should just set my jaw and take it like a good girl?"

She shook her pretty head and waved at the starry sky. "You are not of my world. This is all I know, this tiny patch of rocks and trees. Perhaps fate is different where you come from, if it exists at all. From seeing you and your marvelous friends seize even the gods by the scruff of their necks, I believe you must make your own destiny. If there is a book someplace where your fortune is written, there must be many a blank page for you to fill with a pen of your own manufacture."

Swell. Just what I need. More responsibility fer all this. I was kinda hopin' Fate with a capital F was in charge. That'd take a load off my mind, strange as it sounds.

"Sorry," Jasper said, "no 'Fate Accompli' for Verity."

"Yep, I knew you'd have somethin' pertinent to toss into the mix," I thought.

Me and Ino talked for a while, mostly about nothing important. She described her home village with all the love of a girl who rarely left it. I did the same with both of the places I'd called home, our Maryland farm and our small house in

Washington, down the street from the theatre. Though it'd been several years since we'd lived on the farm, I surprised myself with how much detail I could recall, and with how much warmth it filled me. Right then I promised myself that if I survived the insane quest I was on, I'd take Tommy back there to see how things stood. Somehow I got the feeling that the old place had a lot more to do with who and what I was than Ma had let on. For one thing, I'd bet dollars to donuts that it sat on a woppin' big Chauntline.

There's Ma again. The more I ponder this thing the more I find out she's kept from me.

We stopped twice to rest and get our bearings., and once to set Ino down at the outskirts of her home town. No Maenads, mages, gypsies, Arabes, or windmills came after us. That didn't mean I got to relax. I was jumpy as a rat at a terrier convention. Every innocent sound in the murk made me yelp and start waving Morphageus about, runes blazing. It got so that Ernie and Tyrell would throw rocks near me just so they could fall over laughing at my plight (Jasper, too, of course). Shucks, even Al whinnied with mirth. They stopped real quick when I turned the magick sword into a mousetrap, then into a pot of glue. A girl could only stand so much.

A little before dawn we crossed the border into Gaulle. I only knew where it was because Jasper came near to giving me heart palpitations when he jumped into "The Marseillaise" at full volume. Everybody around me roared with laughter again as my backside left the owl and I clung to its ear tufts for dear life. It's not easy to glare at an invisible spirit living inside you, but I did my best.

"You, boyo, are gonna feel my wrath when we get to the *Kiss*," I informed him with a cold thought.

"Ooh, let's all watch the enchanted sword wet himself with fear," he taunted. "If you hate the classics of music so much, how is that my problem?"

The sky got a little rosy as we swooped low over the coast. To our right the town of Bayonne, which looked about the size of Washington, D.C, snoozed, unaware of the amazing sight just above it. We detoured out to sea a bit when we spotted a couple of Bonaparte's ships skulking about. No need to draw attention to the *Kiss*. A swooping right wheel brought us to a tree-covered inlet. My witched eyes showed me that Pitcairn had towed his frigate, all sails struck, into water only barely deep enough for it. With the aid of some leafy camouflage nets the crew kept for just such a purpose, the sleek vessel was all but invisible from seagoing patrols. Of more concern would be prying eyes on land. Romulus had told me that Bildad had posted sentries a good half-mile inland to watch for unwelcome visitors. So far it seemed we were undiscovered.

Just as we landed the sun came up high enough to throw more light on us than we cared for. We saluted the massive owls, only slightly smaller than Athena's, and thanked them for their assistance. Their leader, a pale gray fellow with eyes that seemed to always be considering you as a meal, nodded at us and said that any day they could inconvenience the Merchantry was a day well-spent. Then they flew out to sea again and left us to our own devices.

With no more sound of wind or wings in my sensitive ears I felt like I was standing—wobbling, rather—in a graveyard. The swoosh of the distant surf was all I could hear. No people were visible on deck, either. *Pitcairn must be keepin' everybody extra-quiet on account of Gaullic patrols. Can't say as I blame him. Scrappin' with the Grand Armee is no fun. Found that out when the Old Guard rushed us in Virginia.* All of my friends jogged up the gangplank and vanished into the bowels of the ship while I stood there admiring our captain's precautions. I shrugged and followed them, hoping that breakfast would be soon. My chow-time in Cumae hadn't been nearly enough.

As soon as I set foot on the teak planks I felt that something was wrong. Nobody kept watch. None of the usual nautical sounds greeted me: no shouted orders, sailors' complaints and curses, the slap of feet, the thrump of lines being hauled on. The *Kiss* felt like a ghost ship. Had she been taken? Did Shades lurk below to capture anybody who came aboard? Did they already get Ma, despite her magick? Was I next?

I yanked my tin cup from my waist and willed it into sword form, holding it high. *Why, fer once, can't I just have a snack and a snooze? Well, I ain't goin' down without a fight, no matter how beat I am.*

The ambush smacked into me from three sides at once. Several heavy bodies bore me to the iron-hard deck, knocking the wind from me. I could hear my attackers' heavy breathing as they restrained me. When I tried to use Morphageus to sweep them away, nothing happened. All I got was a rusty tin cup. Somehow they had a spell that interfered with my mental commands.

Who has that kind of power? Merchantry mages, most likely. This is bad.

A growl left my throat as I struggled against the assailants with all of my Stone-strength. Some of them let go, but before I could take advantage more took their place. Try as I might, I couldn't shed them all. They'd pinned me face-down. And turned Morphageus into a mere theatre prop.

So here ends the quest. Just like that. Sorry, Tommy. Come on, then. Do your worst and get it over with.

Booted feet appeared in front of my snoot. I couldn't raise my head but an inch, so I had no clue who stood before me. Their ruthless commander, no doubt. He let out a low, evil chuckle. Something dropped onto my bare head. Whatever was in my short tangled hair, it moved. It lived. And it slithered toward my helpless face. Probably some devilish fiend from the Obverse, come to suck out my eyeballs.

"Vewy pweased to see you've weturned, Miss Vewity," said an adorable rat with raccoon-like markings on his little face, not six inches from my nose. In one paw he held a tiny riding crop. He twitched his whiskers and gave me a stiff-armed Roman salute.

"We gweet you with gweat pweasure! All hail Vewity, Pwincess of the *Penewope's Kiss*!" squeaked a military formation of rats who stood in formation behind General

Gracchus.

Huh?

Just as it started to dawn on me what was going on, the score of hands that held me down decided to haul me up instead. All the way up to their shoulders. One set of broad shoulders, in particular, I recognized. To make sure, I peered straight down...and grinned.

"Mornin', miss," said Romulus, grinning back. Ernie sat on his brown shaved head, waving at me.

I let the tension flush out of my aching muscles and looked all around. The whole crew, all two hundred of them, filled every available inch of deck space. Roberta, in human form now that she'd returned to the ship, blew me a kiss and winked. Those had been her boots in front of me. Pitcairn stood above her on the quarterdeck, wearing his finest blue brocade coat and gold vest. Elsewhere I saw Bogus and Sham, Fergus, Bildad, Tyrell, Sha'ira. Even tiny Freya with her false eyepatch and wooden sword, getting slurped by the Duke.

I'd been lovingly set up.

"Three cheers fer Miss Verity and her safe return!" cried paunchy little Fergus. Hip-hip..."

"Hooray!" shouted a couple hundred lusty, crusty pirate throats.

After they'd repeated it twice more, to my intense mortification and secret joy, I had only one thing to say.

"I'm plottin' my revenge. Just you wait. You are all dead, dead, dead."

They hooted at me. So much for my carefully-honed acting skills.

Romulus toted me around a bit, bouncing me so much I felt seasick even though the ship was dead still. After he'd set me back down and received a hug that didn't come anywhere near to reaching all the way around him, I gave the same to each and every person I met. My arms ached from that and my face hurt from smiling like a first-class idiot. Back home I had almost no friends, apart from Tommy. Something about the Stone's secret power made kids shun me a little, without their knowing why. That, and my looking and acting like the toughest boy on the block. I had to flee for my life from the worst evil ever to befall mankind to find people who cared enough about me to beat me to a pulp as a loving practical joke. And they were all vicious pirates.

"That's what you call irony," Jasper said. "I'm made of it, you know. Oh, wait. That's iron. Silly me."

"You got that right the first time, buster," I told him. "As fer the iron part, I ain't rightly sure what metal they forged you from. You might have a bit of iron, but most of it is somethin' else entirely.'

"Whips and snails and puppy-dog tails?"

"Don't I wish it were that simple. And don't try to put me off, you. When I tried to make the sword work you just ignored me. Thanks a lot."

The old tin cup flowed from my fist into a small lead soldier, a Napoleonic Grenadier. He marched up my arm a ways and wiggled his oversized moustache. "The rule is that I protect you from imminent deadly harm. A glorified tickle fight don't count. Can't have you loppin' off your friends' heads. Bad for morale, don't you know."

"Why, I declare! That's yet another time you've been right. It's turnin' into a habit. We should alert Horace Greeley so he can get it into his next edition."

After a few more minutes of bein' fussed over and tellin' the story of how I didn't let myself get dead maybe a hundred times over, I found myself up at the wheel with the Dread Pirate Roberta. She squashed me against her generous bosom till I saw stars.

"Glad to have you back in one piece, squid," she said. Knowing how much I hated it, she ruffled my hair. I really needed a new hat.

"Good to be back," I told her.

"Yer mama about drove us all crazy with her worryin' about you."

"There was plenty of occasions where she had plenty of cause fer it. But the fancy-dancy rucksack she gave me saved my bacon a few times."

Somehow she'd managed to retrieve it from under the feet of the mob on the main deck. She held it out to me with a sigh and a get-down-to-business look. "Can't put it off any longer, you know."

I threw it over one shoulder with a heavy nod. "I know. Where is she?"

"Waitin' fer you off the starboard bow. Head down the gangplank and turn left. She's about fifty yards out, under an old willow tree."

Which is just where I found my mother, looking more worried than I'd ever seen her before. It couldn't have been out of concern for my safety. She'd seen us arrive and heard all of the celebrating. No, this was about our impending conversation. I felt amazed. *She's more scared of this pow-wow than I am.*

Ma wrung her handkerchief till I thought drops of blood might fall from it. For the first time I noticed that she had some gray hairs at her temples, though still in her thirties. Lines of strain and anguish creased her eyes and mouth. Had those always been there and I'd never noticed? Or were they due to me being in so much danger lately?

Or from what she was about to tell me?

"You've a right to be upset," she said, looking down at her hands.

I shrugged. "Do I? From where I sit, I ain't been told enough to have an informed opinion."

"Fair enough. I'm sorry for that, honey. But the whole thing is so dashed...complicated."

"More complicated than havin' a talkin' sword in my head? More complicated than havin' the survival of humankind depend on me? Than knowin' that my only friend is gonna die if I don't spring him from the world's scariest dungeon in ...what? A week?"

She shook her head. Strands of brown hair hung down into

her sad eyes like moss on the willow we stood under. "No. Complicated for me, more than you, I'd say. I've been telling myself that you're too young, too naïve about how things are since the Affluxion. I've kept putting this off, hoping things would somehow fix themselves without you and I'd never need to have this conversation."

I set down the backpack. Now it weighed a ton, though I'd already taken out the heaviest object in it.

"Bob's a horrible gossip, you know," she went on. "All the pelicans are chatty, but he's the worst. He's already been here with the details of what you've been through. So I've heard about the gray mage."

"Seems I have an aunt you neglected to mention. I thought you was an only child."

"Oh, don't I wish that were true! You'd be so much safer then. Stay away from her. You don't know how dangerous Maggie is. You were lucky to—"

"Maggie? She said her name was Regan."

Ma snorted and waved that away. "She would. Jumped-up little guttersnipe! Renamed herself Regan the day she left home. Thought it sounded more 'enchantressy.' Her given name is Margaret. I've always called her Maggie. She hates that, of course, and me. Never mind why. Family squabbles. Power struggles growing up. Silly stuff, unless the children involved come from the womb with magical talent. They had to separate us when we reached puberty. Our unstable emotions and bodies threatened to destroy the whole town when we'd bicker. And now she's so enamored of dark magick that her sanity is nearly gone. That's what it does, among other things. Twists the mind until it can't tell fact from fancy. Makes the user see enemies under every bush."

"She called me an abomination. A monster."

If I'd thought Ma's face showed agony before, that'd been nothing to the look that clouded her features when I spoke those words. Gazing at those eyes felt like peering into a well of sorrow. I saw shame, guilt, anger, and denial...all at once.

"Regan just said that to hurt me, honey. She knew I'd hear of it. Another arrow in her ugly quiver, that's all."

Oh, no, you don't. Not when I'm this close. "But why them particular words? She meant somethin' by 'em."

If Ma had been on a rack in the Inquisition's torture chamber she couldn't have looked worse. I thought she'd actually cry out from physical pain. Instead, after a long tense silence she gasped. A tear slid down one cheek. As much as that made me want to rush up to her with a hug, I forced myself to stay put. *This has to happen, no matter what.*

"Open the letter, then," she said in a whimper. "You're ready. That much is clear."

I held it up, the weighty object I'd removed from the rucksack. "It won't zap me?"

"No. Not now. Everything you want to know is there. So read it. I can't bring myself to go through it all again, even after a dozen years."

My dirty thumb pried open the flap of the envelope, breaking the red wax seal. I flinched, expecting a shock or a jolt or something nasty. Nothing happened. Relieved, I pinched the letter and pulled it out. As soon as I unfolded it strange things started happening. Lights and colors spilled from the ink on its surface and swirled into the air in front of me. With a yelp I let go of the paper and hopped back. Rather than a defensive spell on the outside, it contained an illusion spell on the inside.

Like an animated painting in three dimensions, with sound, the vision resolved into a semi-transparent set of images. Ma's voice filled my brain, sort of like Jasper's did. While she spoke her spell showed me the things she described, like a play produced by fairies.

"Since you're seeing and hearing this, Verity, that means you've grown up enough to know about these things. It also means that your situation is so dire that you absolutely must be told. Whether this information will help you in your cause or merely give you a little peace of mind, I can't say. It might very well have the opposite effect. If so, I'm sorry for that, dear.

I'm speaking six months after your birth. You're asleep in your crib while I spin this spell. You may be reading this because I'm gone forever. Or perhaps because I've never mustered the courage to tell you these 'facts of life.' Either way, you'll have to steel yourself and move on. Millions of people are counting on you.

Your father's name is Paul L'Anterne. I met him in January of 1849, in Hagerstown, Maryland, in a dry goods store. He came right up to me, bold as brass, announced that he was buying supplies for his trip to the California gold fields, and would I come with him? He needed a wife. Just like that. I was no shrinking violet, but I nearly fainted with shock."

The motion picture showed me the scene. A tall auburn-haired fellow with a big jaw and freckles tipped his top hat to a very young poke-bonneted version of my mother. His broad shoulders and thick arms weren't in Romulus' league, but they still threatened to bust the seams of his gray frock coat. Such a dark blue they seemed to be purple, his wide eyes had an oddness to them that I can't describe. When he smiled he seemed to give off an energy that may have been a spell, or perhaps just loads of charm. All I knew was that if he'd asked me to travel around Cape Horn with him I'd have been packing my bags in two minutes. Ma's voice continued, accompanied by the vision.

"There was no enchantment. My magick tutor and my mother had both taught me well enough to watch for that. Maggie had just left home after a violent argument. She'd demolished a carriage with her sorcery on her way out. That had left me on my guard, but also alone. This captivating stranger caught me at my most vulnerable and before I could even ask myself what had happened I was married and standing on a Baltimore dock, about to take ship for California.

We never made it there. In fact, we never even got onto the ship. A dark man spoke to Paul just as we were about to board. I didn't hear the conversation, which seemed pleasant enough. But Paul gasped, grabbed my hand, and dragged me into the crowd, leaving all of our luggage behind. Though I'd only known him for three days I could tell that something had terrified him. Two other men we encountered had the same effect on him. All that morning we moved as if pursued by monsters from a fairy tale, peering over our shoulders and dashing from one doorway to the next. That night we stayed in three different hotels, under assumed names. Before dawn we snuck out, our faces covered, and took a hired coach to a farmhouse in the country, miles from anywhere. Only then did Paul relax a little.

I threw so big a fit I feared I'd lose control and use magick to knock him across the room. He had no idea I was a mage. It appeared that we'd both withheld things from one another. In a snit I demanded that he tell me what was going on or I'd head straight back to my mother. All he would say was that he'd got onto the wrong side of some powerful people in a far-off country and he'd had to flee. The man who'd accosted him had been an agent of those men, sent to bring him back. But we were rid of them now and things would be just fine. But going to California was now out of the question.

None of that satisfied me. It was all too vague, too mysterious. I kicked myself for marrying a complete stranger on a whim. So I stormed out of the house and stomped into the barn to think. Once there I got my second shock of my young married life.

There was a Chauntline beneath our barn.

It couldn't have been a coincidence. All of the known lines are familiar to mages. This one was in no book or chart I had ever seen, even though it felt like a fairly strong one. Somehow it had been kept a secret. But how? And why? I knew how to find out, but it would be a betrayal of my new husband.

I did it anyway. Danger surrounded me and I had to discover the truth. I set myself down in the barn and waited for Paul to come looking for me. When he did, I embraced the Chauntline and cast a truth-web over him, a spell that would force him to answer any question I asked.

It didn't work.

Not only that, he shrugged it off with the barest wave of his hand. I'd never seen such smooth defensive magick."

I gasped as I watched the scene in the illusion. Pa—I figured I had to call him that now—held up two fingers as Ma sent a shimmery wave of orange light from both hands. Her spell splashed against it like a weak wave against a rock and faded away. Not only was my father a mage, his abilities made my mother's look like those of an infant.

"The ease with which he blocked that strong spell amazed and frightened me. What scared me even more was how well he'd cloaked his magick signature until then. Nothing in his aura had betrayed him. Not even the most experienced practitioners were able to keep every sign of their energies hidden. A tiny flicker always gave them away at such close range. I knew from my training that there was only one explanation for how Paul could do so.

Your father wasn't human. He had come from the Obverse."

I sagged and fell onto the grass, mouth hanging open like a boxcar door. So I wasn't human, neither? At least, not completely?

"Once I knew that, the affair at the docks made perfect sense. Thinking back, using my mage's sensory recall, I remembered that the first man he'd spoken with had developed a runny nose. He'd not shown as much of a sniffle before then. That was what Paul had seen, too. The man was a demon in human form, telling him a lie. And that far-off country my husband had run away from was no country at all, but the horrifying parallel world that mages mothers used to frighten us into eating our vegetables.

As it turned out, I had no need of the truth-web. Paul sat beside me and revealed everything. At least, I hope he did. Perhaps he held some details back out of fear for me, just as I have from you.

In the Obverse he'd been a warrior-mage, trained in fighting with sword and spell at the same time. Very difficult and dangerous, he said, since it required a split use of body and mind. He wore a charmed stone to make it possible. On a sensitive diplomatic mission he'd uncovered a plot by what we call demons, those whose use of dark magick had corrupted and distorted both their souls and forms. They planned to join forces with the Honourable Merchantry in our world. Their conjoined magickal powers would enslave the Grand Mage and deliver our side of reality to the Proprietor. In exchange, the Merchantry would aid its Obverse allies in rebelling against the forces that held them in check. Armies and secret agents came across to tip the balance in the demons' favor.

Paul was found out. He couldn't be allowed to live with such dangerous knowledge. When hiding failed, and his friends could no longer protect him, he found a portal to our side to lose himself among us until he could warn the Equity and stop the coming storm. That was when he'd met me—by chance, he claimed—recognized my gift, and impetuously decided to join forces with me, hoping he could make the Equity's prophecy come true.

I wanted to leave. Every fiber of my being told me to flee that barn and go back home. But I couldn't. That same mage sense I'd used to recall the demon had also told me that I was already carrying you. For better or for worse, my wedding vows had said. Too true.

So we stayed in that house, posing as ordinary farmers. The Marshals of the Equity looked out for us as best they could, serving as hired hands and such. More than once we had to defend ourselves against minor assaults. Probing attacks, as it turned out. Reconnaissance missions from the Obverse, searching for weaknesses. Their easy repulse also served to lull us into a false ease. When the real attack came we didn't react as well as we should have.

It came the night you were born. While Paul held you in his arms and cooed, we both felt the energy of the whole world tear. Like an earthquake near an undersea volcano. That's how it seemed to me, weak as I was, lying there ten minutes after delivering you. Waves of heat, shock, and terror. My magick winked out, then restored itself. That was the Affluxion, as we now know. The Merchantry and the demons tried to turn all of our world into a vast engine that would fuel their corrupted sorcery. And it worked only too well, except that it also shifted time and space to create alternate realities, as you are well aware.

That's how they found us, enthralled with you and shocked by the Affluxion spell. Paul just had time to hand you to me and cloak us with a charm. A portal opened in the barn, atop the Chauntline. The whole west wall blew out as twenty Darwins and Grotesques appeared, led by half a dozen corrupted warrior-mages. The Equity Marshals engaged them, as did Paul. I was of no use. I had to protect you. Besides, my maiden magick hadn't yet matured into maternal magick. All of my power was in flux. They'd chosen the perfect time to come for us.

The battle was colossal but brief. Your father slew half of them before he was overwhelmed and dragged back through the portal. Many Marshals died to protect us. His final act was to reach through the cloak he'd created, hang the Stone around your neck, and kiss us both. He told me to erase all sign of his presence on Earth, and that if he ever managed to escape, he'd send word to me."

The vision and Ma's voice blew away on the morning breeze. Her enchanted letter dissolved into cinders and did the same. Both of us sobbed. I flung myself into her arms and told her I loved her. She embraced me just as hard and said how sorry she was. Sorry that she hadn't told me sooner. Sorry that I'd been born into such trouble. Sorry that we couldn't just be a normal family like everybody else.

"So I really am abomination, like Regan said?" I blubbered, wiping my nose on my sleeve. "Half human, half…whatever."

Ma held me at arm's length, staring straight into my eyes and fussing with my hair. "No! Only to them, little huckleberry. Never to me. They have to tell themselves that you're some kind of monster, the only child ever to come from both worlds. Because they're afraid of you. They know you can undo all of their awful schemes."

I frowned. "The only child ever?"

"Well, the only one that lived," Jasper gleefully announced. "Usually they're stillborn deformities."

"Oh, gee, thanks fer sharin' that bit of good news," I accidentally said aloud.

My mother let go of me like I was a hot stove. "What?"

"The other abomination speaks," I explained, tapping my noggin.

"Hey!" he whined. "Who's been keepin' the half-breed monster alive, I'd like to know? A little respect, please."

I picked up the rucksack and tossed it over my shoulder. Since the flap was open, I stuffed the tin cup inside and closed the thing up tight. Taking Ma's arm in mine, I steered us back toward the *Kiss*. The party had wound down and Pitcairn had put everybody back to work. We'd get underway when the sun set.

"Hard to breathe in here," Jasper said, muffling his voice as if being in the bag had any real effect on him.

I ignored him and spoke to Ma as we headed toward the ship. "You said Pa's alive. He gets messages to you from the Obverse, then?"

"Yes, once in a blue moon. I don't know how he does it, but tiny scraps of parchment appear on my bedside table maybe twice a year. They burn away like the letter you just read, the instant I've finished reading them. Very brief messages saying that he'd still on the run and that someday he'll find a way to come back. He says that all of the portals are guarded tightly now, on both sides. I can't get any messages back to him, but he seems to know that you're well and growing like a weed."

"You got that right," Jasper said, still muffled. "And not just any weed. Poison ivy. She's quite the little nightmare."

That gave me an idea. "Have you ever considered Dreamwriting to him?"

She stopped dead, staring into space. "Huh! Never crossed my mind. Dreamwriters are so rare. Before Sha'ira I'd never met one."

"We'll see what she thinks. I know she'll do it if she can. But she's sort of a novice at it. Maybe it'd take more skill than she has right now."

"I'll look into it. The Equity may know if that's even possible. If it is, we'd have to guard against the message being intercepted by our enemies. They are terribly good at that sort of thing."

We'd arrived at the gangplank. Roberta perched on it in parrot form, since she was beyond the edge of the hull where the curse began. I asked for permission to come aboard.

"Permission granted, squid," she squawked, saluting us with a scarlet wing. "Looks like you two are flyin' the same colors again."

"That we are," Ma said with a smile, tugging me onto the main deck.

Pitcairn held up the same pair of bated smallswords he'd planned to use three days ago, before the Furies had interrupted our fight practice. "Miss Verity, you are behind in your training."

I took the blade he offered me, setting the rucksack on a bench. Jasper let out an over-acted *oomph* sound. "And I'm behind in my fresh air allowance!"

With my free hand I undid the flap. Out popped a jack-in-the-box, tongue lolling, gasping as if half-suffocated. I smiled at it and bowed to Pitcairn. "Ready when you are, sir."

He came on guard, the white ostrich feather in his hat dancing in the breeze. All of my friends—pirates, pelicans, rats, Marshals of the Equity, parrot, and assassin-turned-Dreamwriter—turned to watch us go at it.

"I should warn you," the ship's commander and legendary duelist said, "since you went into Europa I have been in continual practice."

I thought of Tommy, waiting for me to come free him like I promised. I thought of all that Ma had just told me. And I thought of Pa, on the run in another universe. The Legacy Stone grew warm beneath my shirt as I embraced the frigate's meagre Chauntline. My hair lifted from my scalp as my feet floated free of the deck. Jasper shimmered into the sword Morphageus, red-orange runes flaring along its blade. With a thought it flew through the air into my hand. Blue-white energy sparkled along my arm and out of my eyes.

"And I should warn you," I told the whole ship's company, "I'm my father's child."

"Maybe I would've been safer in that rucksack," Jasper sighed.

This is the end of *Jasper's Foul Tongue, Part 2.*
Book Three, Part 1, *Jasper's Magick Corset,*
Convergin' on the Ridiculous,
will continue Verity's adventures.
(an excerpt appears below).

If you enjoyed this book (or even if you didn't), please
leave a brief review on Amazon, Goodreads, etc.

Thank you for reading.

www.terrykroenungink.com

From *Jasper's Magick Corset, Part 1:*
Convergin' on the Ridiculous

"Scorn...oomph!"

Four to go.

"Defiance...urrk!"

Three now.

"Slight regard...yow!"

Only two. I can do this.

"Contempt...aack!"

Last one. Don't let 'em see you sweat.

Jasper, the voice of my magick sword that only I could hear, snickered. "What on earth are you mumblin' about?"

"Shakespeare," I grunted between clenched teeth. "*Henry V.* We studied it in school some."

Ma yanked on the laces that were threatening to crunch my ribs into dust, her knee in my back. Jasper kept on yapping in his thirteen year-old boy tones. "And this is helpin' you...how?"

"I'm dreamin' up all manner o' tortures-vile," I hissed. "Poison toads fer breakfast. Itchin' powder in his underwear. Dearth-demons munchin' on his wretched innards. Prussic acid pourin' down from the heavens as he begs fer mercy from every woman in the States United and Europa."

"All this misery is for...?"

"Fer the misbegotten bastard what invented the corset!" I

yelped as Ma hauled in on those lines as if she was trying to land some great fish.

"Language, dear," Ma purred, knowing that I'd heard a whole lot worse since coming aboard the *Penelope's Kiss*. What she didn't know was how much worse, mostly from Jasper. Our salty privateer crew could really burn your ears when they got goin'. Jasper loved to imitate them. Boys will be boys, even if they're disembodied spirits.

"Ain't you done yet?" I whined, trying to peer over my shoulder to check Ma's progress. All I could see out of a corner of my eye was a veil of my short red hair. Blowing at it did no good.

"Just getting ready to tie it off. Take a deep breath and hold it, please."

"Will I be able to let it out or is this the last breath I ever get to take?"

She smiled, the crinkles at her eyes looking like starbursts. "Oh, don't be so dramatic, little huckleberry. It's a corset, not an iron maiden."

Jasper, resting on her sewing table in the form of an old tin cup, melted and reformed until he became a miniature torture rack. A rag doll was lashed into it, an expression of agonized horror on its little face.

"Aiee!" it wailed in my head. "Do your worst, Torquemada! You'll never make me a slave to your dark fashion sense!"

I felt it a pity that Ma couldn't hear him. She was the costume designer at Ford's Theatre and had no truck with what passed for *La Mode* among some of our lady patrons. Enormous cage crinolines that made women resemble walking lace mushrooms. Over-trimmed hats that made your head look like a confection. Magenta silk fabrics that gave you a pounding headache to look at. Ma would just shake her head and mumble to herself. Most of the time she wore a simple blue or gray cotton work dress and a cotton snood for her dark brown hair. No fiendish devices to slim or reshape her. All natural, that was her motto.

But I had to travel incognito through Gaulle and into the Scepter'd Isle, so dressing like a native would be required. Walking about Napoleon's time of 1804, to say nothing of Queen Elizabeth's 16th century, dressed in my preferred overalls, straw hat, and bare feet would attract the kind of attention we couldn't afford. Our do-or-die mission to rescue my friend Tommy from a Merchantry dungeon in London was going to be hard enough without getting arrested as a lunatic or a witch.

So Ma had decided to train me for the kind of disguises I'd have to use. Stays and corsets, along with Empire waists, farthingales, and shoes designed by the Spanish Inquisition were all part of it. I'd have preferred a vizard glamour spell that would let me wear what I liked but fool onlookers into believing that I wore the local rags. My mind got changed by Jasper's gleeful explanation of how much I'd have to pay him for such a long-term use of magick. A whole bunch of whiskey, cigars, skinny-dipping, and even shoplifting would just about cover it, he'd said. After considering the disadvantages of sneaking through hostile territory staggering and upchucking I'd decided to take my chances with the corset.

A snooty voice whoofed at me in a Parisian accent. "You can dress up le pig, they say, but it will still make the oink." The big floppy basset hound lying on the bunk rolled his eyes as he spoke. A pompous aristocrat from the losing side of the 1789 Revolution, Jean-Luc D'Arcy Evremonde, Le Duc du Ponteau, had a difficult time letting go of his imperious attitude towards us 'peasants.'

"Look who's talkin'," I shot back with as much force as my constricted lungs allowed. "The Merchantry dressed you up as a pooch, permanent-like."

"But I am still every inch a peer of the realm, even in this tres ridiculous shape. It proves my point." He lifted his long wet nose and posed as if David was painting his portrait.

Jasper turned himself into a six-inch long Roman ballista, bolt aimed at the Duke's wide rump. "Just say the word and I'll make my own point."

"Naw," I said with a shake of my head. "That'd just give him a bigger excuse fer his 'poor little me' act. He's tough enough to tolerate as it is."

"What is your ill-mannered toy saying about me now?" the Duke wanted to know, one eyebrow raised. "It never ceases to amaze me that you two are supposed to be civilization's only hope."

With a thought I returned Jasper to his natural self, the ancient sword Morphageus. Holding it up as high as I could while stuck in the corset, I let him see the black recurved blade covered in fiery runes. "Hey, it weren't no bright idea of mine, believe me, Drooly. I just fell down a hole one night and here we are."

The same night three weeks before that a grotesque dearth-demon named Venoma had tranced poor Tommy and then disappeared with a green flash into the half-built Washington Monument. I'd been heading to London to spring him ever since.

So far I'd been attacked by giant ravens, zombies, Furies from Hellas, the Assassins Guild, Furies, the Hellfiend Legion, a cast-iron submarine, my own insane sorceress aunt, twelve shiploads of disguised demons, the god Dionysus himself, and those creepy corrupt mages who look like little blonde boys, the Bullies.

Oh, yeah...and poop-monsters. Loads of poop monsters.

Welcome to my world, y'all.

ABOUT THE AUTHOR

Terry Kroenung taught literature for 30 years, mostly at Niwot High School in Colorado, where he inflicted his Shakespeare impersonations and love of Eeyore collectibles on tomorrow's leaders. An Advanced Actor/Combatant with the Society of American Fight Directors, he owns more swords than any sane human has any need of and spent countless hours choreographing fights with his students (thus, the gray hairs and nervous twitchings of his poor principal). As unplanned preparation for writing about Verity's adventures he served as an U.S. Army infantry officer on the East German border, a Confederate Civil War re-enactor in Virginia, and a pirate at street festivals. His youthful cigar smoking and whiskey drinking resulted in just as much misery as Verity feels when indulging.

The smart-aleck dialogue and puns come naturally, alas...more's the pity.

www.ingramcontent.com/pod-product-compliance
Lightning Source LLC
Chambersburg PA
CBHW020916060726
47591CB00004B/1265